OTHER BOOKS BY LAURA BENEDICT

NOVELS

ISABELLA MOON
CALLING MR. LONELY HEARTS

ANTHOLOGIES

EDITED WITH PINCKNEY BENEDICT

SURREAL SOUTH 2007
SURREAL SOUTH 2009
SURREAL SOUTH 2011

DEVIL'S OVEN

Laura Benedict

Devil's Oven copyright 2012 Laura Benedict

Published by Gallowstree Press

ISBN: 978-0-9850678-2-3

Book cover design and interior layout by John Hornor Jacobs

GALLOWSTREE
PRESS

Dedicated to the memory of Howard and Marie Baugh

In Gratitude and Thanksgiving

Cindy Gunnin
CJ Lyons
D.P. Lyle
Ellen Clair Lamb
Jedidiah Ayres
Jennifer Holbrook Talty
Joan Huston
Joe Hartlaub
Joyclyn
Karen Dionne
Kay Russell
Kermit Moore
Maggie Caldwell
Melissa Woods
Michelle Gibson
Paige Crutcher
Sophie Littlefield
Susan Raihofer

Pinckney, Cleveland, and Nora

CHAPTER ONE

I vy Luttrell had pricked her thumb many times while sewing, but this time, watching a drop of her own blood melt into the seam she had just finished - the seam joining the head and neck of the beautiful man whose dismembered body she had found up on Devil's Oven - she heard her mother's voice in her head, a voice that rose from deep in her memory.

"You have to expect miracles, baby, if you want them to happen."

Ivy rested a hand on the man's motionless chest. It didn't feel cold, or dead. Just still. She closed her eyes, squeezing out the harsh overhead light spreading over the trailer's dining room table. She took a deep breath, and waited.

Ivy laid out the body parts on the table as though they were pieces of a puzzle. Her half sister, Thora, was down the hill, in the tidy house they finally built for themselves after living in the rusting hillside trailer for most of their lives. Ivy was a seamstress by trade, but she knew Thora wouldn't understand what she was doing, why she would be stitching together a body she'd found in pieces up on the mountain. Thora wouldn't understand that the body - the man - was a gift from the mountain. It was so much more than the bits of decorated pottery or dull arrowheads Ivy had collected over years of walking the mountain's face. Devil's Oven had taken her mother and father. Now it was giving something back to her.

She had been mushroom-hunting alone, as always. As she bent to inspect a clump of scarlet-headed false morels, she noticed a thick, rounded fingertip - a man's - poking up from the earth. But she wasn't afraid or disgusted. Even after she recovered the rest of the body parts from their small, absurdly shallow graves, she felt more wonder than fear. It had taken her days to find all the pieces. She brought them down to the trailer one piece at a time, secretly.

Never before had she touched a man's body so intimately, bathing each part in the trailer's tub with the same care she would lavish on an infant, drying it with thick towels she had sneaked out of the house. She had avoided toweling the most private parts, averting her eyes. Few of the clients who came to her to have their clothes altered or made were men, and Thora liked to tease her about the ones who were.

"You act like they're going to bite you," Thora said. "I'm right in the next room. What do you think they're going to do?"

Time and again, Ivy told herself that she wasn't really afraid of men. She had been friendly with a few boys in high school almost twenty years earlier, quiet boys like Tripp Morgan. The quiet ones never made fun of her badly repaired cleft lip, or the way she absently chewed her uncut blond hair when she was daydreaming, or her decades-out-of-date clothes that had belonged to Thora. They didn't mock her to her face, at least. But there had been no dates, no parties, no special boy. Worse, she had begun to wonder if Thora was right when she said it was her own choice to be so shy, that she wasn't bad-looking but was just too afraid to let a man near her. Was it possible that it was her own fault she blushed a fierce red each time she had to measure a man's inseam, even as he held the end of the tape against his own inner thigh?

Looking over the body, Ivy knew she had to start with something difficult, something bold, like attaching one of the severed legs to the torso. Her slender hands trembled as she threaded a curved needle with nylon that matched his olive-cast skin, and coated the nylon with a pinch of beeswax. If she was going to get all of the sewing done that night, she had to force herself to be brave about touching the body in those uncomfortable places.

She was glad no one could see her as she clumsily shifted the right leg so that the ragged edges of the thigh and groin would meet. The curtains were pulled shut, but it wasn't like anyone came near the trailer now, day or night. Not even Thora. The shabby building remained tucked against the side of the mountain only because Thora - stubborn Thora - had refused to have it demolished. Outside the curtains, a clear triangle of light illuminated the entrance to the old barn and nothing else. Their closest neighbor was a quarter of a mile away.

There were people who said they wouldn't live on Devil's Oven for love or money, but she could never be one of them. It didn't matter that there were books written about the disappearances and murders that had occurred there since it was settled over two hundred years earlier, and that in the last century, the mountain had seemed to reach out and pluck twenty different airplanes from the sky.

Devil's Oven was Ivy's strength and nourishment. Her home and heart. What was there for her to be afraid of?

It had given her the man lying before her. He could hardly be considered a threat; he couldn't even object if her handling of him was careless. He was dead.

Maybe.

As she sewed a sturdy baseball stitch - it would show a little, but only to someone who was looking for it - she was careful not to pierce the grey-white cauls that had grown over the wounds while he was buried on the mountain. The cauls were taut, as though the flesh and muscle beneath them were under intense pressure. She had run her finger over the one covering the opening to his left hand, tracing the fine, knobby veins woven into the thing like lace, imagining that she might feel a pulse or some movement. She felt only a tepid warmth, but that warmth had been like a faint promise of something to come.

It took her the better part of an hour to do the first leg, and the second took almost as long because it was harder to shift the body. The cauls had settled against one another, staying out of the way of her stitches. She was happy to find that the stitching held when she twisted and gently tugged at it. She rested for a while, flexing her fingers, which tended to stiffen when she did hand sewing. Realizing she had been working in total silence, she turned on the radio. The twenty-four-hour public station was all she could get on FM this late at night. It was playing a quiet symphony, something she didn't recognize. She wondered what kind of music the man had listened to.

He was a handsome man. She had positioned his head on the table so that it faced her chair. His lips were full, the color of cherrywood, the sort of lips she had always imagined would be described as sensual. The morning she lifted his head from its dirt grave, she had accidentally touched those lips, but she had avoided touching them a second time. They had been soft, but firm, like the rest of his skin. This had been a man who cared about how he looked. His hair wasn't too short. It was deep brown and wavy, long enough to have significant curls but not look feminine. He was clean-shaven, too. It seemed to Ivy that almost none of the men she saw in town were clean-shaven anymore. And those eyes. She couldn't help but imagine that his perfect, heavily lashed eyelids might open, and she would find him looking up at her, puzzled yet grateful. *What color were his eyes? Would he be able to see her? Would she be afraid then?*

Finally done with the rest of him, she began to stitch

his head to his battered neck. She thought about how different she was from him, how pale and thin and insubstantial she felt beside him. She pictured them walking down Alta's Main Street together and gave a little laugh, a delighted sound that made the room around her seem brighter. They would be quite the sight! She, only five feet, five inches; he, like an exotic giant beside her.

People might stare, but it wouldn't matter a bit to Ivy. She and the man would be happy. Life would be a dream.

CHAPTER TWO

BUD TUCKER DROVE AS SLOWLY as he dared to the offices of the trucking company he owned. He wasn't sure what he would find waiting for him. Maybe the offices burned down, his employees injured or harassed, or the trucks vandalized. His imagination didn't usually run to the dramatic, but his thoughts had been disturbing of late, full of ugliness and fear. Death. Then again, he had never owed money to the kind of people who caused bad things to happen when you didn't pay them back. He had only ever owed money to his old man, or the local bank, which was happy to take just an asset or two, or make another loan at a higher interest rate. This was new territory, and it was making him sweat in places he wasn't used to sweating.

When they had called first thing that morning, he was getting out of the shower, his six-four bulk dripping like a rain-washed monument. He stood on the warm marble floor of the bathroom, beneath which ran some two hundred feet of water-heated pipes, and watched the little red light on the muted phone blink one, two, six times, then stop. They hadn't called the house before, but somehow he knew - *he knew* - it was them. Later, when he went downstairs, he learned that Danelle, the woman who came to keep house for them during the day, had picked up the call, but the caller had hung up without speaking.

"It wasn't a local number," she said, turning from the refrigerator where she was putting away groceries. "Some people are just plain rude, Mr. Bud."

"Isn't that the truth?" Lila, his wife, his love, sat at the breakfast table paging through a book of patio designs. She had lifted her lightly freckled cheek to him for a kiss without looking away from the book. She was dressed for her morning walk, wild auburn hair tamed into a bulky ponytail that brushed the collar of her aquamarine anorak, her feet clad in white leather walking shoes.

Bud shook an envelope of oatmeal into a bowl of water, then picked it up and put it in the microwave.

Danelle took the bowl and shooed him away. "You sit down and read the paper," she said. "I'll get your breakfast."

"What do you think about slate around the hot tub?" Lila said. Their house had been one remodeling project after another within two years of its initial construction. She wrinkled her nose like a child, thinking hard. "Or maybe it would be too slippery."

She wasn't really asking for his opinion. It was a game Lila played, pretending to include him in her decisions. He usually played along, but this morning he wasn't in the mood to do much more than eat his breakfast and get out of the house. If he was home, and he was in danger, he was putting Lila in danger, too.

"What's the problem with the concrete that's already there?" But even as he spoke, he was thinking that turning the concrete into slate would cost him at least two or three thousand. He wouldn't have to pay the contractor for more than a month or two. By then he would have things figured out. Sooner, he hoped.

"Concrete is just so boring," she said.

Lila hated to be bored. Her need for novelty was one of the reasons they were in trouble.

Lila was his heart. His baby, his one true passion. He had a tough time denying her anything.

Let me do it, please, please. You trust me, don't you?

Lila stuck out her lip like a little girl being denied a special treat, and he laughed. They were living in a tired rental house and had been married for a month. She didn't even wait for him to answer, but made him kneel down on the floor in front of the sink because he was so much taller than she.

She spread the shaving foam thick, smoothing over the top and sides of his head. He liked having her close, liked that something so simple could make her happy. It didn't matter that the floor was damn hard on his knees.

Now, hold still, she said. I can do it better than you can because you can't see behind your big ol' head.

He was tall enough that he could watch her in the mirror as she scraped neat rows with the hand razor into the lime-scented lather. Her clear green eyes were serious, and her breath was light on his skin as she bent close, steadying herself against him. At the end of every row, she shook the lather off into the sink and tossed her head to keep her loose red curls back behind her shoulders.

With her slender legs so near, and her denim cutoffs tickling his back, he couldn't resist reaching behind and running his hand up her delicious sculpted calf. But he paid for it when she jumped, squealing, and the razor sliced his skin.

Damn it, Bud! she said. That was your own fault.

You shouldn't ought to put that so close to a man's face, he said, sliding his hand up into her shorts.

Look, you're bleeding, she said. Her voice was scolding, but she spread the remaining cream over the cut. In the mirror he could see a trail of pink foam above his right ear. It stung, but he would never tell her so.

You're much better at other things, he said, tugging her shorts down over her hips to expose her white lace thong. Things I can't do for myself.

In fact, Bud had a hard time denying anyone anything that sounded vaguely reasonable: Claude and the sales guys at the office, the rig drivers, Danelle the housekeeper. Everyone at The Twilight Club, the strip joint he had bought to diversify things a few years back when he was flush. Dwight, who managed the club for him, and the revolving cast of dancers and waitresses who worked there. They were all under his skin.

He knew too damn much about the women at the club: their childcare problems, eating disorders, abortions, drug habits. He felt for their lack of privilege and worried that they didn't care enough about themselves. If they wept in front of him, as they so often did, he had to turn away so they wouldn't see the emotion on his face. It was his greatest weakness, this emotion, and he knew it.

How many times had his old man mocked him, calling him a *goddamn nelly boy*? When he was a kid, it didn't matter if he was standing at the end of the diving board, ready to show his dad the dives he had learned at summer camp, or suited up in his school uniform - navy blazer, gray wool slacks, shirt, and club tie - he had always felt naked and small around his father. Now his father, who had built a coal business from nothing, was eighty years old, and Bud, at forty-five, stood half a foot taller. He even shaved away his beard and the remains of his wiry blond hair every day so that there was nothing soft about him but his blue eyes and slight middle-aged paunch. But despite being bedridden, nearly deaf, and tended to by a nurse who changed his diapers, his father was still a bully who, with a single word, could make Bud feel like a loser.

If his father would go ahead and die, like the doctors had been predicting for the past three years, all Bud's problems would be solved. Olney Tucker was a bastard, but he had never threatened to write his only child out of his will. Up to now,

Bud had managed to hold out, keeping a reasonable cash flow going to cover the needs of the people who surrounded him, suffocated him. But he had really screwed up this time, and was going to have to get the old man to bail him out. And although he knew it was a stupid and juvenile thought, he wondered if it wasn't what he deserved for all those times he had wished his father dead.

At the trucking office, Bud exchanged nods with Claude Dixon, who was at his desk talking earnestly into his telephone headset. He had hired Claude as a clerk, not knowing he would eventually turn into the best logistics guy Bud had ever had. Claude was thirty-nine, and still looked like a kid. The drivers and clients all liked him, loved his jokes. But his choice of a wife was a hell of a puzzle.

Sheryl Dixon had graduated from Monroe Consolidated the year after Lila, had gotten a job at the Git 'n' Go Mini-Mart and never left. Unlike Claude, who was skinny, tip-nosed, and always energetic, Sheryl was ponderous. She spent most of her time on a high stool behind the counter, maneuvering her bulk through the store's narrow aisles only when she absolutely had to. She was only quick with her gossip. If it happened in Monroe County, Sheryl knew about it first. But when she and Claude stood side by side, they were a sight gag.

Bud closed the door to his private office and dialed Dwight's cell phone. Dwight answered immediately.

"What's up, boss?" It didn't matter what time it was, or if he had spent a whole day and night working at the club, Dwight always sounded alert, ready for whatever came at him.

Sometimes Bud worried that Dwight was a little too alert, too ready to fix things.

"Hate to wake you, man." Bud absently slid the framed snapshot of Lila on the deck of their beach condo out of his direct view. Was there something he didn't want her to hear? To see? Maybe he didn't like the reminder that he couldn't tell her everything. "I'll be out of town for a day or so."

"Sure," Dwight said. He hesitated. "Truck business?"

They both knew better.

"I need to take care of some things," Bud said. "It'll all be fixed up when I get back."

"Did something happen?" Dwight was agitated, as Bud had known he would be. "We can take care of it."

"Just look after the club," Bud said. He liked Dwight, appreciated him. But he had let Dwight's enthusiasm get him in too deep. "When you do the payroll, be sure to slip an extra fifty into Skye's envelope. Her mother's in the hospital."

"Bullshit," Dwight said. "Skye's jerking us around. I saw her old lady at the House of Waffles falling all over some drunk guy."

When Bud didn't respond right away, Dwight sighed.

"A day or two," Bud said. As he hung up, he heard Dwight's regretful *shit* on the other end of the line.

CHAPTER THREE

IVY FOUND THORA SITTING on the front porch swing, smoking her morning cigarette. Thora didn't look at her but kept staring out at the wet highway.

Despite her heavy frame, Thora's face had retained its sharpness. She still had their father's strong nose and blocky jaw. Her eyes were clear, always questioning, always interested. She kept her shoulders hunched forward, as though she were ashamed of her large bosom. With the exception of the fine cotton nightgowns that Ivy made for her, Thora wore mannish, unadorned clothes. Before her weight and diabetes had forced her to start using a cane, she had towered over Ivy, intimidating her both mentally and physically. But Ivy remembered that Thora had been almost pretty once. Certainly far prettier than Ivy had felt before her own harelip was repaired. Thora had had dignity. Thora had carried herself like a queen. The young Ivy had very much admired queens.

Ivy had only had a couple of hours' sleep and she was anxious, but she made herself sit down on the top step and pretend she was getting on with her day and that her pulse wasn't racing, ready to propel her off the porch and up the hill to the trailer.

Anthony (that was his name, surely; the words *Saint*

Anthony were tattooed in ornate blue and gold letters across his back, with a delicate white lily floating beneath them - *how perfect*) had begun to seem like a dream to her, but she clung to a grain of certainty that he was real. She even had the small bandage on her thumb as proof of how she had spent the night. When she left him, just before dawn, she had covered him with a light blanket in case he got cold. She tried to tell herself she was being silly, that he couldn't feel anything. *Still. Just in case.*

"What do you want for dinner tonight?" Ivy said. Sitting, she folded the sides of her wide skirt over her knees so it wouldn't drag on the rain-spattered stoop.

"I miss lamb chops," Thora said. "We never have lamb chops anymore. When Daddy was alive, we used to have them all the time."

"All you have to do is ask," Ivy said. "The grocery lamb isn't bad. We've got a package I picked up on sale a couple of weeks ago. And if you want fresh, the Hutsenpillars are sure to have lambs by now. There's plenty of room in the big freezer."

Thora took a final drag off the cigarette and stubbed it into the sand-filled bucket at her feet. As she blew out the last of the smoke, she began to cough. The brutal sound made Ivy want to cover her ears. It hurt her to see Thora struggling for breath. She had begun to need oxygen several times a day.

So many times in Ivy's life she had wanted to get away, to make a life for herself without Thora around to tell her what to do all the time. But she couldn't leave the mountain. Thora wouldn't leave, either, even though she claimed to hate it. She said she didn't believe the stories, even though she and Ivy - with Ivy's mother's disappearance, and their father's suicide - had *become* one of the stories. Ivy suspected that Thora really did believe, and was just afraid. Afraid to stay, yet afraid to leave. A lot of people felt that way about Devil's Oven.

Thora had been fifteen years old when her father married Ivy's mother, and just twenty-one the year Ivy's mother disappeared up on the mountain and Thora - *poor Thora!* -

found their father hanging from a hickory tree not far off the trail. Ivy hadn't seen it, but she had pictured it in her mind a thousand times. She knew the tree - one of their few maples, just out of view of the house. Her father had helped her climb it many times. Just a few branches up. Not too far.

Hold on, Ivy! Brace your feet. Look ahead to the next branch. And her mother: Not too high! Her father laughing, standing, watching, just beneath the limb where he would later die. He didn't tell anyone why. Left no note.

Thora could have turned Ivy over to Child Services and walked away, but she hadn't. Sympathy had gotten her a job at the Department of Motor Vehicles, where their father had worked, and she had spent the next several years giving Ivy a grudging, reluctant kind of care. Ivy could remember a time when Thora's approval mattered very much.

"It's not like I can't cook," Thora said. "I'll call the Hutsenpillars myself."

Ivy picked at some lint on her apron, thinking. Thora was always telling her she attracted bits of thread like metal to a magnet.

Finally, she got up and went into the house to retrieve her canvas barn jacket and mushrooming bag from the front closet. She had wasted too much time humoring Thora. She needed to get up to the trailer.

Thora watched her come back onto the porch, her brow furrowed in disapproval.

"I'm going for a walk," Ivy said. She pulled her muck boots from the storage bench beside the door, and sat down on the bench to change into them. "After all this rain, there should be plenty of mushrooms. They'll be good with chops."

"What's wrong with you?" Thora said, stabbing a fore-finger at her. "You're acting like a ten-year-old, getting in a snit and disappearing up to the trailer or up on the mountain. You think I haven't noticed?"

Ivy tied the mushrooming bag around her waist and dropped the knife into her apron pocket. "The Phelps girl is coming at eleven so I can fit her wedding dress," she said. "I'll be back before then."

"You can't hide up there forever," Thora said. "Things change. They can't stay the same all the time."

Ivy barely heard her. Looking out over the yard, she saw how the raindrops sparkled on the dormant grass. It was like she was seeing everything with new eyes.

Ivy's heart pounded as she climbed the trail. She knew she could have gone inside the trailer right away, but she didn't want to feed Thora's suspicions. Thora was weak but not stupid. It took every ounce of willpower Ivy had to not look back to see if Thora was watching her.

When Ivy turned seven years old, Thora had finally let her go walking on the mountain alone, as long as she promised not to go past the dirt fire road that ran about a third of the way up the mountainside. After their parents were gone, Thora had refused to take her up there, and Ivy had almost lost her memories of it.

The fire road was about a fifteen-minute climb, but there were no other trails anywhere close to their land, no other occupied homes, only the stone remains of chimneys belonging to long-crumbled cabins, or bits of rough rope tied to trees from which some kind of shelter had hung. The woods were so quiet that she could always hear the state's Department of Natural Resources trucks or hikers coming and had plenty of time to hide from them. As a child, she had pretended that the entire mountain belonged to her and her alone. Of course, it wasn't long before she ventured beyond the fire road, and eventually to the top of the ridge. Over the years she had seen any number of black bears and four or five bobcats. The only things on Devil's Oven that frightened Ivy were the abandoned dogs that roamed in packs, looking for food.

The trail was mucky but passable because the spring

rains hadn't yet begun in earnest. One year, after the rains, she'd had to spend weeks clearing the trail of fallen limbs and debris carried down the mountainside.

She crossed the fire road and walked east a little way toward the cabin site she had gone to so often with her mother. Almost two hundred years of curiosity seekers had kept it relatively free of brush and trees; you could still sit on the cabin's smooth hearthstone. The site was supposed to be haunted, but it was also a good place to hunt for mushrooms.

⟨divider⟩

It was a clump of false morels, dense and red as cock's comb, growing close to a log that had led her to Anthony. They were often poisonous, but they were so beautiful that she couldn't help but bend down to inspect them. The hand lying beside them was loosely covered with dirt. It wasn't hard to tell what it was.

How strange!

And yet…

How many voices had she heard in the wind when she was on the mountain?

How many people - like her mother - had disappeared here, or lost their way, never to be seen again?

Not thirty feet away was the broad rock threshold of the cabin that had burned here, the one belonging to a woman who - well over a hundred winters earlier - had bludgeoned her husband and one of her children. She had gone mad, people said. So mad that she had murdered her infant son and hanged herself in the forest using her own nightgown. Ivy and her mother had brought bouquets of garden flowers here, but Ivy had been too young to understand why. Later, it was Thora who told her the story when she was still far too young to hear it. Some thought the daughter who escaped had hidden in the hollow of a tree until her mother passed by, then walked off the mountain, never to be seen again. As a child, Ivy sometimes hid beneath her own bed, pretending to be the brave daughter who had escaped death.

With the dirt brushed away, she stroked the hand. Maybe it was because the texture of the skin was so similar to the many mushrooms she had handled that she wasn't afraid. She picked it up.

Balancing the thing on her palm, the tips of its enormous fingers resting in the crevices between her own, she held it up to the sky. It was heavy, and didn't look the least bit dead. In fact, it looked healthy and plump, rich with blood. At the place where it should have been attached to a wrist, there was a smooth stretch of something that wasn't quite skin; it reminded her of the lengths of casing her father used for venison sausage. She thought of her father's hands, brown with the life juices of the deer he killed, sawing ribs and sinew away to get to the most tender parts. But there was no trace of blood on this hand. It was a single, perfect thing.

Still, it was a person's hand.

She knew she should run down the mountainside and call the police and lead them back here. It was the right thing to do. If there was a hand, there were probably more parts buried nearby. A person - a whole person, a whole man - belonged to someone: a mother, a father, or maybe even a wife. Someone would be missing him.

Looking around, she saw other clumps of blood-red false morels. It made an odd kind of sense that they would grow where he was buried.

She imagined police. Helicopters. Maybe even news vans. They always came when a plane crashed or someone was lost. For a while, anyway. But never here, so close to her part of the mountain, the only place where she could get away from Thora.

Ivy set the hand on the log and knelt in front of it. She listened to the morning birds in the trees and the trees creaking, settling - sounds that made her think of God walking in the Garden. She closed her eyes and breathed. When she opened her eyes, the hand was still there. It was real. It hadn't been well hidden; anyone could have found it. But she had been the one, hadn't she?

Maybe no one was missing him. Maybe he had always been here. Waiting.

She slipped the hand into the bag at her waist and tied the cord.

Now, the false morels were gone. All that was left were a few faint depressions that the wind had already filled with leaves.

Her head felt clearer now that she was up here. She wasn't so worried about Thora. Why had she ever worried about her? Thora might be at the trailer right now. She might even have discovered Anthony for herself. But Thora wouldn't do anything. She would wait to talk to Ivy about it, because if something happened to Ivy, Thora would be alone. More than anything else, Thora didn't want to be alone.

Emerging from the trail, Ivy saw a second car parked near the house. The Phelps girl was early. Ivy smiled to herself. *Brides.* She felt like a bride herself. Touching her hand to her hair, she pushed it back behind her ear, anticipating. She wanted to be at her best because Anthony was such a handsome man.

Hoping that Missy and Thora weren't looking for her out the living room window, she hurried to the back porch of the trailer. She told herself she just needed to see him completed, to check the stitches one more time to make sure they were as secure as she remembered making them.

The air inside the trailer was musty. She would have to burn some scented candles and crack open the windows now that it was spring.

"Hello?" she said, not really - not in her heart - expecting an answer. If she had gotten one, what would she have done? Fainted, probably.

Anthony was still there on the table, most of his body covered with the blanket. Had she really touched him in those hidden places? She blushed to think how bold she had been.

Standing over him, she marveled at how peaceful he

looked in the morning light. She touched his hair tenderly, as one might touch a sleeping child.

"I'll come back, Anthony," she whispered. "Don't worry."

CHAPTER FOUR

TRIPP IMAGINED LILA UP THERE ON The Twilight Club's main stage with the dancers. She liked to get him worked up by stripping down for him at his cabin, and always insisted on a serious fire so that she could start out in lacy panties and a bustier or bra, and finish naked in his lap. She had the body for it, too, more voluptuous than the dancers who worked the stage, and red hair that she loved to shake in his face when she was on top. When she had come back to town married to Bud, there were rumors that she had been a dancer for a while, rumors that got legs when Bud bought The Twilight Club.

Tripp didn't believe it - not that it would've mattered to him, anyway. It seemed like he had been fantasizing about Lila his whole life, and now he had her. The tiny laugh lines around her eyes didn't matter, whatever she had done in those years she was gone didn't matter, her attachment to Bud didn't matter. He was pussy whipped and didn't give a damn.

He motioned for one of the cocktail waitresses to bring him another beer. Lila encouraged him to spend plenty of time at the club. "So I know where you are," she had said. Did she think she was being cute, putting him under Bud's nose? But Tripp also knew he was supposed to be keeping half an eye on

Bud. There was a twisted kind of logic to it all, but he didn't like to think too hard about it.

It wasn't as though he wanted for female company. He had been a science geek in high school and, despite the shy warmth in his hazel eyes, the glasses he'd had to wear kept the prettiest, popular girls like Lila and her friends away. But he had filled out in college, bulking up alongside more athletic male forestry students, and his current job as a Department of Natural Resources officer meant he had plenty of money for things like laser eye surgery. So what if his coppery blond hair had thinned out some on top? He kept it shorter than strictly required by his superiors, indicating to the poachers and yahoos he ran across daily that he wasn't someone to screw around with. His pseudo-military look also meant that a certain kind of woman - the kind who had no confidence in herself - didn't bother him, either. He knew he wasn't the best-looking guy around, but he was gainfully employed, college educated, and without dependents or a substance abuse problem. In Monroe County, those four things alone meant he could pretty much have any woman he wanted.

He wore jeans and a comfortable sports shirt, but few of the other men in the bar had bothered to change out of their second-shift work clothes. They sipped beer, barely glancing up at the steel-framed stage, as though they were jaded fifth-graders on their latest field trip to the zoo. The dancers, too, seemed to be going through the motions. The newest girl was the only exception.

She looked local to him, pale, dark-eyed and pretty in the narrow-faced way of the girls from up in the hills. They showed up at the consolidated high school with hard manners and a fresh mouth or a Pollyanna sweetness that was tough to fake. He hadn't talked to her yet, but he was sure she would be one of the sweet ones.

Lila was enough for Tripp, but he couldn't look away from the new girl's shining black hair, and the way she caught it with her fingers, hiding her face as though behind a veil.

When she threw her head back in a languorous arch of her body, her hair brushed the tops of the patent leather boots that stretched to the middle of her thighs. Her white G-string and lacy satin bustier gave her an old-fashioned, almost conservative look, far different from the neon-bright and glossy costumes of the rest of Dwight's dancers. Her moves were fluid and natural, as though she had been born to it.

Tripp wandered through the nearly empty tables to lean against the far wall. It was early enough in the week that he had a clear view of the stage.

Watching the girl, he imagined her ivory body on one of the rougher mountain trails, naked to the approaching nightfall, a lock of her hair caressing the curve of her cheek, her knees drawn up like a baby in the womb. Helpless, and at his mercy. The image made him feel guilty and sick and he looked away at one of the other dancers to push it from his mind. Still, the strobing light on the stage was like moonlight flashing through the trees, and he couldn't help but look back at her to see the way it reflected - icy blue, like cold death - off her skin. When the waitress showed up with his beer, Tripp didn't notice her standing there until she finally touched him on the shoulder.

Lately he had been distracted, zoning out for anywhere from a few minutes to an hour at a time. That morning he had even found himself on a petered-out fire road up on Devil's Oven, the truck about to wedge itself between a couple of pole-thin pine trees. There was a long scratch through the gold DNR logo on the passenger side of the truck to prove it. Beyond the trees was a steep ravine.

He knew he wasn't getting enough sleep. He had gotten to where he didn't like to sleep alone anymore, and Lila was almost never with him overnight.

Dwight came over from the bar.

"What're you drinking that pansy-ass crap for?" he said, grabbing for Tripp's imported beer. But Tripp was fast enough to pull the bottle to him so Dwight was left holding air. "I got a G.D. wall full of good liquor and you embarrass me by drinking that foreign shit. What kind of man are you?"

"I thought Bud didn't let you out of your coffin until after eleven," Tripp said.

"Hell, my day never begins, never ends. Son of a bitch is out of town again for some truck lease thing. G.D. trucks. More trouble than women."

Dwight never took the Lord's name in vain. When Tripp had had enough beers to ask him about it one night, Dwight hadn't even looked up or paused as he wiped down the bar with the wet rag he kept next to the coach gun beneath the counter.

"Some things you just don't screw around with, man," Dwight had said. Then he had launched into a rant about Monroe Consolidated's losing football team.

Among the men who kept regular hours at the bar, Dwight, with his paint-white, indoor pallor, looked most like the one who should be running the place. He was only about five foot five and whip thin, not from any love of exercise, but from a habit of constant, anxious movement. The nails at the end of his splayed fingertips were yellowed, and he wore gold-framed aviator glasses that - along with his coal black hair - made him look a little like Elvis. He wore elaborate cowboy shirts, with thin braid and pearl-covered snap but-tons, straight-leg jeans, and canvas basketball shoes. On those days when he came in just after waking up, his shirt snapped wrongways, he reminded Tripp of someone who might live at the group home for mentally challenged adults that had been built right next to the hospital. Lila told him he had the wrong idea about Dwight; Bud considered him to be some kind of financial genius.

That Bud was out of town was news to Tripp. Lila hadn't said anything, leading him to believe she had gone with him. Bud took her away to nice hotels and glitzy shopping malls, plus the casinos. She was always standoffish for a few days after they got back from a trip. He worried when she took off with Bud.

"You look all disappointed," Dwight said. "You miss Bud?"

"Yeah," Tripp said. "I miss Bud. We had a date."

Dwight blinked behind the thick lenses of his glasses, silent, as though he were trying to decide whether to believe him or not. Tripp knew Dwight's glasses must be pretty old to be so thick. What in the hell did Dwight spend his money on? It couldn't all go to those stupid shirts.

He didn't actually dislike Dwight. Dwight was just unpredictable, what locals called "squirrelly."

They both turned at a shout from a guy in the crowd.

"Oh, man. Now what?" Dwight said.

Up on stage, the dark-haired girl was on her knees. Though her hair hung in her face, Tripp, along with everyone else, could see she was vomiting.

Dwight gestured to one of the cocktail waitresses to go and help the girl. But the waitress, the one who had brought Tripp his beer, pretended not to notice him and walked toward the back of the bar. Tripp had heard that the waitresses and the dancers at The Twilight Club didn't get along well, but this seemed particularly harsh.

"Aw, screw me," Dwight said. "It's always up to me."

The other two dancers paused, but as Dwight trudged toward the stage, he made a circular motion in the air to indicate they should continue. He hustled up the metal stairs closest to the sick girl and leaned over, his face averted from the mess, to take her by the arm and help her up. As they left the stage, a couple of men in the audience gave her desultory applause, as though they were encouraging an injured player on the field.

Tripp decided it was as good a time as any to use the bathroom, and when he got back, the dancers had moved on to another song and the busboy was mopping up the mess.

Because the waitress had been such a bitch to the new girl, he ordered another beer directly from the bartender and wandered into the poolroom. There was a silver cage in the corner where Bud liked to have a girl dancing on weekend nights, but it was empty now. The guy sitting in the uphol-stered chair in the corner was getting a lap dance from one of the two dancers named Crystal, though this one spelled her name with a "K." She had told Tripp that more than once.

When Dwight found him again, Tripp said, "How's the girl?"

"Jolene? These girls never eat right. It was all nacho chips and beef jerky. Nasty shit," Dwight said, shaking his head.

"Maybe Bud should start a cafeteria or something," Tripp said, putting the eight ball into a side pocket. He hung the triangle on a wall peg and put the cue on the rack. He couldn't help but be neat. It was in his nature.

So, she's called Jolene. The only other time he'd heard that name was in the Dolly Parton song.

Dwight pushed his glasses up on his nose.

"Screw me," he said. "Like I need some other shit to do."

CHAPTER FIVE

ON HIS WAY OUT OF THE CLUB, Tripp checked his cell phone for the tenth or eleventh time, hoping to see a text from Lila. On the phone's screen was a picture he had taken on Devil's Oven a few weeks earlier, after she had fallen on her butt trying to walk up the long, ice-covered driveway leading to his cabin. He had stomped and slid his way down the frozen gravel to help her, but soon they were both falling and laughing. In the picture, she was leaning on one arm, trying to stay in one place. Her nose was a brighter red than her hair, which the frigid wet had coiled into tight curls. She was smiling like a kid, looking more than ever like how he remembered her in school.

The parking lot was more crowded than when he had come in. The threat of serious snow was pretty much over for the year and folks were ready for some relief, though they would still be getting snow showers at the highest elevations of Garrett's Mountain and Devil's Oven through mid-April.

Flicking on the headlights in his truck, he saw Jolene near the club's front door. Her hair was twisted into one of those looped ponytails that aren't pulled all the way through, and she wore sweatpants and a white jacket that looked like it wasn't much protection from the cold. She had a cell phone to her ear and looked frustrated.

As he watched, she threw the phone so that it slammed into the asphalt and broke into several pieces.

There were times in Tripp's life when he chose to do things that he knew would get him into trouble, and even before he got out of the truck he knew this was one of them.

He stopped to pick up the pieces of the phone on his way across the parking lot. The only piece he didn't see was the phone's back cover. He fitted the battery into its empty slot.

Jolene leaned against the concrete wall as though she were too tired to stand.

"You might want to turn it on and see if it works," he said, holding the phone out to her.

She looked from his face to his outstretched hand. "Sure, thanks," she said. She took the phone and stuffed it into the jacket pocket. "I know that was stupid."

"Feeling any better?" His voice cracked like a teenager's. Embarrassed, he cleared his throat to cover it.

Now that he was close to her, he saw she was much younger than she looked onstage. Without makeup, her skin was as clear as a child's. If it weren't for the half-moon shadows beneath her eyes, she wouldn't even look old enough to drive.

"I need to go back in and find a ride," she said. "The cab people said they can't get me for another hour."

Tripp laughed. "You know they only have two cars," he said.

"Figures," she said, without any hint of suspicion or annoyance. For a local girl, she didn't have much of an accent. She smiled. "Not much call for cabs here, I guess. Maybe you could run me home?"

As they walked toward his truck, Jolene moved slowly, telling him she thought she probably had the flu.

He was surprised to find she trusted him to take her home on the proof of his DNR badge and his word that Dwight knew him well enough. He tossed her backpack into the backseat of the king cab and helped her in, reminding her to buckle her seat belt. Shutting the door after her, Tripp found himself smiling, but the smile quickly faded when he saw Lila's white SUV jerk to a stop in front of his truck.

Shit.

He walked up to the SUV's passenger window, which came down.

"Hey," he said.

Lila was wearing her favorite oversize sunglasses even though it was pitch-dark outside the glow of the parking lot lights. Her face was turned toward him, but because of the glasses, he couldn't tell if she was looking at him or past him and into the cab of his pickup. Something about the set of her well-lipsticked mouth told him she had already gotten a good look at the girl.

"Missed you," he said. "I wish you'd called me today."

She didn't say anything.

"Bud out of town? Want to come up to the cabin?"

Lila took off the glasses. Sometimes she wore them when she had been drinking, but now she looked dead sober. The coyote collar of her jacket nestled against her jaw, and she had her hair clipped at the crown of her head so that just a few curls spilled down. She definitely hadn't been sitting at home all evening, but her silence was starting to get to him. Despite the presence of a teenage stripper in his truck, he hadn't actually done anything wrong.

"You going to talk to me, or what?" He was getting cold standing there. It was warm in the truck and the kid was waiting, sick.

Lila's lips moved a bit and he thought she was going to speak. Instead, she spat at him. It didn't hit him, or even make it to the window.

"Now, why did you want to go and do that?" he said, fighting a sudden urge to laugh. Even when she was being a flat-out bitch, Lila was beautiful to him. If she had been angry before, now she was embarrassed and angry. Not a combination likely to increase his chances of seeing her at the cabin anytime soon.

"Just so you know, Bud says those girls are always getting crabs," Lila said. "Enjoy."

She hit the gas hard enough that Tripp had to jump back or else be thrown to the ground. Once she was out of the parking lot, she gunned the SUV. He hoped for her sake that the county cops weren't hanging around, watching for DUIs leaving the club. She was pissed off now, but he was pretty certain she would call him, if not in an hour then the next day. The make-up sex would be killer.

When the SUV's taillights had disappeared, he went back to the truck.

"Ready to go?" he said.

"She was mad," Jolene said.

"Just a misunderstanding. It'll blow over." He shut the door and put the truck in gear, hoping he was right.

She shifted on the seat so she could rest the back of her head against the passenger window. "Really? I hear Mrs. Tucker holds a pretty mean grudge," she said.

He could feel her watching him as they left the lot, driving west up the highway, directly opposite from the direction Lila had gone. Of course she would know who Lila was. That meant she probably knew exactly who he was, too.

CHAPTER SIX

JOLENE STUFFED THE CLASSIFIED AD she had torn from Alta's weekly paper into a pocket of her jeans, and shut the front door of Charity's trailer behind her as softly as she could. Outside, she lifted her face to the sky, welcoming the morning's misty rain. Pulling her mane of coal-black hair around so that it fell over one shoulder, she put up the hood of the white winter jacket she had bought with part of her first paycheck from The Twilight Club. Most of the rest of the cash had gone to things like toothpaste and makeup - including several sets of false eyelashes - and a card that added minutes to the pay-as-you-go cell phone she had tossed in the parking lot. She had twelve dollars left in the zippered change purse in her back pocket.

Walking, she kept her head bowed, and stuck as close as she could to the parts of the road covered with more gravel than mud. There were homelier places than Windswept Holiday Park on and around Devil's Oven, but few of them gave off such strong waves of despair. She remembered it as new, the dozens of trailers painted vivid apricot or robin's-egg blue, and the cheerful, twelve-foot neon sign posted at the entrance. Now the faded paint couldn't hide the auras of gray and maroon and brown and green that bathed the people who lived here. Almost no one was happy.

Most of the trailer park's residents didn't show themselves until noon. But sleep was something different to Jolene, something none of them would understand. She had lain within the rocky flesh of Devil's Oven for three decades, neither waking nor sleeping. Conscious but not breathing, unaware of time passing. It had been just two weeks since she had come - naked and cold - off the mountain, close to the electric co-op facility where Charity's boyfriend, Eli, worked as a night watchman. But already she was feeling penned-in, anxious to get on with what she had come back to do. Whatever it was. *Why can't I be certain?*

Again, she was a different person. Again, nineteen. The face she discovered in the soft light of Charity's bathroom mirror was much thinner than she remembered. Her blue eyes and hair, once as white as a snow fox's fur, had gone dark as chestnuts, as though being buried all those years had caused them to take on the same color as the mountain's scant topsoil.

But how she looked didn't matter to Jolene. She was done with that foolishness. The first time she had been released, confused and terrified, from the mountain's heart, she had called herself Mary, unable to think of any other name. It was the name given to her by her mother, from whom she had fled over a century earlier. It was the only thing she had escaped with. This time, she had chosen Jolene, because of the song.

She did have a mother once, and a father who called himself a preacher when it was convenient. She knew good from evil, and a hundred or thirty years didn't change their definitions. Which one applied to her, she wasn't sure. The choices she made, the things she did, the people she touched weren't really choices. There was a hand guiding her. A strong hand. She was its revelation in the world.

⋅◄ ♠ ◢ ⋅

The Git 'N' Go Mini-Mart was out on the highway, a six - or seven-minute walk from Charity's trailer. But already Jolene's clothes felt heavy with rain. The sullen teenager behind the counter didn't bother to look up from her magazine when she entered the store.

Jolene took a blue energy drink from the cooler at the back, and lingered in the aisle packed with chips and packaged cakes and donuts. She picked up a bag of corn chips and a pair of orange-iced cupcakes and took everything to the register.

"Five eighty-eight," the girl said after ringing it up. "You want a bag?"

Jolene shook her head. "No, thanks," she said.

The girl went back to flipping through her magazine before Jolene was out the door.

If the girl had acknowledged her or been the slightest bit friendly, Jolene might have said something kind to her, or suggested she get to a doctor. The girl's aura was a sickly gray-green, and there were fist-sized spots of black hovering over her liver and lungs. But Jolene didn't consider herself perfect, or even necessarily good. She couldn't save everyone. The only thing she was certain of was that she was here to help Ivy, the girl-now-woman who had been her daughter for five short years.

CHAPTER SEVEN

JOLENE STOOD IN THE GRAVEL DRIVEWAY, adjusting to the timbre of the land that had been her home so many decades earlier. The rain had finally stopped. Clumps of gray vapor hugged the low spots on the ground. She had expected to feel immediately better, being so close to the mountain. *Being home.* Instead she felt anxious, and just as nauseated as she had been the night before.

The DNR guy, Tripp, had helped her into Charity's trailer, even though they both knew that every moment he spent with her would count against him with Mrs. Tucker. Jolene didn't like it at all that he had taken another man's wife, especially Bud's wife. She liked Bud a lot, and he deserved better. And there was something dark hanging over Tripp, a shadow that seemed to be hunting him. Waiting. But she had more on her mind now than the mistakes of a weak-spirited man.

After she left the Git 'n' Go, a woman in a red minivan had picked her up as she walked slowly west in the drizzling rain. She had barely heard the woman's chatter during the five-minute drive up the state highway. Had Jolene even said thank you? She couldn't remember.

The Luttrell land - the part of it that swept out from

the mountainside - had long ago been cleared of everything except a few stands of oak, and a single weeping willow tree whose winter-stripped branches hung limply like skeletons' hair. Two rows of poplar seedlings lined the driveway leading to a tidy ranch house that didn't look more than five or six years old. A flag, painted with spring flowers bursting from a basket, fluttered from a pole attached to one of the porch pillars. In the center of the lawn, a quaint white sign painted with deep blue letters swung from a post: IVY LUTTRELL, FINE SEWING AND ALTERATIONS.

Let me help, Mommy! Little Ivy, usually so timid, pressed against her as she added a few final hand stitches to the pocket of the jumper she was making. She could feel Ivy's steady breath on her cheek - honey and pretzels, the afternoon snack Ivy had made all by herself. Cartoon music streamed from the television in the bedroom, but Ivy had been drawn away from it by her mother's work. Ivy's small fingers, still plump with baby fat, anxiously patted the dotted Swiss cotton as though it were some kind of pet. Ivy the star-wisher, Ivy the careful reorganizer of kitchen drawers, Ivy of the solemn tears. Ivy, who would soon go to kindergarten, where her harelip would make her the object of fear and derision. Her mother stopped sewing. She settled Ivy in her own chair, laid the jumper on her lap, and watched as Ivy, her face a picture of pleasure and intensity, finished the pocket, never asking once for help.

Not long after, Ivy had made herself a colorful, armless doll she called Lolly Dolly and carried with her everywhere. She had other toys, but her mother saw that the doll was important because she had made it.

The cheerfulness of the house was overshadowed by the collection of tired buildings crowded against the hillside, especially the trailer where she had lived after Byron Luttrell had taken her in.

Jolene knew the ragged, collapsing barn and the copper-roofed smoke shack well. Their painted exteriors, once a promising red - she had picked the color herself - had dulled and peeled so that shaggy stripes of gray cedar showed through. An uprooted tree had crashed down from the mountain, making an open wound in the barn's roof. The trailer she had once lived in was badly rusted now, and clung to the mountain in prostrate desperation.

Mommy, why does it sound like someone's crying?

It's the wind trying to get inside because it's cold out there. Aren't you glad you're inside with Daddy and me?

The muddy path leading from the trailer up the hillside disappeared in the trees.

Jolene closed her eyes. She thought about how she could take that path up, up onto the mountain and keep walking east, through the high, piney section of the forest, then eventually make her way to the eastern face, the part of Devil's Oven she liked best. It wasn't time for that yet, but she liked the idea that she could if she really wanted to. Now, she just wanted to see her Ivy.

A woman with eyes the color of wild blue columbine came silently into the living room, where Jolene stood shivering in her wet jeans. Her milky, fair skin gave no hints of her age. Jolene knew the woman was almost thirty-six, but she might have been in her early twenties. Her chambray dress was cinched at her tiny waist and covered by a pristine white apron with enormous patch pockets. A woman-child.

Ivy.

Thirty years had passed since she had held Ivy in her arms, and Jolene was afraid she might not be able to speak without bursting into tears. Those years away from her child

- a child she couldn't ever claim - crushed her as though she were still buried in the earth. She had to stop herself from reaching out to touch Ivy's white-blonde hair.

"Are you here for alterations?" Ivy said. Her voice was quiet, cautious, but there was no recognition in her eyes. Jolene looked like a stranger to her. Jolene *was* a stranger.

"No," Jolene answered before Thora, the other woman in the room, could answer for her. She tried not to stare at Ivy's changed face. The harelip was now just a crescent scar, a tightness across her upper lip. Jolene was relieved to see that someone - who? - had made sure Ivy got the surgery she needed.

"I'm here about renting the trailer. The one up the hill?" She addressed Ivy. Only Ivy.

Thora lifted her rubber-tipped cane a few inches and thumped it firmly on the rug.

"It's been empty for too long, Ivy," Thora said. "Now's the time."

Seeing Thora had been a shock. The cross, loping teenager who had never been happy with Jolene as a stepmother had turned into a disappointed and angry woman. Her once-strong arms were meaty in her shapeless turtleneck, and her stomach bulged both above and below the waistband of her stretch pants. The only thing that hadn't changed about her was the stony set to her eyes, an instant distrust of anyone and anything that was strange to her. Even her intimidating height was gone, stolen by the crooked angle of her back. But it was Thora's aura - mottled gray and weak - that revealed what was really happening to her: she was dying.

Jolene couldn't help but pity her. As she came into the house, she had tried to keep her inner sight unfocused. There was only so much pain she could stand to witness, and the house was filled with it. Plus, the nausea from the previous night was back.

"Oh, Thora," Ivy said. "Why didn't you tell me? We should have talked about it."

Even in the stifling room, with a space heater humming beside the recliner facing the television, Jolene felt an icy energy between them.

"We had renters up there for a whole year," Thora said. "What's there to discuss?"

"It's not clean," Ivy said. "And one of the toilets doesn't work." She pushed her hands into the front pockets of the apron. Jolene watched as Ivy's lavender aura - the aura she was born with, indicating she was intuitive, sensitive, creative - flushed with waves of deep, troubled blue. She was hiding something.

"It's just you wants to rent?" Thora stared into Jolene's eyes. She had always been suspicious. Jolene had tried so hard to love her. She could see the hurt in Thora, but could never heal it.

"Just me."

"I already told you it wouldn't be ready for a couple of weeks." She nodded to Ivy. "Plenty of time for a plumber."

"Why don't you come back then?" Ivy said. "If you haven't already found a place." Her smile was awkward, as though she didn't smile often, and Jolene wondered if maybe the scar tissue had become inelastic, making it difficult. She didn't want to think that Ivy had nothing to smile about.

"Why should she rent somewhere else when *our* trailer's empty?" Thora said. "Doesn't make any sense."

"It's okay," Jolene said. "I can wait. But if you really don't want tenants…" Despite the tension in the room, she knew she could stay there for hours. Days. She wanted to sit and watch them, to know how they were living. What made them happy, or sad. If she stayed there, she could keep Ivy safe. She might feel truly human again. Love again, and be loved in return.

Thora put her arm out as though she would stop Jolene from leaving.

"No," she said. "I'm going to take you up and show you the trailer. It belongs to me as much as it does to *her*." She lifted the cane and poked it toward Ivy.

Ivy took a single step toward them. "Let's talk about this." She glanced at Jolene. "It doesn't feel right."

"Feelings this, feelings that," Thora said. "We're not made of money. Another two-fifty a month would make a real difference. We've got the power turned on up there for no good reason at all."

Jolene watched Ivy's face. Thora obviously still intimidated her; another few minutes of tension might break her. Thora hadn't dared be so aggressive with Ivy when the girls had been younger. Ivy had been more like an annoying little pet to her older sister. A pet who easily stole the small amount of affection their father had to give.

Now, even Jolene was starting to feel overwhelmed. *So much pain. Fear.* She wanted to run for the shelter of the woods.

No. Not this time. This time I'm staying.

Ivy was almost begging. "I've got bills out for two wedding dresses, and two more ready to go. We're fine for money."

"Really," Jolene said, anxious. She hadn't wanted to bring them strife. She had just wanted to see them. "I'll go. I can come back."

Thora was limping toward the door. "I'll get my jacket," she said.

Jolene felt a sudden rush of something - heat? - from behind her. The movement in the air made her dizzy. She turned to see Ivy, her face a mask of false serenity. The blue-gray aura cloaking her was misty, but it fluctuated, strengthening.

"If you take her up there, I'll leave," Ivy said, no longer sounding fretful. "Someone else will have to move in here and take care of you."

Thora's hand dropped from the closet's door handle.

Jolene was suddenly aware of all the medical equipment around them: a tank of oxygen on its wheeled base, the packaged syringe on the television table beside the recliner, the box of disposable gloves on another table.

Now Thora was looking at Ivy as though *she* were the stranger in the room.

Sunlight pushed through the clouds as Jolene started down the highway, not back to town, but west, to where the Luttrell land met a thick stand of trees. The wind had warmed some and she unzipped her jacket. Within a few minutes, she had made her way up into the woods, following the rise until she was sure no one in or near the house could see her. Then she took off her too-noticeable white jacket and laid it at the base of a dogwood that was thick with tight brown buds.

Ivy had offered to drive her back into town as an apology for Jolene's wasted trip, but Jolene had demurred. As much as she would have liked to spend time with Ivy, even as a stranger, she had needed the excuse to leave on her own. Ivy, who as a child had never been comfortable with a lie, was definitely hiding something. She didn't want anyone near the trailer, and Jolene suspected she had a dangerous reason for both her fear and secrecy.

The ground above the trailer wasn't as soft as it had been down near the house. She squatted in the leaves, loving the familiar scent of the wet woods, watching the house to see if either of the women would come outside. The morning's raindrops slipped from branch to branch in a rhythm as familiar as her own breath.

When she decided it was safe, Jolene half-ran, half-slid down to the trailer's back porch, keeping her head low as she went.

The curtains were drawn, but she pressed herself against a window to peek through the narrow gap between the curtain panels. She could see outlines of furniture - a broad, high table in front of a couch; a bookcase; a chair. She relaxed, allowing what little she could see to make an impression on her mind. The light was faint and the shapes diffuse, but everything shared the same flat, dull quality. When she had lived here, she had tried to make it a bright, happy place, with covered pillows and houseplants in the windows. That was all gone.

The wind picked up, spreading gooseflesh over her exposed arms. A few feet away, the storm door squeaked open a few inches, then banged shut. Unafraid, Jolene moved away from the window and put her hand on the door's tarnished handle.

She went inside.

CHAPTER EIGHT

SQUATTING BEHIND THE DUMPSTER of the Git 'n' Go, he scratched the tender skin surrounding the stitches at his left wrist. He was careful not to worry the fragile bits of thread, somehow understanding that he might damage them.

He could make out each distinct odor coming from the Dumpster - rotting lettuce and sausage, crusted nacho cheese, soiled diapers and tissues, soggy cardboard, stale beer, and sweet pop of some kind. But none was the scent he had been wanting, waiting for, the scent he had been searching for since leaving the trailer, keeping to the edge of the woods and shadowed walls and fences, until finally picking it up near the Git 'n' Go. At first he had been drawn to the blue car parked behind the store, but no one was inside so he followed the scent right up to the store's back door.

He rolled back on his bare heels, hardly feeling the bits of gravel and glass beneath them. Once his senses had been in almost perfect balance, dulled very occasionally by fine whiskey and, even less frequently, a particular blend of soil-brown hashish, but now they were warped or heightened or shrunken, depending. He didn't know the difference anymore.

He closed his eyes and time passed. He breathed in,

breathed out.

The back door scraped open.

"Ain't my fault if she chooses to be late. I'm fine with the overtime."

He caught the woman's scent as she passed between the Dumpster and the door. She wasn't the one, but she carried the scent of the one he was waiting for. She flung something heavy into the Dumpster and went back inside.

He closed his eyes again, remembering a woman's fingers on his skin. He remembered the close smell of the room where he first opened his eyes. He remembered *hungry* and, for a fleeting moment, thought about food.

The second time the door opened, he covered his ears with his hands to protect them from the hideous grating sound it made against the pavement. He didn't need to hear the woman's voice to know she was there and that she wasn't alone.

"Slide that stack of pallets this way, Claude," she said. "Those morons don't know the difference between the left and right sides of the stupid door."

"So what does all this labor get me, is what I want to know."

He breathed in, opened his eyes. He moved.

"*Somebody* has to take care - Sweet Jesus!"

The woman stared up at him. She was short but a yard wide, wearing a black-and-white-splotched tunic. She spread her arms, palms away from him, as though she was shielding Claude, who stood slack-jawed behind her.

His eyes fixed on Claude, and he smiled. He swept the woman out of his way, not for a second feeling the bulk of her. When she hit the security door of the Git 'n' Go, her shoulder cracked.

Claude didn't even see what happened to her, didn't hear her

low-pitched oooomph of pain. He could only stare at the thing in front of him, the smiling, shirtless hulk of a man. The man's torso and arms were covered with curling black hairs, and the memory of a swimming instructor he had when he was seven flashed into Claude's mind. Then the man's hand was on his neck and his back was against the wall and before he lost consciousness, he saw that the man's smile looked frozen on his broad, handsome face.

He ran. Claude was slung over one shoulder. He didn't like the heat of Claude's body against him, and the way Claude's head and arms flopped against his back. Something about it repelled him, but he knew he had to keep running and stay to the edges of town until he could get up the mountain. There was no map to follow; he only knew he had to keep going up, up, up. But there was something happening inside him as he ran. It wasn't a feeling, but a vibrant memory that drove him forward. It was the memory of happiness. The memory of a job well done.

CHAPTER NINE

TRIPP PULLED THE PICKUP AROUND his state-issued vehicle and parked beneath the cabin's carport. The cabin's windows were depressingly dark. Just like every other time he returned late at night, he thought how nice it would be to have a lamp on a timer or something. A dark house looked too empty. Not frightening - he couldn't think of a single thing that really frightened him - but soulless.

Ten or eleven years earlier, he had even had a girl named Darla living with him. The sex was good, but she had used his money to buy so many tiny, absurd beanbag animals that the shipping boxes had crowded them out of the living room and half-filled the bedroom. But before the spring was over, she had gone back to her home in the next state, disappointed he wasn't going to marry her and let her add on to the cabin to make room for all the toys.

The trouble was, once he had seen Lila again after a dozen years of almost forgetting her, he couldn't see beyond her. She still made him feel weak inside, desperate to have her look his way, embarrassed at his raw need to put his hands on her. He had bided his time, though, eased himself into her view. She had never been the kind of girl to sleep around, despite the fact that no man with a half-working dick could see her and not want her. And she loved Bud. She swore it nearly every time they were together. Tripp wasn't a man who believed in taking another man's wife, but all bets were off with Lila.

Inside, he turned on the lights. Anyone who had been in the cabin before Lila started spending time there would certainly know the difference. Now there were taupe pillows on his army green couch, a couple of prints of masculine paintings of dogs, and dead game on the wall instead of the sports-car-and-beer-girl posters he'd had since college. There was also a cappuccino maker on the kitchen counter. He didn't even like coffee.

He set his wallet and keys beside his holstered .44. Lila gave him hell about keeping it out in the open, but he had gotten very good at changing the subject with her. Usually it entailed telling her how glad he was to have her there or just putting his mouth on hers.

Taking himself out to dinner at the mall in the next county over had done nothing to cheer him. Lila hadn't answered her phone or any of his texts all day long. Knowing Bud was out of town didn't help. What the hell was she doing? Was she with another man? The thought made his body tense. It was bad enough that he had to compete with Bud, but he had learned to handle it. After all, she was married to Bud, a situation he hadn't been able to convince her to change. If she was punishing him by screwing someone else, that was bad. She didn't get to do that.

After getting a beer from the refrigerator, he cued up an episode of a cop drama on the DVR and sat down in front of the television. But the show didn't hold his interest, and he fell asleep thinking not of Lila but the dancer, Jolene, and how she had seemed out of place entering the single-wide in which she was staying, like she was some kind of princess in disguise. He wanted to forget how he had thought of her the night before, hated the part of him that had imagined her hurt and helpless on the mountain trail. He had never had threatening

thoughts about a woman before, and certainly had never actually hurt one. Ever.

Tripp startled awake at the sound of three beeps from a car
horn down on the road - Lila's signal that she was on her way
up the hill. There were no lights for at least half a mile around
the cabin, so even on clear nights like this one, when the
moon was high, she wanted him to come out and meet her. As
he stumbled out of his chair, he knocked over the half-empty
beer bottle, spilling flat beer all over the coffee table. Swearing,
he grabbed the fuzzy brown throw Lila had brought on her last
visit and soaked up as much as he could. The show had ended.
It was ten minutes before midnight.

Had she decided to forgive him? Or was she just there
to bust his chops? Assuming it was the second choice, he took
a wide stance on the front porch to show her he wasn't at all
concerned that she was angry. *Where did she spend the day? Who
has she been with?*

The lights of the big SUV bounced as it came through
the rut at the front of the driveway. But before it was halfway
up the five-hundred-foot distance to the cabin, Tripp saw, in
the truck's stark halogen beams, a flash of movement in the
woods to the west. There was a rushing noise as well, as though
an animal were about to break out of the trees, but the sound
disappeared in the roar of the truck's engine. Tripp stiffened.
Lila wasn't driving fast enough for a deer to do serious damage
to the truck, but it wasn't going to be pretty. He could only
watch, helpless, as something burst into the open and landed
thirty feet or so in front of the vehicle.

Had Lila seen it? Tripp ran toward the truck, waving
his arms and shouting for her to stop. What the hell was lying
in his driveway? A deer? And why wasn't it moving away? The
SUV stopped just a few feet short of whatever it was, and sat
idling.

He raised his arm to keep Lila in the vehicle. "Stay back!" he shouted, hoping she could hear him in the truck's quiet interior.

The headlights cast the thing on the ground in vivid detail. At first the bloody mass at one end confused him, but he made out a sport shirt and dark blue jeans easily enough. Realizing it was a man - a small one, but still a man - he took two steps back and had to fight the urge to vomit.

"Tripp?" Lila called. She had the SUV's door open and had stepped onto the running board. "What in the hell?"

Unable to speak, Tripp just looked up at her.

"Tripp?" Leaving the door open, she got down and came around to the front of the vehicle.

Then the screaming started.

When Lila stirred on the couch, Tripp came right over to her side. He had the phone in his hand, but laid it on the coffee table so he could keep her from trying to sit up. An angry bruise had started to form on her left temple, where she banged it against the truck when she fell.

In his lifetime - particularly in his job as a Department of Natural Resources officer - Tripp had seen many bodies, some burned so thoroughly that the bones crumbled to gray dust at a touch, others melted into the earth where they had fallen. He didn't like to think about this one at all, though. He had never seen that kind of violence done to a human being, and hated that Lila had witnessed it, too.

"Baby," he said, brushing her hair back from her forehead. "Can you open your eyes?"

Her lips moved and she seemed to whisper. Tripp bent closer to her face.

"Lila, you need to wake up," he said.

When she finally opened her eyes, she stared at his face, but seemed not to know him. Then she put her hand to his jaw and pushed him away with a cry. Before he could react, she jumped up from the couch.

"I have to get home!" she screamed. "I have to find Bud!"

The patterned silk blouse she wore beneath her suede jacket gaped open at her chest, the button lost. Her lipstick was smeared and the ends of her hair were dusty from the driveway. Tripp held his hands out to try to touch her, to calm her.

"Shhhhh," he said. "Baby, it's going to be okay. You don't want to go outside. Just stay here with me. We'll get this sorted out. You hit your head."

"There's a freaking *person* out there," she said. "I didn't dream it. I'm not asleep!" She was shaking, holding herself as though she were freezing in the heated cabin.

Tripp grabbed the throw from the couch. "Listen, Lila." He tried to put the beer-damp throw around her but she edged away.

"No," she said. "We've got to get somebody. We've got to see if he's alive."

"You need to stay warm. I don't want you going into shock." He knew he was probably in shock himself, but he could only fall back on his professional training. Training was supposed to kick in when your emotions were on overdrive, when there was a gun in your face, or a firebreak that wasn't holding. Why in the hell hadn't anyone trained him for a mangled - *hey, that's a good word, but hardly sufficient* - body in the driveway?

He didn't know what did it, but he saw the fight drain out of Lila's eyes. Her shoulders dropped.

"God," she said, "who was he?"

Tripp put the blanket around her and pulled her close to him. They held on to each other. He buried his face in her hair, and the smell of it broke the pressure inside him. He knew if he pulled away from her, if he saw her tears, he would break down as well. His training against doing that was damn solid, but there were things that even training couldn't get you through. He told himself it was just his concern for Lila that had him feeling like this, that he could get a grip on himself and everything would be okay again. But the truth of it was, everything had changed the minute he walked out onto his porch and there wasn't a damn thing he could do about it.

CHAPTER TEN

"IVY! IVY!"

Ivy woke to see Thora bent over her, her thinning hair pushed back by the black elastic headband in which she always slept. For just a second Ivy was confused, thinking it was her father trying to wake her. Thora's grip on her arm was tight and painful.

"Where's the shotgun?" Thora said.

"What's wrong?" Ivy said, twisting her arm away. Thora let her go. Outside the window, the only light came from the fixture over the entrance to the barn. It was still night.

"There's somebody up at the trailer," Thora said. "I bet it's kids. I bet they're up there drinking. Remember when I found that rubber in the driveway a few weeks ago? I told you I didn't like those band kids coming out here for uniforms. Get the shotgun!"

Ivy, now fully awake, knew it wasn't teenagers. She had to keep Thora from panicking.

She had lain sleepless in bed for over two hours after she said good night to Thora, who liked to stay up and watch the late-night comedy shows.

After supper, in defiance of Thora's morning judgment, she had gone back up to the trailer, wanting to be near Anthony, to touch him. The air felt heavy, like the rain might start all over again, and her feet seemed to drag as she walked up the hill. Something was wrong. She could feel it. She almost turned and ran back to the house.

Maybe it had been a dream after all.

Anthony was gone.

Her sewing materials sat in a neat pile on the kitchen counter where she had left them. The door of the master bedroom closet stood open, but she might have done that herself and forgotten. Thora was always complaining that she was careless that way. Walking from bedroom to bedroom and back to the kitchen, her panic skyrocketed. Had someone found him and taken him away? *Impossible.* Thora couldn't have managed it, and even if she had, she certainly wouldn't have kept it a secret. Also, the blue jeans she'd bought for him even before she had sewn him back together were gone.

The only answer was that Anthony had left on his own.

The idea both thrilled and frightened Ivy. She managed to get through Missy's final fitting, but the girl had what Thora called "bride's brain" and hadn't noticed anything beyond her own image in the mirror. After the girl was gone, Thora watched Ivy carefully, so she had retreated to her workroom to sew. Her mind was busy, worrying. Wondering. Marveling.

What have I done?

"Go back to bed," Ivy said. "I'll take care of it."

Thora shook her head. The unadorned nightgown Ivy had made at her request caused Thora to look even larger than she was, like an overfed ghost.

"Those kids aren't going to be afraid of you," Thora said. "We'll both go. Or maybe we should just call the sheriff."

Now it was Ivy's turn to grab her sister's arm.

"We don't need to call the police," Ivy said. "Just let me take care of it. You stay here."

"Why?" Thora said. She stood up to her full height, dwarfing Ivy. "Who's out there?"

Ivy heard the familiar note of suspicion in Thora's voice, that reminder of Thora's deep need to be certain she wasn't being cheated out of some useful bit of information, or missing out on some advantage. Hours earlier, Ivy had been hopeful that her threat to leave would keep Thora compliant. Now she understood that Thora could spoil everything.

But as miserable as that possibility was, the truly important thing was Anthony had come back to her!

Glancing at the clock, she saw it was almost four a.m. Dawn was only a couple of hours away. She turned on her bedside lamp.

"You'll want to put on some clothes," Ivy said. "We'll take the car up to the trailer so you don't have to walk. I know where the gun is, but we won't need it."

CHAPTER ELEVEN

HE THREW OPEN the trailer's kitchen cabinets, looking for food. But only the scent of it remained, and his frustration grew as he searched. As he moved through the kitchen, he left the cabinet doors standing open, their handles smeared with clotted blood. He needed food to stop the pain in his gut. Claude, whose scent was so rich and inviting, had piqued the hunger that had started when he sat waiting behind the Dumpster, but he understood that Claude wasn't food. Food was something else and there was none of it here.

The food from his past came to him in vivid images: meat, red and thick and dripping on colorful plates; fish, cold, raw fish handed to him on blocks of wood by smiling, dark-eyed women; bread stuffed with sausage and red tomatoes and onions. Strawberries smothered with white whipped cream, and plates of noodles and sharp cheese and olives. Warm red grapes plucked from vines curling around their wooden staves. He couldn't name these things, but he could think of them, see them, but not touch. It was maddening, and he slammed the cabinet doors, busting one in with his knee so that the flimsy wood buckled at the force. This need for food was even stronger than his need to find the man called Claude had been. He would have to go in search of it, too.

The woman had been here, leaving behind her scent of
garden flowers and something else, something that reminded
him of steam-covered windows and noisy machines and freshly
pressed clothes. He put his hands to his chest, as though the
answers were there. He left the kitchen to go and find her.

It didn't surprise him to discover two women standing in the living room. Surprise was no longer in his catalog of
reactions.

One of them cradled a rusty shovel in her arms and he
knew she meant him harm. Her scent was acrid and offensive
to him, but there was something sweet in it, too, like the smell
of something cooking.

The second woman, the smaller one, was the woman
he was looking for, the woman he knew. He was compelled to
be near her, though compulsion was now just instinct to him.
She held food out to him, in one hand something brown that
smelled of cinnamon and oranges, in the other a banana.

"Put the shovel down, Thora," she said, her voice soft.

Was *Thora* what he was called? It didn't sound right,
but he wasn't sure. He looked down at his hands and looked
back to the smaller woman for some answer.

"He's got blood all over him," the other woman said.
"Sweet Jesus, he's done something. I know he's done something and he means to kill us."

"He's afraid of you. Please go outside."

"I'll be damned if I will." But she took a step back,
toward the door.

He wanted to jump at the food, but knew he
shouldn't.

The other woman made another slight move toward
the door. Now she gave off a smell like Claude did just before
he put his hand on Claude's neck. He knew the smell. She
wanted to run away.

The smaller woman, the one with the light hair and
twisted smile, set the food on the table and stepped away.

"Stay out of his way," she said.

Then she smiled at him.

"Go ahead, Anthony." She still smelled of garden flowers and he thought about her hands and how they had felt on his skin. It gave him pleasure to think of it, but his hunger overwhelmed him and he grabbed for the food.

He forgot the women as he ate, filling his mouth with the rich brown bread. It tasted like nothing he had ever eaten before.

CHAPTER TWELVE

"IT'S SICK, is what it is," Thora said. "He's not some stray dog. Good God, Ivy. He could kill us in our sleep. What's in your head?"

She was following Ivy up the front porch steps. The monster her sister called Anthony had devoured the loaf of spice bread, shoving it into his mouth in huge, crumbling chunks. After drinking two tall glasses of water that Ivy filled for him, he sank onto the couch. She had watched as Ivy helped him stretch out on the cushions, and then tucked a throw pillow beneath his head. This man - if that's what he was - was possibly the biggest one Thora had ever seen. He was so long that his lower legs and feet hung over the arm of the couch. He had looked up at Ivy, his eyes expressionless, but his chapped, full lips curved in a drowsy smile. His eyes were mahogany brown, like his hair. Through it all, he hadn't said a word, making Thora wonder if he could talk at all.

"But he's like a child," Ivy said. "We have to help him."

"I want to know how he came to be living in our trailer," Thora said. On the porch, she propped the shovel against the railing, thinking, *We should have taken the shotgun.*

They went inside.

Dear Lord, there's a monster of a man in our trailer cov-

ered in blood that's not his own. And Ivy is delusional.

"He came off the mountain," Ivy said, continuing toward the kitchen. "I'm hungry. Are you?"

Thora, too, had awakened hungry; she always did. But her mouth had gone dry and she was so shaken that she thought she might be sick if she tried to eat or drink.

"What do you mean?" Thora said. "Ivy! Stop, now. Tell me!"

Ivy shrugged like a recalcitrant teenager. Outside, dawn was breaking and the first rumbling string of trucks from the quarry a dozen miles away had started its run out on the highway.

Thora had never liked to be rough with Ivy, but now she grabbed her by the shoulder to hold her still. "What do you mean, *he came off the mountain?*"

"I never ask you for anything," Ivy said quietly. "Can't you let me have this? Can't you let me have *him?*"

"You met him up on the mountain? Tell me!" Thora said, shaking her. Despite the controlled tone of Ivy's voice, Thora knew her sister wasn't begging. She had already made the decision to have this...whatever he was. Ivy wouldn't be moved.

Thora stared at her, feeling Ivy's thin shoulder through the wool sweater she had thrown on over her pajamas. Maybe she had always doubted her half sister's sanity. All the hours Ivy spent alone. All the hours she spent sitting behind her sewing machine, creating just the right shape of a wedding dress for some slut whose parents were able to come up with the seven or eight hundred dollars to fraudulently clothe their daughter in one of Ivy Luttrell's innocence-white wedding dresses. Ivy, who had never to Thora's knowledge been on a date with a man. Ivy, who had never displayed anything but shy deference, or a calm, businesslike attitude toward men and women alike. Ivy, who was almost pretty. Ivy, who wouldn't say *boo* to a goose. There was something wrong with Ivy that had to have come by way of Mary, the slight, strange young woman who had seduced and married Thora's father. Whatever that something was, it made Thora afraid, and had kept her from - did she dare even think it? - loving either Ivy or Ivy's mother.

Ivy stood up straighter beneath Thora's hand.

"His name is Anthony, and I made him," she said. "I found him buried on the mountain, and I put him back together." She held up her hands. "I stitched him back together with *these*."

Thora looked more closely into her half sister's angry face, at her lips with their sad, jagged scar. She looked closely, thinking it might help her understand what she had just heard. She saw only madness. She let her hand drop from Ivy's shoulder. *What has Ivy done?*

"You don't believe me," Ivy said, shaking her head. "I knew you wouldn't. Nothing I do is ever good enough for you."

After Ivy's mother had disappeared, and Thora had discovered their father hanging in the woods, Ivy had retreated deep into a private world, making up stories about her mother coming back, about creatures she met up on the mountain. Thora knew she bore some responsibility. She had been too young to take on a child. Far too young. But hadn't she tried? Hadn't she done what their father would've wanted her to do? Now, if Ivy had truly gone mad - and *oh, yes*, it seemed that she had - Thora would have to do something. She felt a headache growing in the back of her skull and knew it was going to be a bad one.

"It's not right, Ivy," Thora said. "You can't own people. I don't know what you think you've done. That man is all wrong. He's dangerous."

"I knew you wouldn't understand," Ivy said. "You've always hated all men except for Daddy. *You're* the one who's afraid."

Before Thora could stop herself, she slapped Ivy's cheek. She had never hit Ivy in anger before, and the act left her shaking and afraid of what she might do next.

Ivy didn't run from her, or even jerk away. Her lips just tightened with resolve.

"I'm going in to work for a while," she said. She started toward the workroom, but then turned back to Thora. "Don't do anything to Anthony."

Thora felt her body go cold.

CHAPTER THIRTEEN

"**C**HRIST ON A CRACKER, Tripp. Something popped this guy's head like a bean."

Tripp knew most of the troopers who worked this part of the state, but he considered Keith Caldwell a friend. When he had called Keith's cell phone around six thirty, waking him up on his day off, Keith had told him it was no problem. Six foot two and a fit two hundred sixty pounds, Keith had been a talented lineman at the state's technical university, but a knee injury had prevented him from moving on to the pros. When he got a few beers in him, he didn't mind talking about his football career, but preferred to talk about coaching his son's Mini League team. Tripp had waited for him down at the entrance to the driveway, watching a gray dawn spread through the sky and pushing away thoughts about reality in the harsh light of day.

"So you woke up this morning, came outside, and found him" - Keith swept his hand over the body - "just lying in your driveway? Seriously?"

Even as a kid, Tripp had been an unconvincing liar, so he tried to meet Keith's eyes in a sincere, unblinking manner. If he couldn't pull it off here in his own driveway, how would he hold up at the trooper station or in front of his own boss, who would soon be there as well?

"I don't know what to say," Tripp told him. "I came out to take a leak, you know, to wake up. I thought it was a dog or a deer or something." He'd had the entire night to think about what his story should be and had decided to keep it simple.

"You know him?" Keith said.

Tripp shook his head. "It's not like I could tell if I did."

Staring down at the body, Keith gave a grunt of assent.

"Maybe check his ID?" Tripp said, hoping to take Keith's focus off of him. He didn't like the way he had to weigh every word against the lies he had already told. He had only been at it in the hour or so since he had called Keith, and he was already weary of the whole thing. It wasn't even like he had murdered the guy or was hiding anything significant. That Lila - or anyone else for that matter - had been with him when the body had basically fallen from the sky and onto his driveway was irrelevant. They had been in the wrong place at the wrong time. Period.

"I've got gloves in the cruiser," Keith said. "Don't suppose you could come up with any coffee there?" He nodded toward the cabin. "Somebody got my ass out of bed awfully early this morning."

"I could probably dig some out of the freezer," Tripp said, thinking about the instant he kept for his very occasional visitors. Then he remembered the machine on his counter. "Or, hey, I can do cappuccino."

Getting Lila calmed down and into some kind of shape to drive herself home had been tough. As they walked past the body she had held tight to him, hiding her face against his shirt, and he had stayed at the truck with her for another ten minutes before letting her drive away. He had watched the taillights of the truck disappear into the dark, then reappear briefly as the road curved away and down the hillside.

Walking back up the drive, he had shined his flashlight on the body, not really wanting to look but feeling compelled. There was no way even to tell what color the guy's hair had been. It was as though the skull had been sucked out the top of the head, leaving behind flaps of lumpy, chewed-up skin. The neck was twisted and stretched, longer and much thinner than it should have been.

Tripp stared, trying to imagine it wasn't human, that it wasn't real. But despite the hash atop the body's shoulders, it was obviously a man. One of his arms had broken at the elbow and lay at an impossible angle. Tripp could only think it had happened as the body landed. He had knelt to take out the wallet whose shape had worn a faded square in the back of the man's pants, but stopped himself, knowing he would be better off not touching the body at all. Later, as he lay in bed not sleeping, he thought he should have covered the body with a tarp or something. That would've been a bad idea, too. If only a bear or pack of coyotes had come through and dragged the thing away. It wasn't a thought he liked; it just would have made everything easier.

Lila called him around four a.m. She had taken a sedative and sounded better, calmer, but wasn't able to sleep, either.

"What will we do?" she said. Her voice was soft in his ear. Tripp hated that she might have been there beside him all night, if it hadn't been for…well, if it hadn't been for a lot of things.

"It's handled," he said. "You can forget about it."

"Sure," she said, giving a rueful laugh.

"Go to sleep," he said. "I love you."

"You sleep, too," she said.

He held the phone to his ear, wanting to hear more, but there was only the sound of the call disconnecting.

"The body" turned out to be Claude Dixon, a dispatcher at Bud Tucker's trucking company. When Tripp came back carrying the steaming cup of cappuccino, Keith showed him Dixon's ID card with its two-inch-square photo. A grinning Claude Dixon hunched forward, squinting at the camera so that his narrow, freckled face loomed. But the eyes beneath his bowl haircut were bright and intelligent, and one got the sense he was born with a sense of humor.

Bud Tucker's company. Lila's husband's company.

Tripp wasn't even able to process the implications before the next thing Keith told him turned everything upside down in his head a second time.

"You're not going to believe this shit," Keith said. "I just found out that Dixon's wife - works at the Git 'n' Go down in Alta - she called in around eleven thirty last night screaming that some giant hairy guy had beaten the crap out of her, assaulted Claude, and then ran off with him."

"Ran off?" Tripp said.

"Threw him over his shoulder like a sack of potatoes, she said. Smiling like some kind of freak. And he wasn't wearing a shirt or shoes."

Tripp shook his head, lost in both relief and confusion. "So how did he - Claude Dixon, I mean - get up here? You think somebody brought him all the way up here to do *that* to him?"

"All I can say, Tripp, is you should be damn grateful that you're under six feet tall and not covered in black hair."

Within the half hour, the hillside was crowded with uniforms and flashing red and white lights. Tripp shifted into professional mode, and with the shift came a huge sense of relief.

He was no longer Keith's sole focus and the area around the body in the driveway was an official crime scene. Everyone there - the state investigators, his DNR co-workers, and even his supervisor, Denise - could be counted on to keep the emotions to a minimum. His palms were still sweating, but he was finally sure he could handle things the way he knew he needed to.

For now, Keith seemed to have his back and was sticking close to the state investigators. He had also sent away the guys who'd shown up from the county-licensed ambulance service. Word had spread about the mutilated state of the body. As people came and went all through the morning, Tripp's front yard took on the air of an impromptu carnival, with Claude Dixon's exploded head as the five-dollar sideshow attraction.

Finally, Burns and Johnson, two of the state's investigators, got around to questioning him. Tripp led them to the front porch where they could have some privacy, and he was glad neither of them asked to go inside. He was fairly certain he had hidden Lila's things, starting with the bra she had playfully left hanging off the back of a chair a few days before, but he didn't want to take any chances.

Burns, sixtysomething and with the relaxed manner of a man who was only a year or two away from retirement, asked the questions. Johnson lounged against the porch railing, picking clean his nails. Easily twenty years younger than Burns, Johnson wasn't as clean-shaven as the state liked their boys to be, and his jacket was badly wrinkled. When he leaned forward to introduce himself, Tripp had noticed a citrusy smell that reminded him of the cologne his kid sister had worn when she was a teenager.

He had also seen Johnson more than once at The Twilight Club. Somebody young like the Jolene girl would appeal to him. The whole Investigator Johnson package was distasteful to Tripp. He was glad it was Burns who spoke, asking him the same questions he himself would have asked of someone with a dead body in their front yard: Had he heard anything in the night? Had anyone been hanging around the cabin? Did he know, or had he ever met, Claude Dixon? Where had he been the night before and with whom? Tripp made sure to mention the name of the restaurant where he had eaten, and that he had stopped to fill up his truck on the way home. Was it his imagination, or did Johnson give a disbelieving snort when he said he had fallen asleep in front of the television before ten? *Believe what you want, asshole. As long as Lila's name stays out of it.*

When they were done with him, the investigators moved off into the woods nearest the drive, and Denise came up to the porch with Keith. Keith asked if he could use the facilities and Tripp waved him inside.

"You doing all right?" Denise asked him when the door closed behind Keith.

Denise was good people. A thirty-year DNR veteran, she had survived six different governors' administrations and an investigation into her alleged use of state money to finance a sweet house on Lake Norfolk. Nothing was proven, and six months later she had melted back into bureaucratic obscurity. Despite being a grandmother of six, Denise, only about five foot two, was compact in her gabardine pantsuit and tailored navy trench coat. The damp had caused her closely trimmed gray hair to curl slightly and her faded blue eyes were concerned. She cared about her people and liked to surround herself with those she felt she could respect and trust.

Tripp nodded. "Hell of a way to wake up," he said.

"I imagine you don't get much excitement in the neighborhood," she said. "How long have you been up here again?"

"Almost twelve years," he said. "As soon as I could afford it." He didn't mention how cheaply he had gotten the place, or how he had bought it off a doctor whose kids had been so spooked by the density of the nighttime woods, and the sounds of coyotes and owls they heard when they came up on the weekends that they refused to ever come back.

"Spotted a timber wolf last week up near the wood pile," Tripp said. "He took off, but he looked pretty well fed."

"Livestock around the place?"

Tripp shook his head. Even small talk felt weird to him, and Denise was always slow to come around to her point. "Nope, I think he was just marking territory."

"You need to take a couple days off to clear this out of your head," she said, gesturing to the uniform-surrounded body. "I can get Becker out of mothballs to cover for you. He's had a good two months since his shoulder surgery. Plus he's driving me crazy at the office." She eyed him closely. "You sure you got some sleep last night? You don't look like you rested very well."

"I'm good," Tripp said. "There's been a lot of activity over on the western boundary. I need to follow up." He knew he probably looked like shit, and it would be like her to notice. "But it can wait."

"Works for me," Denise said. She gave his upper arm a light squeeze. "Keep me posted. Get your beauty sleep."

Tripp watched her walk down the steps and out to her state-issued SUV. She didn't stop to talk to any of the investigators or troopers, but nodded to them as she turned the vehicle in the grass and drove out. He liked Denise. He didn't like to lie to her.

"I don't think the big boys need me hanging around," Keith said behind him. "Ginger and I like to have some alone time while the kids are at school. But I guess I ought to look in at what's happening at the Git 'n' Go first, see if the Jolly Green Giant returned to the scene. Hell of a mess. I wonder where the rest of the poor bastard's head is."

"You know I appreciate you coming up here, man," Tripp said, meaning it. "It was good to see a friendly face after…"

"No face at all?" Keith grimaced. "Sorry. Couldn't resist."

They stood in silence for a moment. Tripp noticed that the bank of bird feeders he kept on the rise in the side yard was completely empty. He had overlooked more than a few things since he started seeing Lila. He felt sometimes like he had let his own life drift away from him while he took on another.

Keith started down the porch steps. When he reached the stone walk, he turned back.

"Hey, did you say you were dating a dancer a while back? What was her name again?"

Tripp said. "Not me, man."

"Damn. Could've sworn you told me you were dating a redhead from the club. Or maybe someone said they saw you out."

"Must have been someone else," Tripp said. *Bullshit. No one saw me with Lila. We're too careful.* Then he remembered what Jolene had said about Lila. "I gave one a ride home the other night. But she had black hair, and I wouldn't call it any kind of date."

"That's what they all say," Keith said. He grinned.

Tripp shook his head. "Plus, if The Twilight Club had a redhead, I never noticed."

Keith laughed. "You wouldn't," he said. "I'll let you know as soon as I hear anything, but I think the big boys will stay in touch. By the way, you make a helluva cappuccino. Don't let anybody tell you different."

As much as Tripp wanted to follow Keith off the mountain and drive straight to Lila's place, he knew he had to stay where he was. Lila, and probably Bud, were themselves certainly dealing with the sheriff's deputies and Bud's trucking employees. In fact, Tripp was kind of surprised that Bud himself hadn't shown up to take a look at Claude Dixon's body. Bud was that kind of guy - big and big-hearted and stubbornly honest. At the club, he was surrounded by half-naked girls any given time of day or night, but despite Lila's paranoia, there was never even a hint he was screwing around with any of them.

No, Bud didn't deserve the kind of treatment he was getting from either Tripp or his own wife. But Bud didn't deserve Lila, either.

The coroner's SUV, the state investigators, and the crime scene team were gone by four in the afternoon. As Tripp watched the last vehicle drive off, the exhaustion overtook him and he could think only of crawling back into the bed he had abandoned so early that morning. Instead, he made himself a bologna sandwich with mustard and ate it in front of the sliding glass door that looked out on the primitive backyard. The doctor he had bought the house from had cleared the yard of stumps and tried to plant some grass, but there was way too much shade from the surrounding forest and it had never taken off. The yard was also smaller now than when he had bought the place. Mindful of fire hazards, he kept the brush away, but he had nurtured the few oak trees that had managed to start themselves. Taming nature had never been one of his interests. He liked a certain order to things, but the mountain had its own rules and he never fought those rules. Sometimes, though, he found it difficult to live with them.

He had tried to leave the mountain more than once, first by going away to college a thousand miles away, a place where the mountains were too vast, too unfamiliar. And two years earlier, he had taken a winter's leave of absence and half his savings to find out what life would be like living in a rental near his folks' place near the beach. But he was back on the mountain in eight weeks. Now, there was Lila.

The daylight faded behind his closed curtains. He lay in bed, thinking of her. She was down there in that enormous house with Bud to comfort her instead of him. What was she telling him? Did Bud even know she needed comfort? He probably did. Lila had never been good at hiding her feelings.

As much as he despised the thought of Bud touching Lila, holding Lila, his weariness won out and he could no longer hold her face in his mind. He found himself remembering the distant sound of snapping tree limbs and the frantic rustle of fallen leaves, the sound of whoever - whatever - had been wandering the mountainside carrying the body of Claude Dixon through the darkness. The troopers had found no footprints in the woods and somehow that seemed right to Tripp. Whatever had killed Claude Dixon might have found him in Alta, but it had surely come from the mountain and was still somewhere on it. Tripp was strangely comforted by the thought. Terrible and dangerous as the thing was, if it was from the mountain he refused to be afraid of it. It would be like being afraid of himself.

CHAPTER FOURTEEN

THE FRONT DOOR WAS ONLY A FEW feet from where Jolene slept, so she woke at the sound of the first knock. Her mouth and throat were so dry, she could hardly swallow. Thirst was no small thing to her. Thirst was a memory of being buried deep in time-hardened soil, caressed by tree roots that searched year after endless year for hidden water. Thirst was proof there was some human part of her left, even though she couldn't see or feel or hear until she had been thrust from the ground and into the world once again.

Instead of answering the door, she ran to the bathroom, desperate. Filling the plastic tumbler on the sink with tap water, she drained it then refilled it and drank again. It didn't matter that the water tasted like rust and chlorine. It soothed her tongue and throat and cooled her skin as some of it ran onto her chin and dropped onto her chest. *One more glass. Always just one more.*

She leaned against the sink, breathing hard. In the mirror, the skin beneath her eyes looked blue, translucent. After coming back from Ivy's house, she had started to feel worse, and Charity had offered to cover her shift so she could rest. She had expected to feel better on waking, but only wanted to go back to sleep.

Out in the hallway, Charity was yelling at whoever was at the door.

"Eli, that better not be you!"

The milky light coming through the window above the shower told Jolene it was no later than seven thirty in the morning, and Charity awake after only three or four hours' sleep wasn't a nice thing to hear.

Eli had forgotten his front door key twice since he had brought Jolene to stay at the trailer. Both times Jolene had been the one to let him in, and Charity was always threatening to throw him out for waking them too early. If he and Charity were going to fight, they would do it in front of her. Dancing or not, Charity liked an audience. Then there would be at least an hour of noisy sex, also loud enough for Jolene's benefit.

Charity's aura was always a passionate red that flared directly over her heart. Jolene had trusted her from the moment Eli led her from the trailer out to his truck, where Jolene sat naked and not yet able to speak, wrapped in the sleeping bag he kept balled up behind the seat.

≈ ≼ ♦ ◢ ◂

Shrouding her shoulders with the quilt, Jolene shuffled back down the hall toward the living room, hoping she might be able to sleep for another hour or two.

Charity swung open the door. "Jesus Christ," she said. "What the hell's on fire?"

Bud Tucker stood on the step looking chagrined. Taking off his fawn cowboy hat, he ducked his head unnecessarily as Charity stood aside so he could come in. Jolene felt the rush of cool air that came with him. Despite the cold, Bud's face was flushed and his forehead wore a sheen of sweat.

The hints of gray around his chest worried Jolene. Otherwise, his aura was a rich indigo she had never seen waver; he cared deeply about the people around him. There were pictures of him in younger, healthier days on a wall in the club's office - pictures with a governor; with a slightly gap-toothed woman who had signed her picture *Carly* in a tight, loopy scrawl; and with a smiling actor in front of a *Barbarian Master* poster. Both men wore tight-fitting suits and skinny neckties, and it was one of the few pictures in which Bud wasn't the biggest person in the shot. Bud didn't have any hair back then, either, but he'd had a more athletic build. She had never seen him smile as broadly as he had in the pictures, but his moss-green eyes were never threatening, even when he was dealing with the club's roughest customers.

"Breakfast." Bud held out two stiff paper sacks and gave Charity a conciliatory smile. Noticing that Charity's satin robe had fallen open to partially expose her triple-D breasts, he glanced away. "I can't stay long, but there's some coffee and blueberry muffins for you and Eli, and I had Lori Ann at the diner pack up some of her chicken noodle soup for Jolene."

Charity's irritation softened at the mention of coffee. She pushed a hairspray-stiffened lock of blond hair behind one ear and then took the sacks.

"Yeah," she said. "Some guy who worked at the trucking company, he got dragged off or something last night?"

Bud shook his head. "I don't know what happened, but I'm on my way over to the office. It's Claude, my dispatcher. Dwight called me, but I couldn't get back in town until now."

"That's horrible," Jolene said. She sank down onto the couch and wrapped the quilt tighter around her. A couple of the drivers hung around the club. They were nice guys, good tippers. But she had never met Claude.

She hadn't even been in Alta two weeks and some-one was dead of violence, or as good as dead. *Did I bring the violence with me?* Every time she closed her eyes, she saw the world as it might become: its edges seeping black, all its life drained away.

"I hope they find him alive," Bud said. "I don't have the whole story yet. I haven't even told Lila. She's probably still asleep."

Jolene stopped herself from telling Bud she had seen Lila two nights earlier. Lila couldn't see that the kindness Bud showed everyone around him cost him a hell of a lot. He couldn't help being as trusting as he was. Deceiving him was too easy, like deceiving a child. *Deceit meant death for the soul.*

"I heard the guy looked like some kind of ape," Charity said. She looked at Jolene. "I was going to tell you, but you didn't even move when I came in this morning, and Eli said you were totally passed out when he left. You still look like hell, by the way."

Realizing that Bud was also staring at her, Jolene got self-conscious.

"It's not anything," she said. "I'll be okay to work tonight if I rest today." She knew she hadn't done herself any favors spending so much time in the rain, but it had been worth it to spend an hour on the mountain. The very air there restored her.

And now she knew who/what Ivy was hiding. The huge man with the strange stitches on his skin. But Jolene didn't know what to do. There was no voice, no helpful set of instructions written in the air. He had been dead on that table, hadn't he? No aura at all, just the blank absence of life. The idea of Ivy hiding a dead man in her trailer had puzzled her, but she saw now she had been wrong. He hadn't been dead. He was as alive as she was - if the tenuous connection she had to the earth around her could be called *life*.

One of Bud's employees was probably dead, and she might as well have killed him herself.

Charity glanced up at the sunburst metal clock above the couch. "Eli's on his way home. Sometimes he goes to his mom's for an early breakfast," she said. "You can bet I'm going to make sure he has the .38 loaded and out on the dresser when we go back to bed, just in case."

Bud cleared his throat. "Maybe you could warm up that soup for Jolene?" he said, fidgeting with the brim of his hat. "And have Eli drop you at the club tonight, or give Dwight a call. I'll make sure there's someone keeping an eye out on the parking lot. At least until we know what's going on."

Charity looked from Bud to Jolene. She had already told Jolene she thought Bud had a thing for her.

"Sure," Charity said.

Bud watched after her as she carried the bags into the kitchen. When she was gone, he eased a peeling vinyl ottoman closer to the couch and sat down.

"I can't stay," he said. "You think you've got the flu? You don't want to mess around with the flu."

Jolene was touched by the concern in his eyes. She tried to smile back at him. "You need to get to your office. Really, I'm okay," she said.

"Dwight said you got sick in a pretty big way." There was finally the hint of a smile on his face. "It's not easy to make an impression on Dwight. Must have been spectacular."

"Dwight's so sensitive," Jolene said, and they both laughed. Dwight was about as sensitive as a dead snake.

Dwight was hard for her to read. Everything about him was dirty gray, obscured. His body wasn't sick. His sick was in his soul. She didn't trust him, and someday she might be close enough to Bud to tell him so. There were so many things she could tell Bud, just because she knew he would listen. He would understand. He had chanced to be in the office that day when she had first come in with Charity, and he had hired her over Dwight's objection that she didn't have any experience. She'd been nervous during her brief audition on the stage, but she had let Charity's excellent coaching and the music take her over. Dancing for even just those few minutes, she'd felt a sweet release of the pain that had been building up inside her since she came out of the woods.

Bud lowered his voice.

"I have to go, but did you think about it? With Claude gone, we'll need even more help in the office…" The words faded into silence and he looked away.

Jolene wanted to touch him, to heal the worry in him. She watched him struggle with what to say next.

They heard the *beep beep beep* of the microwave and Charity cursing the too-hot bowl.

"You wouldn't have to start right away," he said. "Things are up in the air for a while. Messed up."

Out of the blue, he had offered her a job filing and answering phones at the trucking office. He hadn't said why he had chosen her out of all the other girls - or anyone else in town, for that matter. Who hired a dancer to answer phones?

"I like dancing," Jolene said. She wasn't sure it mattered where she spent her days or nights. "Plus, I don't really know anything about computers, except for what Eli's shown me."

Bud was about to speak when the cell phone in his jacket began chiming a tinny version of "You Are My Sunshine." He pulled it out of his pocket and answered.

"Lila. Honey," he said, his voice full of emotion.

Charity came in bearing the bowl of soup on a metal baking sheet. Bud held up a hand to keep her from speaking.

"I know, baby," he said. "I'm almost to the office right now. Meet me there, okay?...They what?...Holy Christ."

Jolene wanted to push away the darkness she saw seeping into the blue surrounding him.

"Don't cry," he said. "I'll come right home to get you...I love you, too, baby."

Bud stood up and snapped his phone shut.

"Troopers want to talk to me," he said. "They found Claude's body way up on Devil's Oven."

CHAPTER FIFTEEN

LILA MET BUD JUST INSIDE the door leading from the garage. The vacant look on her face told him she had taken more than her usual dose of sedative. Dressed in a simple cotton sweater and blue jeans, with her curls pulled back into a loose ponytail, she looked young and vulnerable. He was a little surprised to find her so devastated. She rarely took much of an interest in his trucking employees, but then nobody they knew well had ever been murdered.

"They're in the living room. Danelle's giving them coffee." She let him pull her to him, and rested her head against his chest. "I missed you so much," she said.

He stroked her hair as he held her, wishing he could take her upstairs where they could be alone. She needed reassuring. What happened to Claude was a terrible thing, but it didn't have anything to do with them.

When she pulled away, he touched the quarter-sized bruise on her head with a careful finger. "Hey, what happened here?"

She raised her own hand to it. "Hit my head getting into the truck," she said. "I'm okay."

"Poor baby," he said. He kissed the bruise. "You don't have to go in there with me if you don't want to."

She shook her head. "I don't want to be by myself."

"I'm sorry I had to leave you alone," he said. "Financial stuff. They wanted me there in person." It was enough of the truth. He never wanted her to see him chastised the way he had been by his father.

"Next time," she said. "Promise?"

"Red, you sure you're okay?" he said. He had seen her shaken before, but now she seemed to have undergone a complete personality change. Her confidence was gone. She seemed defeated. Maybe he needed to take some of the money he had brought back and get her out of town for a few days. Nothing was more important than making sure she was all right.

But even as Bud looked into her face, he knew they couldn't do it. The money thing needed to be handled. Dwight had been trying to help him, to protect him, but now the people to whom Bud owed money were getting close. As much as he wanted to believe the best about people, Bud knew he had screwed up. Dwight's money friends weren't going to wait anymore.

"We don't know anything about this. About Claude," Lila said. "Why do you think they're here?"

"Damned if I know. Maybe because he works - I mean, *worked* for me." He shook his head. "Damn, I can't believe he's dead. Such a good guy. I sure as hell hope he wasn't into drugs or anything like that."

Panic spread across his wife's face. "If it's that, then there might be more of them. They might not stop with Claude," she said. "What if they come looking for us?"

"Hey, take it easy," he said. "Whoever killed Claude isn't going to come after you. Or me. Unless you've been hiding a habit I don't know about."

"What?" she said. "I don't understand."

She seemed afraid. Lila was never afraid.

He put his arm around her and led her down the hall to the kitchen. She didn't resist.

"It was just my piss-poor excuse for a joke," he said. "I'm sorry. Claude's dead, but it doesn't have anything to do with us. I promise."

She didn't look convinced. Pulling away from him, she went over to the stove where a kettle was simmering. As she poured the water into a waiting mug, her hand shook, spilling water on the counter.

"No. I don't think I want to talk to them if they don't need me," she said.

"Sure, baby," he said. "I don't know why they would."

Over on the kitchen table, Lila's cell phone buzzed. They both looked over at it.

"You want your phone?" he said. "Might be your mother. She probably heard about Claude."

"It's nobody I want to talk to," she said. She picked up the mug and headed toward the back stairs.

He stopped her before she could pass. She looked less afraid, but he knew she was worried. He tried to think of something to say that would make her feel better.

"Get some rest," he said, and kissed her on the cheek. He would die before he let anything happen to her.

CHAPTER SIXTEEN

"ANTHONY! WHAT HAVE YOU DONE?"
Ivy dropped the linen napkins she had gotten from the closet in the guest bathroom.

Thora had spent the afternoon staring at the television or out the window, uncharacteristically quiet, the tension coming off her in waves. Ivy had understood she was trying to decide what to do about Anthony. Two different people had called with news about the murder at the Git 'n' Go. Ivy had answered the phone herself, but the murder had also been on the news.

Now Thora lay at Anthony's feet, her body jerking without rhythm, blood welling around the knife blade protruding from the front of her neck and streaming onto the vinyl floor. Her mouth was slack, lips and chin dotted with blood. Her eyes, wide with shock, stared up at Anthony.

Ivy wondered if this was what she had wanted all along. Maybe Anthony had looked into her heart and granted her unspoken, unacknowledged wish.

Anthony stood over Thora wearing his corpse-stupid grin. It was the only thing about him Ivy couldn't bear. She felt afraid when she saw that smile, and she didn't want to be afraid of him.

What would he do if he thought I was angry? Or fright-ened?

Finally the gruesome smile faded, and Anthony took an uncertain step back from Thora.

When Ivy had brought him down from the trailer for dinner, Thora had looked on in silent reproach as they came in the front door. Anthony wore the blue jeans and shoes Ivy had run out to buy, as well as a light pink oxford shirt that one of her clients had brought in for repair and never picked up. It was too short and pulled at the buttons, but she had helped him roll up the cuffs so it didn't look too bad. He kept his head down, staying close to Ivy, as though he were a new pet, uncomfortable in the house. But when Thora finally said something under her breath - *animal*, or *criminal*, maybe, Ivy wasn't sure - Anthony's body went rigid and he turned his empty brown eyes to her half sister.

Thora!

Despite whatever was in her truest heart, Ivy couldn't bear to see Thora suffer. Kneeling, she took hold of the carving knife that had been meant for the lamb roast cooling on the table, and pulled it out of her sister's neck. Stunned at the brutal sight of it, she flung it to the floor.

"Thora," she said. "Oh, my God, I'm so sorry, Thora." Without the knife, the wound relaxed, releasing a fresh wave of red, red blood. The skin around Thora's eyes tightened and she focused on Ivy's face.

Once, emerging from anesthetic after knee surgery, Thora had looked at Ivy for a moment with sudden, surprising tenderness. But seconds later her face blanked into her usual indifference and the complaining had begun. Would there be tenderness now? Forgiveness?

Ivy saw only fear in Thora's eyes. Thora knew she was going to die, and Ivy knew it, too. There would be no forgiveness.

What could she give Thora?

She took her sister's trembling hand in her own and

felt how fragile it was, even with its protection of well-marbled flesh. Why couldn't Thora have understood? Why couldn't she have seen how important Anthony was to her? Ivy had saved him from an endless, bleak eternity buried on the mountain. What had he suffered up there, buried in the dirt? What had he suffered before he was put there?

"Look for Jesus, Thora," she said. "Look for Daddy. They're waiting for you. Your mama, too." She squeezed Thora's hand between both of hers, as though she could make Thora see the happy, greeting-card picture she wanted her to see - a vista without shadow and her parents coming for her, smiling their welcome. Did their father even make it to heaven? People said suicides went to hell. She hadn't known him, really. Thora had told her he rarely went to church, and often used the Lord's name in vain. But Sundays at the sparsely attended Baptist church in town were important to Thora, and for years she had made sure Ivy went with her.

Ivy thought Thora might pull her hand away, but Thora held on.

"Please close your eyes," Ivy said. "Just close your eyes."

Thora obeyed. She coughed, her misdirected breath expelling more blood from the wound, spattering Ivy's white apron.

Ivy had never seen anyone die before, and her body trembled with equal parts terror and fascination. She studied Thora's face as Thora choked for some particle of air that wasn't filled with blood. Watching Thora die was like watching her own life twist into some strange, unknown shape. All Ivy could do was wait until it was over.

For the second time in as many weeks, Ivy found herself confronted with violence and death. Both times, she had neglected to call someone for help. No, not neglected - *chose* not to. Worse, she had a murderer in her kitchen who had settled himself in a chair to eat the lamb and potatoes and green beans that had been meant as a kind of peace offering to the woman he had just killed. Had Ivy always been so cold, so

selfish? But if she was so horrible, why couldn't she stop crying?

She looked up at the man who had caused her to
betray the one remaining person in the world she actually
loved - or at least tried to love. Anthony, whose only apparent
emotion seemed to be an eerie, charmless glee. His massive
shoulders hunched over one of Thora's grandmother's antique
china plates as he stabbed a table knife into the softened stick
of butter. Freeing a good-sized chunk from the stick, he spread
the butter on the roll with the slow deliberation of a six-year-
old child.

Taking one hand away from Thora's, Ivy wiped her
tears away and focused more closely on Anthony's left hand.
He held the knife at an awkward angle. Appraising his hand as
she might a piece of clothing she had repaired, she could see
that something about it was wrong. For all her care, she had
sewn it on badly.

Ivy Luttrell, maker of pristine, flawless wedding gowns
and sewer of perfect seams, had failed at the most important
project of her life.

She began to laugh, and couldn't stop. Anthony turned
to look at her, blinking, the hard roll still in his not-quite-right
hand, the knife in the other. A smile spread over his face.

When Thora's last breath whistled through the hole in
her throat, Ivy didn't hear it for the sound of her own laughter.

CHAPTER SEVENTEEN

TRIPP PULLED ONTO THE HIGHWAY from the sheltered driveway in which he had been waiting, and brought the truck up to the SUV's quickly increasing speed. Lila was alone. He flicked on the emergency lights behind the truck's grill. She took so long to pull off onto the shoulder that he thought she might be ignoring him.

"What in God's world do you think you're doing?" she said when he walked up to the window. "What if Bud was with me?"

So she was all right. She wasn't lying in a hospital or her bedroom, sedated out of her mind, or being questioned by the police with a lawyer sitting next to her. He was relieved to see her even if she was pissed off. Which she definitely was.

A sedan slowed as it approached them so its elderly driver could get a good look at what might be going on. Tripp gave a terse nod and waved it off.

"Baby, if you'd answer your phone, this wouldn't be necessary," he said. Standing on the side of the road, he wasn't about to go into how he hadn't been able to get her off his mind, how he had spent another night alone, alternating beers with aborted calls to her cell phone. He had left four or five messages, and as it got later and later he had gotten more and more worried. By the time he fell into bed, he had felt like a fool.

"I want to talk," he said.

Lila took off her sunglasses. Her vibrant green eyes were red, strained. She looked exhausted.

"Shit," she said. "Not today. Please, Tripp."

"You want me to get in, or should I follow you?" he said. "Doesn't matter to me."

≈≺♠≺≀

Hawk's End was one of the lesser-used hiking trails on Devil's Oven. Tripp parked his state truck in the lot and unlocked the gate to the service road so that Lila could drive on through. He got in the passenger seat of the SUV, and she didn't say anything as they drove the half-mile to the place where they had a habit of parking. And having sex. This morning, she put the truck in Park, but left it running.

He knew he should be careful with her, but his head still ached with the memory of Claude Dixon's body. He couldn't let it go.

"What did you tell them?" Lila said, staring ahead at the trees. The ten-minute drive had calmed her. "Nobody asked me anything. Not even Bud." At her husband's name, did her voice get that much quieter, or was Tripp imagining it?

"Poor sonofabitch," he said. "That psycho killed him and brought him all the way to my place. Why all the way up there, do you think?"

She turned to face him.

"I bought Christmas presents for his kids every year. Bud dressed up like Santa, and the little girl got scared and hid in the break room," she said. She put her face in her hands.

He knew then that she couldn't get the image out of her mind, either.

With her head bent, he could see more than a few silvery roots along her purposely messy part. It occurred to him, for the first time, that they were almost exactly the same age. For some reason he had always thought of her as being younger, even though they had known each other forever.

"You ever seen a dead body before?" he said.

"What?" She looked up, letting her hands drop to her lap.

"They aren't supposed to look like that," he said. "Somebody blows his own head off, it doesn't look like that. His neck was, I don't know, it was like taffy, like it came off one of those pulling machines they used to set up at the fair." He imagined the killer's hands like the metal arms of the machine, stretching Claude Dixon's neck until the skull broke out of the top of his head. It was fascinating somehow, animal in its brutality. "I don't know why it reminded me of that. It was like the killer thought it was some kind of joke. Like he was showing off."

"Jesus, Tripp," she said, shifting away from him, putting her back against the door. "That's not funny."

Reading the fear in her face, he knew he had let his mind drift too far into the dark places he had visited over the past fortysome hours.

"No. No," he said, shaking his head. "I didn't mean to scare you. But doesn't it seem like we were meant to see what happened to Claude Dixon? You and me?"

"You're reading way too much into this," she said.

"It can't be a coincidence," he said.

"I'm not talking about this anymore. I'm not talking about Claude Dixon," she said, her voice rising. "Is this why you've been calling me, because you want to *talk* about it? Did you take pictures, for God's sake?"

"This happened to *us*," he said. "You can't pretend like it didn't."

He understood she was vulnerable. He knew for damn sure she was afraid. A person couldn't walk away from that kind of trauma without being affected by it. But why wouldn't she let him help her? She was on the edge of something, maybe breaking down in front of Bud. Maybe she had already told Bud. The thought twisted Tripp's guts. They had to get through this together, to keep it between the two of them. He reached for her.

"Stop it," she said. "Don't even."

He recognized her tone. Once, when they were high school seniors, he had seen a freshman boy trip with his lunch tray, sending chocolate pudding and lasagna flying across the ten feet separating him from where Lila sat with her clique. The sleeve of Lila's white sweater had been splattered with brown globs of pudding. When the trembling boy tried to apologize and offered to clean it up, she didn't even look at him, but ordered a girl beside her to get the backpack from her locker and meet her in the bathroom. It was the girl who looked like she was about to pee herself.

"Treating me like shit isn't going to help you get over this," he said.

"Why don't you get that I'm already over it?" she said. "Starting now, as far as either of us is concerned, I wasn't there."

"You're making a mistake."

"No," she said, jabbing a finger at him. "*You* made the mistake when you let that slut get into your truck. That's where you stand. I'm just married to the boss of a guy who happened to get murdered. Get out of my car."

Shit. It was back to the girl, Jolene. She had been the reason Lila - a mad-as-hell Lila - came to see him that night.

"She needed a ride," he said. "She was sick." Even as he said it, he knew it sounded like a lame excuse. The kind of excuse guilty men gave their wives or girlfriends every day.

"Oh, yes. They're all sick, aren't they?" she said. "Or broke." She began to tick off on her fingers. "Or pregnant. Or twelve-stepping. Or lonely. And just like Bud, you're the knight in shining fucking armor."

He winced at her profanity. His mother had never cursed, telling him that women who cursed lacked imagination. He wasn't worried about Lila's imagination. She was inventive enough when he got her alone in his bed, or on his couch or in his backyard under a starry sky.

"She's also one of Bud's employees," he said, unable to curb the edge in his voice. Sometimes she pushed him too far. He turned sarcastic. "Thought you cared about all of them."

"Get out," she said, shoving him away. "Out!"

"I'm sorry," he said. "That wasn't fair."

"Get away from me or I'll go out to the road and flag down the first trooper I see and tell him there's a psychopath who won't get the hell out of my truck."

He wanted to tell her that she had a good chance of making it all the way down to Alta before she would see more than two cars of any kind. He wanted to grab her and hold her and make her understand that she needed to trust him. Only him.

Before he could say anything more, she had the door open and was out of the truck, her purse bouncing against the doorframe as she hoisted it onto her shoulder. She slammed the door.

"Lila, wait!" He tried to climb over the console separating the two front seats and fell, jamming his chest against the steering wheel. As he righted himself, he accidentally hit the horn, sending its cheerful blast into the surrounding woods. By the time he was able to get out, she was a good way down the road.

"Listen to me, please."

She turned around, walking backward for a few steps.

"You think you know every damn thing," she shouted back at him. "We all knew you were the one who snitched about us having the answers to the chemistry final. You always were a loser! I don't know why I ever let you come near me."

Every step was another hammer pound on his headache. Why wouldn't she listen? He'd just wanted to see her, to comfort her. But he'd ended up sounding like a needy idiot. What was she saying? She was running now, unsteady in the heels she wore with her snug-fitting jeans.

Tripp began to run, too.

"Damn it," he said. The sun glinting through the trees was pure and white as moonlight.

She took a sudden right into the woods. If they had been farther up the mountain where the fallen pine needles swallowed every footstep, her detour would have been silent and he might have lost her. But down here, he could hear her rustling progress through last fall's sodden leaves.

"Stop," he called. She was headed for the trail, but he knew she could easily lose her way. The trees weren't crowded here, but as he ran, the sunlight faded so that he couldn't see more than twenty feet ahead. The day seemed to be moving backward, the two of them running toward the early dawn.

Tripp stopped, listening. Knowing how the first hundred yards of the trail paralleled the service road, he took a hard left, almost colliding with a boulder that rose up without warning in the dimming light.

When he could no longer hear her, he guessed she might have reached the trail. He thought of the wolf he had seen near his cabin. Worse, he thought of whoever had killed Claude Dixon. Where was he/it hiding?

"Lila!" His voice sounded hollow in the silent woods. *No birdsong. No quarreling squirrels.*

He jogged a little farther and the trees thinned even more. The bright blue bench that sat just a few hundred feet from the trail's head broke out of the gloom. He slowed, breathing hard. His footsteps were silent on the trail's hard-packed dirt.

Why couldn't he see? For a moment he wondered if it wasn't his eyesight. Maybe the headache had burst some blood vessels in his eyes.

He called her name again. By now she might even be back at the SUV.

Rounding a hard curve around a blistered oak tree, his foot caught on something and he nearly fell.

A woman lay in the middle of the trail. The pure, waxing moonlight spread over her alabaster skin. A lock of thick black hair curled against her cheek, and her eyes were closed. She hugged her knees to her chest as though for comfort.

"Jolene," he whispered, wanting to wake her, but knowing at the same time that he shouldn't.

She opened her eyes, which were as black as her hair, and turned her head just *that much* so she could look up at him. She smiled the smile of an angel and extended her arms to him like a child.

Tripp was certain he had been here before, but he couldn't remember when.

He knelt to take her in his arms. Sliding one arm beneath her neck - her skin was as cool as marble against his arm - and the other beneath her knees, he lifted her. She weighed almost nothing, as he had known she would. Beef jerky and corn chips, Dwight had said, and obviously not much of either. She nestled against him, resting her head on his biceps. As he carried her down the trail, he breathed in the scent of her. She smelled of the woods - green, fragrant, deep woods - after a heavy rain. But there was something else, too. Woodsmoke.

Neither of them spoke.

He wasn't sure where they would go. He only knew there was a building sense of urgency in his chest.

The trees fell away behind them as they reached the trail's head. Tripp looked to the sky, stunned to find it was once again filled with bright sunlight.

The girl tensed in his arms and began to struggle. When he looked down at her, he saw that her eyes were now green and she was no longer smiling. Her hair, which had been soft like ebony silk, was now red and coarse against his skin.

"Put me down," Lila said.

CHAPTER EIGHTEEN

BUD GRABBED THE OSTRICH-LEATHER briefcase he had never much cared for from the truck's passenger seat. Like any gift from Lila, he made generous use of it and kept any unflattering opinion he had about it to himself. But given that it contained a hundred and fifty thousand in cash at that moment, he would have preferred it to look less expensive, less conspicuous.

He felt like hell after the long, restless night with Lila. After the troopers left, she had spent most of the day in bed, watching television and reading. She had no interest at all in what the police had asked him. It was as though she wanted to pretend it hadn't happened. But when they both went to bed that night, she had struggled in her sleep, constantly talking beside him as she slept. The words were unclear, but she sounded angry, sometimes frightened.

The scene at the trucking office was similarly chaotic. The two secretaries were doing their best to keep up with the tight logistics schedule that Claude had set up for the week. Everyone was grateful at how organized Claude had been, but it didn't make them feel any better. Claude was the guy everyone liked.

Bud crossed The Twilight Club's back parking lot, anxious to get inside. Beneath his jacket and sport shirt, his skin wore a layer of cooling sweat. If the manager of the Mountain Fidelity Bank's main branch weren't one of his hunting buddies, he knew he would have been in much rougher shape. Not just anyone would have cashed that kind of check with only a day's notice. Another bank officer would have hinted that Bud should get caught up on the loans the bank had already made to his businesses before he walked out of the building with that much cash.

In many ways he felt lucky, despite the fact his entire life was imploding. He had even gotten the money from his old man with a smaller-than-usual amount of bullshit harassment. His father's low-key response might have had something to do with dropping testosterone levels and his shrinking frame. Old age wasn't being kind to him.

He let himself in the club's back door and found Dwight headed into the office with a box of lightbulbs. Dwight squinted against the flare of sunlight from the open door.

"Dwight, buddy!" he said. "How's it hangin' today?"

"Three overheads burned out," Dwight said. "Everything working out at the truck office?"

"I got the best people in the world working for me," Bud said, meaning it.

He followed Dwight through the doorway and laid the briefcase on his desk casually, as though it contained nothing more significant than his lunch.

"Anything in the mail?"

"Crap," Dwight said. "Some wholesale dildo catalog, like we're one of those G.D. bookstore places. Models and everything. Who buys that shit?"

Bud grinned. How did someone like Dwight stay so naïve? Dwight always cracked him up, even when Bud felt like six kinds of hell.

"I hear they sell them at parties," Bud said. "Like Tupperware."

"Screw me," Dwight said. "Ignoramuses. You won't see *my* grandma passing one of those things around a martini party." He set up the ladder and arranged the bulb boxes on its protruding shelf.

Bud sat down behind his desk, watching the smaller man work. Dwight had just shown up one day, like an answer to an unspoken prayer. Where would Dwight go if Bud had to close the club? He knew he probably should have turned over the club's financials to Dwight two years ago - he had certainly proved himself trustworthy enough early on. Since Dwight came on board, the cash drawer had never been short more than might be expected for an operation like The Twilight Club, and the cops had to break up fights less often. Despite his brusqueness, he took good care of the girls. They needed someone like Dwight.

But it was that kind of thinking, Bud had been told, that made him a poor businessman. *A piss-poor businessman* was the exact phrase. Still, he didn't know how to do it any other way.

"What do you say I get us some coffee?" Bud said. "You got any made?"

Dwight looked down at him from the ladder, the light of the first bulb he'd changed bouncing off his glasses.

"You don't drink coffee," he said.

Bud fiddled with an envelope on his desk.

"I need you to take care of a thing for me," he said. "I've got some cash - not all of it yet - and I need you to get it to your friends."

Bud couldn't see Dwight's eyes from where he sat, but the look that swept across his face hinted there might be some kind of problem.

"What is it?" Bud said. He knew he could handle whatever Dwight told him. He'd had enough bad news lately that more wouldn't be any kind of surprise.

"Have they been on you already? You need to keep me in the loop, Dwight. This is my problem, not yours."

"It's fine," Dwight told him. "Is that it?" He pointed to the briefcase.

"They've been calling my house," Bud said. "I want to get this to them before something happens. You know, to Lila, God forbid. Or around here." He massaged his temples, trying to fight the headache coming on. "I can't believe I ever let it get this far, man. And I hate that you've put yourself in the middle of it."

Dwight guffawed. "Just call me the tasty crème filling." But when he saw the misery on Bud's face, he stopped.

"Seriously, boss," he said. "It's handled. I already told you it's not a problem." He climbed down the ladder, careful not to catch the pointed toes of his boots in the steps. He leaned over the desk and stuck his hand out for Bud to shake.

Bud didn't trust himself to speak. He took Dwight's thin, soft hand and shook it firmly, like men do.

＊◄✦◄＊

It took Dwight the better part of an hour, but by the time Bud left, he'd seemed more relaxed and less like he was going to freak out right there in the office. On top of his financial problems, the troopers were still harassing Bud with questions about the murder of that poor bastard Claude Dixon. Nearly all local murders were of the domestic abuse or pay-up-for-the-shitload-of-meth-I-fronted-you-asshole varieties. The troopers were probably enjoying the novelty. Dwight was a fan of monster-of-the-week television himself, and this death had all the titillating marks of one.

In another life, he had specialized in setting up similar puzzles for the cops. He had been too good at it, and it had gotten boring. Alta was a place he thought he could get away from all that, but it had followed him here like dog shit stuck to his shoe.

As juicy as it sounded, he wondered just how reliable the Dixon woman's story was. Exaggeration was her specialty.

Half the people who stopped at the Git 'n' Go to buy a tank of gas or a frozen pizza or cigarettes had to hear about her hemorrhoids, her Peekapoo, or which male member of the county supervisor's board took his wife's lingerie and high heels with him when he traveled alone out of town.

He put the ladder and box of bulbs away in the closet and returned to stand in the doorway of the office.

"Screw me," he said. What was he going to do with Bud's cash? He didn't know for sure where Bud had gotten it, but had a reasonable guess. The guy must have had to dig his balls out of one of Lila Tucker's thousand-dollar purses to get it done. Dwight didn't want to blame Bud, but it sure would have helped things if his boss had found the money a little sooner. Dwight pushed his glasses up on his forehead and rubbed his eyes. He had to think. There were messages on his phone asking him questions he wasn't ready to answer. Throwing money at some of those questions might help, but there was no guarantee. The former associates he had helped Bud borrow the money from were businessmen, and handing them less than half of what Bud owed them wasn't going to cut it. Already they were looking for more than just the money. Bud just didn't know it yet.

What Dwight really wanted to do was go home, throw some clothes into his suitcase, and leave this godforsaken place, with its crazy-ass hillbillies and too-dark nights and mountains that slumped on the horizon like worn-out beasts. He wanted to sit on a concrete stoop where he could watch the traffic and shoot the shit with the mailman or a bag lady, and then wander down the block to a bar where he could enjoy a cold, non-alcoholic beverage even on a Sunday afternoon.

Instead, he went to Bud's desk and opened the case. He counted the money, shuffling it back into neat piles with brisk efficiency. Bud had probably counted it himself. Bud was nothing if not honest. Too G.D. honest, as far as Dwight was concerned.

He closed the briefcase and tried to think of where

he might keep it until morning. He couldn't leave the club because he was waiting on a beer delivery, and the safe was too small to hold the case. Later he asked himself why he didn't just take the money out of the case and put it in the safe. But that was much later. By then, money had ceased to be the big issue.

He took the case down the hall to the supply closet. It fit nicely into a fold of a rust-stained tarp in the corner, and he arranged the tarp's edges to make sure the case was hidden. Taking out his keys, he locked up the closet and went back down the hall into The Twilight Club's high-ceilinged bar-room.

For the first time in a lot of years, he considered going behind the bar and pouring himself a couple fingers of scotch. Things hadn't been this bad in a hell of a long time. But just before he reached the shining black and chrome bar with its mirrored rows of attractively labeled bottles, the back door buzzer rang.

Dwight stopped and looked at the big neon clock above the bar. The beer guy was early.

"I'll be damned," he said. "Saved by the G.D. bell."

CHAPTER NINETEEN

"**Y**OU'RE GOING TO HAVE TO PUT the phone down. Stand up as straight as you can," Ivy said. "Please, be still." She stretched a measuring tape across the freckled V of skin that began where the back zipper of the third bridesmaid's dress had gotten stuck.

The girl - maybe sixteen years old - tried to look over her shoulder at what Ivy was doing, but Ivy pressed her fingers firmly on the girl's back to get her to look forward. It was supposed to be a final fitting, but the girl had shown up with a belly that was three or four pounds heavier than it had been at the first fitting six weeks earlier.

"You won't say anything?" the girl whispered.

"About what?" Ivy knew she was being too short with her, but she had far too much on her mind to worry about a stranger's secret, a pregnancy that wouldn't be a secret for much longer anyway. Far more important to her was that no one find out that Thora's body lay rolled in a clear plastic tarp in the big freezer at the back of the house. Or that the periodic snores coming from the guest room down the hall belonged to a once-dead murderer.

So much to hide. Soon, people would be asking where Thora was. Ivy already had to cancel a doctor's appointment that morning. How natural she had made her voice sound! She'd even joked with the receptionist as though her heart weren't broken with grief. And Anthony. She had tried to get him to go back up to the trailer, which she'd stocked with all kinds of food he might like, but he had just sat down in Thora's chair and turned away from her to stare out the window.

"I'll fix it so you'll get through Sunday's wedding," Ivy said. "Tell Missy there was a problem with the zipper. Come back and get it Saturday morning." She almost added that it would have helped if she had been told about the pregnancy at the first fitting, but the girl was so young. How could she know whom she could trust? Ivy was only just realizing there was no one else in the world *she* could trust.

She should have trusted Thora more. Thora hadn't told anyone about Anthony. *But she would have. Eventually.*

The girl sighed, letting her shoulders relax, and Ivy saw that the dress was going to need yet another extra half-inch. Out in the living room, the two bridesmaids who had already been fitted burst into a fit of noisy laughter. When it subsided, Ivy heard the jingle of the tiny bells she had hung on the door of the guest bedroom down the hall.

"Go on and change," Ivy said, tossing the measuring tape on the table. "We're done." Propelled by fear, she rushed out to the hallway to stop Anthony from coming out of the room - or someone else from going inside. She slammed the workroom door behind her.

Ivy pressed her hand against Anthony's chest and urged him back into the room as firmly as she dared. He was naked and looked like a very tall, sleepy child. Late morning sunlight framed his body in gold. How was it that she could touch him so intimately? Before Anthony, she had only seen men naked in films.

"You can't, Anthony," she whispered. "There are people

in the living room."

He looked down at her. She had learned to recognize when he understood her.

"They'll be gone soon," she said. "I promise."

The air in the guest room was close and unpleasant. She had washed his bloody clothes and laid them on Thora's hope chest at the foot of the bed, but she hadn't been able to coax him to take a shower. One of his hands cupped his penis and his forehead wore a deep crease. He obviously had to use the bathroom.

"I'm sorry," she said, shaking her head. "You'll have to wait."

He seemed to understand and moved back from the door. But when the girls started laughing again, he turned his head toward the sound.

"Anthony," she said, trying to keep his attention. She knew she had been foolish to let the girls come today, but there had been no other time. Sunday was the wedding. Even in crisis, she felt compelled to finish her work, to make sure her clients would always come back to her, especially now that Thora's disability benefit would stop. Though she would have to tell someone Thora was dead for that to happen, wouldn't she? Otherwise, the checks would continue. For a while. Until the questions started.

"Get dressed." She tried to sound as though she wouldn't take no for an answer. Taking the clothes from the top of the chest, she pushed them into his arms.

While he seemed distracted by the clothes, she stepped out of the room and shut the door. She felt surreal, like she was taking part in some kind of dark, comic farce that was fated to end badly. It had already ended badly for Thora. The right thing to do - the only thing - was to send the girls away, call the police, and tell them Anthony was here and that he had murdered Thora and threatened Ivy. No one would blame her for being terrified of him. His eyes said everything. And nothing.

But Ivy's heart was pounding and she felt more alive than she had in many, many years. She didn't know what would happen next. The only thing she knew was that she had to shelter him, to protect him. There was no one else who would.

"Miss Ivy?" the pregnant girl, now dressed, stood in the workroom doorway.

"What?" Ivy said, louder than she intended. "You're finished. What do you want?"

"Should we take the other dresses with us?"

Ivy wanted to scream at her to just leave, but the girl already looked worried. She managed a tight smile. "I'll get them and bring them out."

When she heard the car start in the driveway, Ivy hurried back to the guest room. How could she convince Anthony to stay up at the trailer? It was too much, worrying about him running into the clients she had coming in and out of the house. They were used to Thora, who had mostly ignored them. But Anthony? They could never see him.

She opened the guest room door, expecting to find him lying on the bed or sitting in the room's single chair. Instead, he was standing in the corner near the window, still naked, his back to her. About two feet up the wall, the paint was darker and looked wet.

"Oh, Anthony. No," she said. "Stop!" She was too late.

He didn't turn around until his bladder was empty. When he did, he seemed much less agitated than when she had left the room.

"This isn't right," she said, pointing to the urine-soaked corner. "You need to do that in the bathroom. You used it yesterday, remember?" She had even heard him get up around one o'clock when she was still scrubbing Thora's blood from the kitchen floor. Afterward he hadn't flushed or washed his hands, but she was keeping her expectations low. Who knew what he had been like before? Thora had always insisted that men were pigs.

Was it her imagination, or did he look the slightest bit sheepish, or perhaps embarrassed?

"Come on," she said. "Now you really do need a shower."

She left the bedroom, hoping he would follow. He did.

As they started down the hallway, she felt something tug at the ponytail hanging down her back. Her pulse quickened. This time, the tug was more insistent, even playful. She looked back over her shoulder. Anthony wasn't smiling, but his head was tilted slightly, like he was trying to concentrate. He reached for her ponytail again.

"I'm sorry. I-I forgot my phone."

Ivy stopped. She leaned around Anthony's bulk to see the pregnant bridesmaid standing at the opposite end of the hallway. Anthony turned at the girl's voice as well, and the girl's eyes widened, taking in Anthony's naked form. She didn't look away until Ivy pushed around Anthony to stand between them.

"You didn't ring the doorbell!" Ivy cried. "Why didn't you ring the doorbell?"

"I didn't mean…" The girl started backing away, but her eyes were drawn back to Anthony, who filled the hallway. She stared as though she had stumbled upon some rare animal in the forest. "It's my phone," the girl said. "I didn't mean to come in. Everyone's out in the car."

Behind her, Ivy could hear Anthony breathing heavily. She almost looked back, but she was afraid to see the look on his face.

"Wait," Ivy said. "Go wait on the porch."

After the girl fled, Ivy realized she had been holding her breath and let out a long sigh.

The very worst that could happen had happened. She had no idea if the girl even knew anything about the murder at the Git 'n' Go. If she did, it was all over. Ivy closed her eyes against the image of Thora lying on the floor, limp as a doll. *What in God's world am I doing?*

Maybe the girl didn't know. Or didn't care. Teenagers were like that - ignorant. Ivy was an adult. Why shouldn't she have a man in her house, even a naked man? It was her right, and nobody's business but her own. Women she knew were always having affairs. They couldn't keep their mouths shut about them, telling her about their younger, older, sex-crazed, or drunken lovers as she hemmed their designer blue jeans and or let out their dresses, confiding in her as though she were a hairdresser or bartender. Even Lila Tucker, one of the area's most visibly married women - a woman Ivy had known almost her whole life - had dropped hints. But of course, no one would expect it of Ivy Luttrell. The virginal Ivy Luttrell. The motherless, harelipped Ivy Luttrell.

What people thought of her didn't matter. It never had. She looked up at Anthony.

"It's not right, Ivy," Thora had said. *"He's all wrong. And I think he's dangerous."*

The girl seemed to have had no effect on Anthony at all. Did that mean he didn't want to kill just anyone? Maybe killing people was just a periodic need he had. Was it possible he chose his victims for a reason?

He turned away from her and continued down the hall to the bathroom. As he walked, he reached out one finger and trailed it along the wall until he came to the bathroom. Ivy was still amazed by the muscularity of his body, the physical power that seemed to ripple beneath his skin. He was beautiful.

He disappeared inside the bathroom and she heard the water come on in the shower.

･⋖♠⋗･

The pregnant girl stood on the porch, staring up at the mountain. When she heard Ivy open the door, she came to meet her on the threshold. Bass thundered from the neon blue compact car idling in the driveway behind her, but the girls inside weren't paying any attention to what was happening on the porch.

Instead of immediately taking her cell phone from Ivy, the girl reached for Ivy's wrist. Her fingers were ice cold, and Ivy instinctively tried to pull away. But the girl held her fast, her dark brown eyes looking directly into Ivy's. Her oval face was free of makeup and, Ivy thought, as plain as an old shoe. The only thing even vaguely exotic about her was the delicate silver ring at the pointed end of one over-plucked eyebrow.

"The Lord Jesus Christ Our Savior doesn't call me to judge you." The girl spoke with a confidence that astonished Ivy. "Judgment comes from Him. Not me. Okay?"

She let go of Ivy and took the phone. "We're all sinners, but we're forgiven by His grace." A wide, sympathetic smile transformed her face into something lovely.

Ivy stared after her as the girl hurried down the porch steps and got into the waiting car. She waved at Ivy as they drove off, the pounding music fading as they turned onto the highway.

Ivy woke in darkness, the prayers she had been dreaming on her lips. She needed forgiveness. She needed luck. She needed patience. Most of all, she needed patience. Anthony was as thoughtless as a seven-year-old, and more dangerous than she could have ever imagined a man to be. She held tightly to the hope that he would change, that he would become something better. What was wrong with wanting someone she might love unconditionally, someone who might be kinder to her than Thora? And the way to teach Anthony kindness was to show him kindness.

When she heard the far-off jangle of the Christmas bells she'd hung on the front door, she knew she hadn't awakened soon enough. She had propped open the bedroom door and worn comfortable clothes to bed so she would be ready if he tried to go out. But she had slept through his leaving the guest room, and he was already gone. Had he even bothered to get dressed?

She rushed to the front of the house to find the front door standing open and the porch dark. Outside, her breath fogged the air. The temperature was freezing, or dangerously close to it.

Grabbing a flashlight, she slipped on her rubber gardening clogs and ran into the yard. She looked toward the highway first, knowing he probably hadn't gone that way.

Up on the hillside the trailer was dark, but that didn't mean Anthony wasn't inside. He never seemed to mind being in the dark.

She was only halfway up the hill when she heard the hysterical yipping of a dog or coyote off to the east. She stopped and changed direction. Never before in her life would she have followed such a sound, especially at night. But it worried her. Worried was her new second nature.

She battled with the voices in her head - a chorus of voices, Thora's among them - about whether her worry made any sense. They told her that Anthony couldn't be hurt, that he couldn't feel anything because he was already dead. Dead, like Thora. But no! *She* had restored him, restored his life, hadn't she? *Her* blood, *her* life. Anthony was a part of her in a way that no one else in the world could ever be. He had come from the mountain as a gift, and she had done her part.

Could she have helped Thora? Did she have that kind of power? Every time she thought about Thora lying in the big freezer, she flushed with shame. It had happened too fast. There hadn't even been time for an ambulance, let alone thoughts of something less...normal. *No, there was nothing.* Nothing she could have done.

Now, with the mountain rising above her, dark against a deeper darkness, she understood what she might have done. Could still do. Bury Thora on the mountain.

Ahead, she saw a terrible vision - the majestic outline of a man, an animal flailing at the end of his outstretched arms. The animal's yipping had become a strangled, desperate whine. Ivy could feel its terror in her own gut, as though she were the one dying, she were the one whose panicked eyes were quickly draining of light and life.

She dropped the flashlight, screaming Anthony's name.

Before she could reach them, Anthony gave the animal a final shake and let it fall to the ground. Silhouette hid the details of his face, but she knew he was smiling.

Without looking back, Anthony ran for the shelter of the mountain's blackened forest.

By the time she reached where he had been standing, he was gone. The winter-starved coyote at her feet was still. She knelt, laying her hand on its ragged coat. Nothing.

"Anthony," she said. The word hung in the air, but there was no one else to hear it.

Giving Anthony life had only brought more death into the world. *Unintended consequences* was a favorite phrase of the pastor at church. *Damn dangerous things.*

The coyote's back legs gave a sudden kick and its body shuddered, releasing a foul odor. Ivy felt a sharp pang of guilt, but there was nothing she could do. The vultures or, God forbid, other coyotes would take care of the carcass.

She shushed her way through the grass to retrieve the glowing flashlight. Her stomach was upset and her hands shaking when she picked up the thing, so the beam bobbed as she walked. A hundred feet or so from the dead coyote, she heard a rustling in the brush above her. Cutting the beam up the hillside, she called Anthony's name. More rustling. But the light only revealed a pair of flat gold discs - an animal's eyes.

"Go!" she shouted. "Get!"

The animal stared for a moment, but when she feinted

toward it, the eyes blinked, and disappeared.

Inside the house, Ivy slipped off her clogs and started to lock the front door, her hands still shaking. But she thought better of it. Anthony was certain to come back. This was his home now. He would soon be hungry. Tired.

She went down the silent hallway to turn on the light in Anthony's room. *It's not fair to call it the guest room anymore.* He had formed a kind of nest on the floor with the blankets and sheets from the bed. The room smelled of urine, but so far he hadn't defecated anywhere but the bathroom. Most of his clothes lay in a pile on the room's single chair, and nine or ten plastic water and soda bottles stood in neat rows on the dresser. A cupcake wrapper and an empty peanut can sat in the middle of the bare mattress. It was like a young boy's room. A boy who had bad, indulgent parents.

Surely he would come back.

Glancing again at the pile of clothes, she realized he had been wearing pants and a shirt when she saw him running into the woods. Progress? Maybe.

Inside, she was still nervous. Worried. But as she walked back to her own bedroom, she smiled.

CHAPTER TWENTY

JOLENE WAS SO GRATEFUL to be out of the trailer, she didn't care that the coffee Lori Ann's daughter brought to the table tasted like ashes. She emptied two more sugar packets into the sturdy porcelain mug and stirred until the amber crystals melted. Charity and Eli had dropped her at the diner on their way out of town for the day, even though Bud had made Charity swear to keep her in the trailer until she looked better.

Charity had taken her temperature that morning. When she saw there was no fever, she told Jolene she needed to get up off the couch and get some air no matter what Bud said.

"Come to the mall with us," Charity had said. "Eli's picking up his monkey suit today. That stuck-up bitch his cousin's marrying is costing everyone a freaking fortune."

Jolene had begged off going to the mall even though she was curious. There were so many things she didn't know, hadn't seen. After thirty years the world was different - again - but the people were always the same. Naïve. Hopeful. Sometimes they were weak or cruel. Sometimes, like Charity, they surprised her. Strong, vibrant people like Charity didn't need to be saved.

But it was Eli who understood Jolene. His family had settled on Garrett's Mountain almost two centuries earlier, even before Jolene's first life had begun on neighboring Devil's Oven. The legendary crimes - the vile murders of her father and baby brother - that her mother had committed back then were part of Eli's familial memory. Nothing that happened on Devil's Oven surprised him. Jolene was grateful it had been Eli who found her the night she came off the mountain.

Tripp walked into the diner just before nine looking preoccupied, like he wasn't sure what he was doing there. He wore his DNR uniform with a gun snugged into a black holster on his belt.

"Hey," Jolene said. "I remember you."

At the sound of her voice, his face cleared for a second and she knew he had been looking for her. Then he was on guard again. He was so different from Bud. Warier. Bud could never be cruel; Tripp wasn't safe. Through the confused green of his aura, Jolene could see how he wrestled with himself, and that he had no clue as to what was really happening inside him. His aura was at war with itself, surging blue one moment, overcome with sickly gray the next. His turmoil saddened her. There had been a time in her long, long past when she would have been afraid of him. There was weakness in that confusion. Chaos.

He sat down on the other side of the booth and slid over. "You having breakfast?"

"I ate already," she said. Another girl might have been flattered that he had been looking for her. Jolene knew it was just a step. Something that had been decided long ago.

He waved at Lori Ann's daughter and she nodded.

"Lori Ann doesn't have corn chips on the menu, I guess," he said.

She laughed. "No. But she does have blueberry pancakes with whipped cream." They had been wild blueberries, once frozen, but still tiny and tart. She loved the feeling of food passing her lips, tasting salt, sugar, bitter lemons, and the thick sourdough bread that Eli's mother sent over. Any food, really, except for meat. Charity had even found her standing in front of the refrigerator eating hot sauce from a spoon. All Charity had said was, "Ugh. Gross."

Charity never asked her any questions, never even wanted to know where she had come from or if she had any people nearby, let alone why she had eaten hot sauce from a spoon. Jolene wondered what Eli could have told her that made her willing to take in a naked stranger as her roommate, then help that stranger get a job.

Tripp Morgan, though, was full of questions. She could almost see them in the air between them. She started first.

"Is she still mad? Mrs. Tucker?" she said.

Then Lori Ann herself was there setting a cup of tea in front of him and asking if he wanted his usual omelet. They talked for a minute as though Jolene weren't even there, Lori Ann asking questions about Claude Dixon. Jolene listened to him describe coming out of his cabin in the morning and seeing something that looked like a pile of laundry in the driveway.

His aura flickered as he talked. Clouds of black - an absence of light - bled into the green and brown and gold. Death was breaking through. He was lying! But why? She didn't really need to see his aura to know that the picture he was painting for Lori Ann was all wrong.

Lori Ann left the table, finally satisfied. She hadn't acknowledged Jolene at all, but turned around when she got close to the kitchen.

"You ready for more coffee, honey?"

Jolene shook her head.

They sat for a minute, Tripp staring into his tea. Jolene noticed how rough his hands were. A pair of loaded coal trucks broke the quiet, rattling the picture window as they passed.

Tripp sat back and took his watch from his wrist. "It's this kind of stuff I don't need from Lila," he said. "I need *her*."

He slid the watch across the table and Jolene caught it before it slid off the edge.

She held it close so she could see the diamonds beneath each numeral on the watch's face. She had never worn diamonds before. Byron, Ivy's father, had given her a narrow rose gold ring that bore a single fashioned heart at their Justice of the Peace wedding. It was the sort of ring high school boys gave their girlfriends, but she had worn it lovingly until the day he chased her into the woods. She had thrown it back at him, frightened, tired of his insane accusations. It was the last day she had seen Ivy.

"Why are you telling *me* this?" she said.

"I don't know why I'd tell you anything," Tripp said. He leaned closer to her and lowered his voice. "I don't even know why I felt like I had to come and find you today. When you're riding in my truck or we're sitting across from each other in a public place like this, I think I'm okay." Jolene saw fear and something else - hate, or passion, or both - in his eyes. His aura surged. "But when you're in my head, you scare the hell out of me. And I want to know why."

Jolene wanted to look away, but found she couldn't. She knew why she frightened him. She just couldn't tell him. Not in words.

CHAPTER TWENTY-ONE

HE WOKE CURLED in an earthen pocket beneath the base of an uprooted hickory tree, his skin still damp from the morning mist. The sun was high overhead, but the niche was sheltered, still shaded. As he stretched his legs to climb out of the hole, a sluggish blacksnake that had been sleeping at his back broke ahead of him. He watched it muscle its way through the roots and into the brush.

He was hungry again. The woman's food had become a habit, but he was nowhere near the house now. Standing outside the hole, he unzipped his pants to urinate. When he was finished, he went in search of the creek he had heard running during the night. He found it a little farther down the mountainside, near the uppermost branches of the fallen tree. The creek was shallow and rocky. He lay down on his belly and splashed the cold water on his face, then drank his fill, his mouth to the water's silver surface. Resting there, the smell of dirt and water and new growth filling his nostrils, he knew he could get up to follow the creek and eventually come close to the town. There was no telling how he knew this. Some things he knew, some things he didn't. In between there was no frustration, no worry. There was simply a need to go forward, to follow a path whose destination he couldn't see. He would get there soon enough.

The shoes the woman had given him were too small. He had only been walking a few minutes when he had to stop and sit down on the ground to pull them off. He bent and twisted them in his massive hands, trying to make them larger, or at least more comfortable. But they weren't good shoes and when he put them back on, they still wouldn't yield. With a great cry - *Gaaaaaaaaaaaaaaa!* - he took them off again and threw them into the trees, out of sight.

He hated to wear shoes, especially the white vinyl ones his mother brought home from the thrift store. Everyone else, even some of the girls, wore expensive basketball shoes with famous logos or players' names stitched on them. Today he would just wear his boots. He would have to sit out P.E. and get a zero, but that was fine with him.

He lay on his stomach, sliding the shoes with his fingertips as far back as he could beneath the bed. He heard the school bus's brakes sigh at the corner, then the grind of the engine as the bus pulled away without him. Then came her footsteps. He gave the shoes a final push and eased himself over the gritty carpet. By the time she appeared in his doorway, he had pretty much brushed all the cat hair and crumbs off his navy blue shirt.

"Hey, Ma," he said. "I missed the bus. Can you take me?" He smiled at her because sometimes it worked and she would just laugh and tell him to get in the car. For someone who almost never laughed, her laugh was pretty. Contagious.

But she already had the thing in her hand. It was just a handful of unbent wire hangers tied into a bundle. They didn't need a name for it.

"Uncle Abram said I'm too old for that," he said.

"When your uncle starts paying my bills, I'll let him tell me what to do for five minutes. Maybe." She gestured with the thing. "Hurry up. You're not going to make me late for work today."

Which meant she had someone coming to the house be-cause she didn't work at the nursing home on Thursdays. He had

heard Uncle Abram warn her about the men who came to their
apartment. Uncle Abram didn't like the way it made their family
look. Maybe Uncle Abram needed to know she was back at it.

"Sure, Ma," he said. "Whatever you say." He smiled again
and his acquiescence confused her for a second. But she didn't
leave. He unbuttoned his blue jeans.

As he crossed the mountain, he was watchful for
anything that might be food. It wasn't until he had gone almost half the distance he needed to go and the sun was much
lower in the sky that he found a single, intact apple tree in the
remains of an orchard. The other trees had long since crumbled, their insect-eaten trunks lying in pieces. The tree had no
leaves, but its fruit - four perfectly shaped apples, each about
the size of his fist - shone bright yellow in the hazy sunlight.

Saliva warmed in his mouth. The apples were too high
for him to reach, so he climbed the tree's fragile lower branches, snapping several as he went higher. Anyone watching
would have seen the smile on his face. It was a different smile
from the one the woman was used to seeing. Bracing himself
in an elbow of the tree, he reached out with both hands and
picked two at the same time.

Once he was back on the ground, he put one in the
pocket of his pants. He pressed the other against his nose to
smell it before opening his mouth and biting into its tender
flesh.

A handful of March flies, drawn by the scent of the
unseasonable fruit, dove at his head, biting wherever they
landed. Their bites on his neck and ears were painful, and he
stood up to slap them away without losing the apple. Finally,
he slammed one against the back of his left hand, dropping it
onto a pale leaf at his feet. With two flies still crawling on his
neck, he stooped to examine the dying fly, which was on its
winged back, waving its bent legs in the air. He flicked it onto
its abdomen with the ragged edge of a chewed fingernail, but
it didn't stir from the leaf. Picking up the leaf, he held it to his
face. When his tongue met the fly, its wings stuck to him. The

thing buzzed frantically in his mouth. Even mixed with the sweetness of the apple, it tasted bitter. Foul. He spat the thing out onto the ground and finished the apple.

He stood on the mountainside looking down at the blue rectangle of concrete sitting in the center of the parking lot like some kind of giant, ugly cake. There was a sign, a glowing white figure of a large-breasted woman--her face featureless except for a pair of pouting red lips--astride a yellow neon star. It wasn't the image of the woman that stirred something deep inside him. It was the building itself, and what it contained, that aggravated the small semblance of feeling he had left. It wasn't anger. It was something more substantial, something elemental. It was a slow-burning, constant hum like the buzzing of the flies. If he had words for it, he would call it rage. But he couldn't go down to the building. Not yet. He was following the path. He couldn't veer from it.

CHAPTER TWENTY-TWO

TRIPP WAITED FOR JOLENE to put up the passenger window before he released the key from the truck's ignition. She had spent the entire drive up the mountain pressed against the door, her face to the wind.

"I had a dog that used to ride that way," Tripp said.

"What did you call her?" Jolene said. Already she looked better. Her cheeks were chafed pink from April air and she looked more awake, less tense than she had seemed down at the diner. When she'd asked if he would take her up on the mountain, he didn't question why she wanted to go there. There was a new kind of understanding between them. Not a comfortable understanding, but something.

"Peaches," he said.

"Peaches."

"She was small and kind of - I don't know. Kind of a brownish peach color."

"Oh," Jolene said.

"I didn't name her," he said, embarrassed.

He saw she wasn't listening anyway. From the truck, she headed straight for the sad mix of moss and yellowed grass filling his front yard. Dropping to a squat, she ran her hand over it thoughtfully, as though it were fine silk. He had to look away from the inch-wide stripe of porcelain skin that appeared between the top of her jeans and her black cotton pullover.

"I want to take a walk," she said, standing. "Will you come with me?"

She looked young and untouched. He had the feeling she would go on without him if he told her no.

"Nowhere I need to be today," he said. He was officially off the clock, and it suited him to stay away from the post, where they would all be talking about Claude Dixon. Burns and Johnson, the detectives, had said they wanted to talk to him again, something he definitely didn't want to do. "It's cold up here. I'll get you a jacket from inside."

"Sure, thanks," she said, turning away toward the woods.

He had never hurt a woman before.

Tripp held on to the thought like a talisman as he followed her over the mud-slicked trail. It seemed like it had rained almost every day since Claude Dixon was murdered. No big storms like the previous month, but a continual pattern of morning showers that left each afternoon draped with a dull silver sky. The air was heavy all the time. Even his legs felt weighted and reluctant to carry him.

They hiked across the mountain's southern face on a trail that eventually dumped out on a state road on the other side of the mountain. Every so often it branched off and led to smaller, less-traveled trails. They talked little, and always about what was around them. Not about Alta or Claude Dixon or Lila or even the club.

Where was Lila in all this? Lila was still his. Lila was his love. This girl was something altogether different. This girl felt *necessary*. Like breath. Like air. But if she was like air, why did he feel as though he would suffocate if he got too close to her?

Unlike Lila, there was no feminine scent trailing her, no perfume of roses or lilacs or other summer flowers. Today her hair was loose like it was when she danced. Before she put on the navy wool jacket his sister had sent him for Christmas, she had pulled her hair over one shoulder so that it framed her face like a satin hood. What would that feel like spread over his face, caught between his fingers? His lips? Along with hundreds of other men, Tripp had seen almost every inch of her skin under the stage lights. She was here now and he could reach out and touch her shoulder or her waist if he wanted to. He tried to keep his voice under control when they did talk, and not be distracted by the way her ass moved in her tight-fitting blue jeans or the tilt of her head when she laughed, the sound spilling through the trees like music.

"Here," she said, slowing.

At some point they had taken a branch of the trail that joined the old logging road the department used - *he* used - to access this part of the forest. He hadn't noticed when the ground beneath his hiking boots changed. They had just kept moving. Time seemed to be closing in on him again, just as it had when he was last with Lila.

"Ah, this place," he said. They stood at the edge of the remains of a cabin site. He had heard the story repeated his whole life - how a woman had gone mad at the end of a starving winter and murdered her husband and two children, one of whom was an infant boy. If he remembered correctly, though, the daughter's body had never been found. Jolene was naïve, and young enough to believe any story, of course. There were plenty of them, but none got to the heart of what he believed was wrong with Devil's Oven. He was certain it had to be some kind of mineral buried here, perhaps something magnetic. The ground was somehow dead. Murders had happened here, yes, but he was always careful to differentiate between causalities and correlations.

Where did Claude Dixon fit in?

"You don't believe in ghosts, do you?" he said.

"No. Not ghosts," she said.

"How'd you know about this place?" He left her on the road and started through the brush surrounding the cabin site. "I can't imagine how hard it was to live up here - what? A hundred, a hundred and fifty years ago."

"Maybe they didn't know it was hard," she said. "It sure had to be lonely." She walked around the eastern edge of the site, disappearing behind the small stand of wild rhododendrons.

He waited for her to appear again.

It was part of his job to remind people to stay on their guard when they were out in the woods. Snakes, bears, wolves, falling branches. Now there was whatever the hell had killed Claude Dixon to worry about. He never worried for himself. He knew every acre of his territory and knew, for the most part, where the dangers lay. Others depended on *him* when they got lost or injured or too drunk to find their way out.

When he broke up parties, or pairs of indiscreet lovers at other sites on Devil's Oven, people often got belligerent with him. But not here, not at this place. They always went without argument. And if any of them noticed how quiet it was - that it was always empty of birds and squirrels and other animals - they never said anything to him. Was he the only one who noticed? It was definitely quiet today.

"Jolene," he said. "Hey!"

Silence.

"Shit." He glanced around the clearing. Why was she playing games with him? He was the one who had brought her up here. Wasn't it his game?

"Jolene," he whispered, wanting to wake her, but knowing at the same time that he shouldn't.

After a moment, she opened her eyes, which were as black as her hair, and turned her head just that much so she could look up at him. She smiled the smile of an angel and extended her arms to him like a child.

He sank down on the hearthstone. What the hell was

he doing here? It felt dangerous to be alone with her here.

"Here I am," she said. Her voice came from behind him, near the ruined chimney.

He turned to give her a hard time about playing hide-and-seek, but the words wouldn't come. There was something different about her. A fragile shell of light surrounded her body. He had always known it was there, hadn't he? That was how it was between them.

She touched his shoulder and knelt down in the dirt in front of him.

When he reached out to stroke her cheek with the back of his hand, she didn't pull away, but tipped her head back to let his hand trail onto her neck. He ran his fingertips behind her ear and into her hair. He thought she might close her eyes, waiting for him to kiss her, but she stared back at him. For days he had been plagued with the image of her on the trail - lovely but weak, corpselike. A broken woman-child. The way seeing her like that made him feel, he knew he might have injured or even killed her. He hated that feeling, hated himself because of it. But while she was here in front of him, he felt different.

He leaned forward to kiss her, and she let him.

The hearthstone was unpolished granite, free of moss and dirt because of all the hikers who had rested there and the lovers who had coupled there. He thought it would be too hard and tried to ease her onto the soft ground, but she told him *no*. This was the only place, she said. Her hair spread over the stone so that they seemed to be lying on a dark blanket.

Time felt suspended in that place, but he found he couldn't hold himself back from her. Her mouth was malleable and warm, but he wanted more. He wanted to turn the whole experience around. He wanted to be inside her first, and do the other later.

When he began to strip her of her blue jeans, she didn't resist, but helped him. Her shoes were off, and then his. They were finally naked below the waist, and though at another time he would have taken a moment to touch her smooth, muscled legs and taste the salt of them, now he just wanted her. He wanted - *God forgive me and Lila forgive me* - to find the depths of her. He wanted to be in the place where he ended and she began and neither of them could tell the difference.

Jolene's hands, though small and slight, held on to his arms with a surprising, gentle strength. As she eased her way from beneath him, he found himself lying back on the cold, smooth stone. She straddled him, caressing his member with the hot interior of her thighs, but didn't let him inside her. Not yet. Something in his mind was screaming for him to overcome her, but when she pressed her lips against his chest, his shoulder, and made her way up to his neck, the screaming faded. He felt her breath on his cheek, close to his ear.

When she raised her head, he saw her face. So calm. Her eyes were closed, her lips wet. The air between them was cool with the strange, pearl light surrounding her. He moved lower beneath her so he could put his mouth to her breast. Unlike Lila's small and freckled athletic breasts, Jolene's were heavy with the promise of nourishment. Satisfaction. He suck-led and bit her nipple gently, insistently. She responded with an approving moan and pressed her breasts, her groin, harder against him. He was so lost in the taste of her that they might have remained there for hours. He found he couldn't be satis-fied. He wanted more and more of her.

Jolene didn't resist when he gripped either side of her rib cage and pushed her slowly away from him. As soon as they were sitting up, her pelvis still fitted to his, Jolene put her hands to the back of his head and pulled him close again. She kissed him deeply, as though she wouldn't let him go. She was so small in his arms. He felt as though he might break her with his need.

He ended the kiss.

Jolene opened her eyes.

In them, he saw someone else, someone who wasn't

Jolene. Someone who was far more fierce. Terrifying. He
understood then that she wasn't real, that he could never really
know her. But that didn't matter. It was Jolene in his arms, and
Jolene he would have.

The screaming need started up again in Tripp's brain.
He pressed Jolene onto her back, onto the hearthstone that
had been warmed by their bodies. As he entered her, Jolene
grimaced for the briefest of seconds, and he wondered for
just a moment if he had hurt her. He closed his own eyes so
he didn't see the unfamiliar, knowing smile that spread across
Jolene's face. He was already lost.

Lost in a flare of light, he could no longer feel her
body, but only a stinging wind that passed through his skin. As
the blazing light faded back into day, he saw a mass of treetops
below him, a white sun over his head. A dream? The air was
too cold, his body weightless. His arms were no longer arms,
but feathered extensions of the rest of his body, now coal black
and sleek. Shifting quickly from one broad ribbon of wind to
another, he felt powerful, like a threat. It was a feeling he could
get used to.

The trees below him were coming on fast, but he didn't
panic. With a tilt of a wing, he righted himself, and drifted
through a tangle of branches to land on a naked poplar.

Below, a man's body lay sprawled on a rude dirt trail,
eyes open and arms thrown wide as though to receive him. He
lifted from the poplar branch and landed beside the bloodied
head. He was close enough to tip forward and peck at the
man's open eyes - a sudden temptation. Instead he pinched the
scalp above the ear with the point of his beak and tugged away
a chunk of oily brown hair. He took a few steps, picking at the
soil with his delicate feet, then rose into the air. Effortless.

He coasted above the forest's stark canopy for a moment, and saw a woman climbing the trail, a hatchet swinging
at her side. *I know her, know why she's here. She is my purpose.*
Seeing his shadow race ahead of her, she looked up and stumbled after him for a few steps. He heard her cry out but kept

on, up, up the mountain.

There was a certain tree he was looking for, the path to it seared into his brain. The forest thinned as he flew along the mountain's ridge, the clusters of hemlocks and oaks separated by scrub and rock.

Spotting the cedar, he landed on the ragged edge of an eagle's ruined aerie that clung to a single upper limb. The scorched remnant of the second limb that had supported it for fifty years had wedged itself among living branches a few feet away. His treasures looked lonesome in the basin of the five-foot-deep nest. A rock-hard green beetle's carapace, a rusting bell that looked heavy enough to pull him to earth as he flew, a broken rattlesnake's egg. He hobbled among them, stopping to duck his head beneath a wing to root a mite out of his silver-black underfeathers. He rested, protected from the winds by the weave of twigs and glut of rabbit, fox, and mice bones, but when he felt his energy return, he covered his treasures with crisp brown leaves and took off again.

The woman wasn't hard to find. She moved slowly, dragging her feet in the dirt. There was nothing bright about her, nothing interesting or remarkable. No buttons or buckles on her heavy wool cloak or the front of the bloody nightgown on which it opened. Her black hair clutched at her face in the wind.

He called out to her. She stopped.

When he spoke the woman didn't raise her head, but only her eyes, one clear and moist, its black iris round and perfect, the other weeping red from infection.

"You're not finished," he told her. "If you don't hurry, they'll wake. You don't want them to wake." He felt his own heart quivering against his breast.

"I can't," she said, sounding uncertain.

"They've touched evil," he said.

"Innocent," she said.

He dropped down to a branch on a level with her weary face.

"His seed," he said.

The man's body was well out of sight down the trail, but she looked over her shoulder as though he might appear beside her at any second.

His hearing wasn't as good as other birds' - *where are the other animals? We seem to be the only living creatures here -* but he could hear her blood whispering through her body.

"He took the salt this time," she said. Now she brought a roughly finished box with a black iron catch from beneath her cloak. "He wasn't coming back. We made it through the winter, but he meant to leave us without salt. He meant us to die." There was passion in her voice. She was remembering.

"His seed," he said.

He flew from the rhododendron, leaving the branch bouncing gently behind him. She stared at the space where he had been.

⚜

It was only late morning, but the forest was filled with a lead dusk. After going back once more to check on his treasures, he flew to the cabin and perched on a bit of branch protruding from the roof.

The woman hadn't wasted any time.

The wailing from inside the cabin sounded no different to him than the distant cries of a family of rabbits or opossums set on by coyotes. He listened.

The black-haired girl came out of the cabin, naked, falling once, twice, as she tried to run. An endless, feral scream rose from deep in her undeveloped chest. Her face and arms were streaked with blood.

He could hear the angry murmur of the woman's blood before he saw the woman herself. But the girl could see her. Finally the girl's voice came, filling the tidy clearing and the woods beyond.

"Mamaaaaaa! Mama, no!"

She stared at her mother, frozen, the gash along her jawline weeping red.

The woman came into view, shrieking obscenities. The girl turned to run.

At first he could only see the top of the woman's head and the shoulders of her raw linen gown, which billowed in the rising wind. She cradled some small thing in the crook of one arm, and carried the hatchet - now purple with blood - in the other hand. The smell that rose up caused a shudder in his wings.

Beyond them, the white of the girl's skin flashed in the trees.

The woman looked to the sky and howled. When the sound faded into the wind, she swung around and looked up at him.

"You!" she said. "For you!" She dropped the hatchet and used both hands to thrust the thing out to him.

He bowed his head and absently groomed the nearest chest feathers. He didn't need to look at the thing in her arms. Its smell alone threatened to overwhelm him.

Giving out a shattering *caaaaaaw*, he swept from the roof, flying close enough to her head to catch one of her long black hairs on his foot.

As he rose in the sky, she started after him, pressing the pitiable thing in her hand firmly onto the pointed fencepost at the front of the yard.

The girl was stronger and faster than the woman. He followed, dodging trees as he flew. He tried calling after her, but only the woman could hear his language, only the woman could act. And she was falling farther and farther behind them. He could no longer hear the sound of her blood. Disappointment wasn't in his nature, but he sensed he was about to fail. The girl would be lost to him.

He dove at her head and she tried to beat him away as she ran. The second time he dove, she glanced his wing and he wheeled to the ground, stunned. The girl fell as well.

She sobbed, her breath coming short. He kept an eye on her as he righted himself, wary that she would try to hurt him again. She was a pretty thing, pale as dawn. Her eyes were as black as her hair, as black as her mother's. In another life she might have made a pet of him, letting him sit on her shoulder and eat from her plate.

The woman appeared, tearing through the bracken to reach the girl.

He waited. Watched. There would be more blood, and it would end.

The girl didn't run or stand to try to subdue the Fury that her mother had become. Lying prone, she turned with a languor more suited to a bed of down than one of brittle leaves and twigs. She scraped a portion of earth into her hand, then put it to her lips, mixing it with the blood already there.

He could hear her whisper even over her mother's screams.

"Mountain, hide me."

He felt the ground beneath him shudder.

The woman stumbled and fell, her voice silenced.

The girl held on to the dirt, letting the spasms of the earth move through her body. She looked apprehensive but not afraid, as though she knew what was coming but not what to think about it.

He flew to a low branch well away from her.

The ground beneath the girl swelled, prying tree roots and rocks from the dirt. The roots snapped free; half-dead branches fell like heavy rain around them. It might have been the birth throes of a second mountain on the face of Devil's Oven. Even the tree in which he was perched began to tip and fall. He flew to a second tree farther away. The earth crested, groaning, and lifted the girl as high as a full-grown dogwood tree. Trees continued to break and fall, but none of them touched the girl. From this distance he wasn't distracted by the bloody violation of her body. She was white against the dirt, soft against the crust of the mountain.

Then the risen land began to fall back onto itself. The girl held fast.

He flew from the branch to circle above her. He saw the look of calm acceptance on her face.

At the last moment, before the ground covered her completely, she raised one hand to the sky. To him.

CHAPTER TWENTY-THREE

LILA STRIPPED OFF her nightgown and panties and put on the delicious spa robe Bud had bought for her on their last trip out west. She checked the bedside clock - she was way overdue for another sedative. Her back and neck muscles were tight with stress, but a good hour in the hot tub would help with that. Though she had begun to think it was possible she would never feel clean, never feel human again.

Her cell phone sat nearby in its charger. Bud had reminded her to turn it on, and she had, but as soon as he was out of the room, she turned it off again. Her parents were freaking out, begging her to come and stay with them in the city "until that horrible killer is caught." God knew how many messages she had from Tripp.

Every time she closed her eyes, she saw one of two things: Claude Dixon's lump of a body in the blinding relief of her headlights, or Tripp's face - or what was supposed to be Tripp's face staring down at her as he carried her from the woods. But that pinched mask, with its unfocused eyes, creased jowls, and gray, hollowed cheeks, couldn't have been the man she had been sleeping with off and on for the past year. The man she trusted almost as much as Bud. What in the hell had happened to him? He had called her by that slut's name. *Jolene*.

In her heart she knew he hadn't messed with the girl, but she suddenly wanted to be free of him. It was as if Claude's murder had woken her from some spell Tripp had cast over her.

He had always been on the strange side, with his computer geek friends and the way he'd stayed away from sports in school. If any of the girls she had hung out with at school found out she'd been sleeping with him, they would laugh. *But then.*

She couldn't help herself after he pursued her for almost a year, showing up on her walking route, at the few restaurants in the area, at the grocery store, at the gym. Never pressuring her, but letting her know she was looking good, that he was there. Ready when she was. As old school friends in a small town, no one seemed to think it was unusual that they would spend fifteen minutes chatting, having coffee. Not even Bud. When she finally let herself fall into it, fall into *him*, it had felt familiar and wonderfully new at the same time. She didn't even have the excuse of being unhappy with Bud.

Tripp had been good to her, hadn't he? Almost as good as Bud, in his way. She had been a shit to them both.

It didn't matter now, though. *This* Tripp was a different person.

If she dumped him completely, would he tell the police in revenge that she'd been at the cabin that night? And if he was a different person, had he become the kind who might murder someone? No, she didn't think so. He had been standing on the porch when Claude's body came shooting out of the woods. But if she hadn't seen it for herself? *Maybe he was still capable of it.*

In the kitchen, she pinched off a still-warm corner of the banana nut bread Danelle had baked that morning, and made

a snack of wheat crackers and honey with a few baby carrots
on the side. She ate more when Bud was around because he
seemed to worry if she didn't eat as much as he thought she
needed to. Since she'd hit the down side of her thirties, she had
begun to notice she couldn't eat like she had only a year earlier.
But she was hungry even now, stressed out as she was.

She called for Danelle, just wanting to know where
she was, and that she was working. When she got no answer,
she padded from room to room in the spongy terry slippers
that matched her robe. Tripp had bought her a pretty red silk
robe at a lingerie store in a mall. She hadn't had the heart to
tell him that, like many redheads, she didn't much like to wear
red.

She found Danelle hanging sheets on the clothesline
that was hidden in the corner between the maid's tiny apartment - they never were able to find a decent live-in - and the
back of the garage. Air-dried sheets were among Lila's favorite
things. Because Alta was well away from any coal plants or paper mills, the air around Devil's Oven was always clear. Always
perfect.

She left Danelle to her work. The woman was distract-
ible enough, and Lila wanted to get some time in the hot tub
before she had to meet Bud for lunch. He had told her that he
didn't think it was right to be seen out enjoying himself after
what had happened to Claude, but she had convinced him it
was okay. It wasn't like he killed Claude or they were related or
even that they would run into Claude's poor wife (that shrew
- Lila felt mean thinking Claude was probably better off now
without her). Getting out was for Bud's peace of mind. And
hers.

She went into the backyard, balancing her plate, a dec-
orating magazine, and a mug of tea. When she was settled, she
pulled up some Sarai on her mp3 player, rested it on a towel,
and put in her earbuds. Finally, there was some sunshine, and
she could feel spring trying to break through. It seemed that
the days since Claude's death had been filled with fits of mist

and rain and cold. She was desperate for more spring. For light. She leaned her head back and closed her eyes.

He saw her from the trees. She sat in the water with her eyes closed, all but a few stray curls of her red hair wrapped in a chocolate-colored towel. The breeze brought him the smell of her sweat. It was nothing like the sour smell of Claude Who Was Not Food or the stench of sickness that came off Thora. It was sweeter, like something from the woods. But as much as it attracted him, it was the smell coming from the kitchen that drew him past her and into the house.

He walked in an arc behind her, keeping to the bushes, not because he was concerned she would see him, but because it was the easiest way to the kitchen. She was what he had come for, but she could wait.

The house felt familiar. It was more than the smell of the nutty loaf he found cooling on the kitchen counter. It was the feeling of space - of tile and painted walls; rich cabinetry; vast, open ceilings; and shining floors. He recognized these things and found them pleasing. He picked up the loaf and broke it into halves. He bit into one half, then stuffed his mouth full of its sweetness. But as he ate, his hunger grew instead of faded, as though his gut were being quickly emptied. By the time he was finished and licking the last few crumbs from his fingertips, he was trembling all over. Thirsty, too. He looked around for something to drink.

"What the hell are you doing in my kitchen?"

A woman - not the one he had come for - set the basket of laundry she was carrying on the floor. She was much shorter than he, reaching only to the middle of his chest. With her gray hair and lusterless white skin, she was like Thora. The tang of her fear made his nose itch.

"You get yourself out of here," she said. He watched her eyes slip to the knives hanging above the massive stove.

He caught her in the front hallway, first grabbing her by the shoulder, then getting hold of the roll of fat around her neck. She died quickly. He had taken one of the smaller knives, and, standing over her, he thought of the other yellow apple in his pocket, of peeling the skin from it with the blade, and raising the blade with the skin of the apple to his teeth.

⬩ ◂ ✦ ▸ ⬩

He could hear the teacher calling from maybe a hundred yards away at the other end of the orchard. The three of them - Anthony, Marcus, and David - made an awkward triangle around Allan. Shy Allan who couldn't speak, and would only sign with David, or his aide, who was home sick that day.

"You're it, Allan," Anthony said, right into Allan's face. "You know how to count to a hundred, don't you?" He thought hide-and-seek was stupid and that they were too old to play it, but the field trip was boring and the teacher had left them on their own for the last twenty minutes. Anthony hated the country. There were probably killer snakes around the orchards - copperheads, the pit vipers the science teacher was always talking about, or maybe someone's escaped pet python.

"He's deaf, not stupid, you moron," Marcus said.

"Bite me, asshole," Anthony said.

Marcus was always out to make him look stupid. Marcus wasn't afraid of anything because his older brother Nikko always came around to settle his problems. He had seen Marcus, his girly pink lips pressed together in a smug smile, stand behind Nikko as Nikko beat the shit out of another eighth grader who had cut ahead of Marcus in the lunch line.

"Take a joke, moron," Marcus said. "Anyway, it's your turn. Allan goes last. He always goes last." Marcus wasn't going to let him make an issue of it.

Allan folded his arms and croaked out something that might have been "yeah." But he wouldn't meet Anthony's eyes.

David didn't say anything, either, which meant he was

with Marcus. As always.

"I'm only counting to fifty," Anthony said, turning around. "And don't even think about leaving me here, assholes."

They had been climbing up into the trees to hide from both the seekers and the orchard staff, who had lectured them about staying close to their classmates or the farm store when they were done picking their bucket of apples. Anthony had already given his apples to Leeza, a sixth-grade girl he liked.

Anthony walked slowly through the orchard, listening, but at the same time keeping a watch out for snakes.

He found David easily because he had been dumb enough to try to hide without taking off the bright red down vest he was wearing. Sometimes Anthony wondered who was dumber: David or Marcus. He was pretty sure David's old man had dropped him on his head when he was a baby. The two of them found Allan in a graying wooden crate the pickers used to dump the apples.

This time they heard the teacher's whistle blow, which meant it was the last call.

"I'm done with this shit," Anthony said. "Let's go."

"We gotta get Marcus," David said. "Where's Marcus?"

"Screw Marcus. I'm going to get some more of that cider stuff," Anthony said.

Allan shook David's arm, signed, and pointed to the western side of the orchard, which ended in an overgrown field.

"Allan says Marcus is over there."

"You find him," Anthony said.

"You're such a pussy," David said. "Marcus always says you're a pussy."

Anthony knew David was baiting him, but he bit anyway. He'd been thinking he might be able to take on Marcus's brother if he had to. There was a hunting knife he had lifted from a sporting goods store that he'd been practicing with. It was big, though. He would have to be wearing his boots to get it into school.

David and Allan watched him go into the overgrown pasture. The grass and weeds were all at least two or three feet tall *and hid everything except the top of a rusting sedan and a piece of farm equipment that was in similar shape.*

"Marcus!" Anthony shouted. "Come out, you asshole!"

He looked in the sedan first. All of the glass was broken out and a bush with red, leafless branches grew up out of the backseat floor. He climbed up on the collapsing hood of the car, almost losing his footing on its pitted surface.

David yelled for them to come on. From behind them, Anthony could hear the shrill scream of the teacher's whistle getting closer.

He saw a flash of Marcus's yellow T-shirt against the brown grass and jumped down. He ran. He could get in at least three or four good punches before David or Allan could even get out there.

Later he would hear that the mangled thing Marcus was hiding under was called a haybine. He had heard of combines, but this was something different. It wasn't his fault that some lazy farmer had left the stupid thing half taken apart out in the field, its tines and bale spear hidden in the tall grass.

Springing onto the hitch end of the haybine, he walked along the metal arm like it was a balance beam. When it shifted beneath his feet, he heard Marcus cry out. He froze.

"Shit, oh my god!" Marcus sounded terrified, amazed. "I'm dead!" Then he made a croaking sound that made Anthony want to laugh until he realized it was the real thing.

Anthony couldn't move. The teacher's whistle blew. He heard his name, but who was calling him? Now it came over him. That feeling of happiness. That feeling like warm sunshine that filled him when things were going just right.

Anthony jumped, rocking the busted heap of metal. Marcus was crying. Crying like a baby. He jumped again and again until the haybine shifted again and he fell off. From where Anthony lay in the tall grass, he could see one of Marcus's arms. Finally, Marcus stopped crying and let out a burst of air like a punctured tire. He went silent.

·‹ ❦ ›·

It took Anthony a minute to find the refrigerator, disguised as it was to look like the rest of the cabinets. The smells from inside it rushed at him: meat, asparagus, wine, ripe cheese, sugar. Lots of sugar. He wiped his bloody hands on one of the bright green dish towels lying on the counter before he scooped his fingers into a crockery bowl of pudding topped with meringue.

The pudding was vanilla, and there were cookies and slices of banana at the bottom of the dish. Taking a second scoop, he got cookie crumbs wedged beneath his shallow fingernails, but it didn't bother him. Then he peeled a fleshy layer of meringue off the undisturbed side of the bowl. He put a chunk of it in his mouth and closed his eyes, standing still as it melted on his tongue. Finally, the smell of banana and sugar overcame the smell of the woman's blood coming off his clothes and skin. When the bowl was empty, he opened a jug of milk and drank, nearly choking himself with the flow.

"Red? You home?"

He had never heard the man's voice, but his words brought the smell of him through the big front hallway into the kitchen and he knew. Still, it wasn't time to kill the man. Not yet.

The front door shut and he heard the jangle of keys.

"Danelle?"

Anthony felt the air change. The man had found the woman. Anthony looked out the big glass door that opened onto the backyard. The other woman, the one he had come for, was still in the water.

"Red! Where are you?"

He heard the pounding of the man's feet as he ran up the front stairs.

Anthony took one more drink from the jug of milk and set it back on the refrigerator shelf.

Lila's first thought was that a cloud had drifted between her and the weak April sun. She opened her eyes. The sun wasn't bright enough to put the man standing over her in backlit shadow, so she was able to get a good look at him. It seemed the two of them were locked together there - she, surrounded by water, her body bare, vulnerable, he - well, who in the hell was he, and what was he doing there? Should she be afraid? He was enormously tall, and his clothes were dirty, caked with mud and - *Jesus, is that blood?* Her mind froze. She wouldn't be able to recall until much later that he had initially seemed handsome to her, like someone she might flirt with at a party to make Bud jealous enough to take her home and give her the kind of loving attention she wanted. But by then she had seen his eyes, and the smile that made her want to make herself as small as possible and hide in some safe and secret place.

Before she could speak or move, she heard Bud scream at her to *get down!* His voice came from above her, maybe from one of the upstairs windows.

Thank God. Thank God for Bud, who loves me.

The man was already lifting her from the water when Bud took the shot. She trusted Bud. He would never miss, would never kill her instead of the man whose sure hands were squeezing the breath out of her so that she couldn't even scream. She kicked at him, but she was nothing in his arms, and soon he was holding her in such a way that she couldn't land her foot anywhere on him. She knew if she let him hold on to her, let him take her, she was already dead.

She clawed at his face and neck. His skin was waxy and stiff beneath her nails. They would use a special tool to dig it from beneath her fingernails when they autopsied her. She had seen it on TV, imagined the clink of the stainless on stainless as they finished and dropped the tool into a basin. Finally, she was able to scream, but the man didn't flinch or even try to shut her up.

Then they were moving away from the house and she

was seeing the world upside down and she could hear Bud screaming after them. Poor Bud. He sounded afraid for her. But there were no more shots. Then there was no more Bud. There were only the filthy heels of the man carrying her and the sudden, cold embrace of the forest.

CHAPTER TWENTY-FOUR

B UD PACED THE KITCHEN, unable to sit. He could
hear the troopers out in the hallway. They kept their
voices low, but there was no mistaking the undercurrent
of excitement. Danelle was lying out there, her blood painted
in an almost perfect arch on the wall beneath the staircase. Her
husband, Roy, was on his way to the house.

Bud wanted to roar into the hallway and blast them
all out of there. He wanted Danelle to be alive and whistling
the funny little tunes that drove Lila crazy. He wanted Claude
back at his desk working the phones. He wanted everything
back the way it was.

He had let Lila down. He'd had the chance to save her
and he had let her down. Was she even alive? If she was, what
was the bastard doing to her? Every muscle in his body tensed
at the thought of what she might be going through. Lila
wasn't afraid of much, but he had seen her face as the creature
dragged her out of the hot tub. The word *terror* didn't begin to
describe what he had seen there.

His carry piece sat empty on the kitchen table under
the watchful eye of the patrolman guarding the patio door.
Bud wanted to grab it like a lifeline and run out after Lila.
She was somewhere on Devil's Oven, but the troopers weren't

letting him leave, and they weren't doing anything to find her. The way they had talked to him, he wondered if they thought he was involved. He would be damned if he was going to sit around any longer. He took out his cell phone to call Dwight as he headed for the front hall.

"Mr. Tucker?"

Detective Johnson made a hard stop in the kitchen doorway to keep from running into Bud. "I need another minute of your time."

"I want a hell of a lot more than a minute of *your* time," Bud said. "Do you know what could be happening to my wife while you people are screwing around down here? Where are the damn dogs? Is someone bringing dogs?"

The detective gave a look to the trooper by the door, and the man nodded. He went outside to join the technicians near the hot tub.

"Detective Burns is on his way. We're putting a team together," Johnson said. "Let's you and me sit down for a minute."

"I want your people to get their asses out there and find my wife."

"If they're on foot, they're not going to get very far, very fast. You said the guy was barefoot?" Johnson said. "The Dixon woman said the man who took her husband was barefoot." He absently bit at a thumbnail and studied it. "Hell of a thing to be running around the woods in your bare feet."

"My wife didn't have *any* clothes on, Detective. Her hair was wrapped in a towel!" He didn't like the guy's attitude. Johnson was a pissant downstate trooper, but he carried himself like he had a camera trained on him twenty-four/seven.

Bud could smell peppermint on the detective's breath as he pressed in close. He knew there was a chance he could get the guy's 9mm in his gut, or - if another officer happened to see them arguing - a state-issued, .40-caliber piece pointed at his head.

"A fucking towel," Bud said. "I'll be damned if I see

any humor in that."

Johnson's left eye twitched.

"The aggrieved husband thing only buys you so much patience," he said. "You need to step away."

Before Bud could respond, they heard shouts from the hallway. Roy cried out his wife's name.

"Wait here," Johnson said.

Bud didn't much appreciate the detective's tone. He followed him into the hallway, unwilling to be pushed around.

A pair of troopers held Roy by each arm. He strained forward, his face red and twisted with pain, trying to get to his wife's body in the middle of the floor. He wore his farm coveralls and greasy ball cap, and looked as crazed as any drunk that Bud had removed from the club on a payday Friday night. Only, Roy didn't drink. It was a picture that would stick in Bud's head for a long damn time.

Roy and Danelle were good people. Claude Dixon had been good people, too.

Seeing that Detective Johnson and the troopers had their hands full with Roy, Bud backed slowly into the kitchen, then turned and ran up the back stairs two at a time, his footfalls masked by the thick carpet.

The troopers hadn't yet gotten to the second floor of the house, and the bedrooms were all empty. The master suite opened onto the gallery overlooking the foyer, so he had to take care to prevent them from seeing him go in and out. It wasn't like he was easy to miss, either. Fortunately, they were still dealing with Roy, and Roy wasn't getting any quieter.

Bud found the 9mm in his bedside table, just where it was supposed to be, and made his way back downstairs.

With troopers and technicians in both the front and back of the house, the only safe ways out were the garage and the side door leading to the yard where Danelle hung the laundry.

The garage was closer to the woods.

Bud bent forward as he climbed, carefully negotiating the muddy incline that was glutted with trees from some long-past storm. The loafers he wore were no good for a run up a mountain, and after ten minutes they were caked with mud and leaves. He kept his eyes open for a sturdy branch or limb to brace him, but everything he tried to pick up crumbled in his hand. All he had was the gun, and it was more of a hindrance than anything at this point. But he couldn't leave it behind. He had to be ready to take the shot.

Raised east of the Piedmont, not far from the low-country, he was wary of the mountains. He never could understand why Lila had changed her mind about coming back after they had been married a couple of years. They had made a life here, but he felt the presence of the mountains too fiercely. Their shadows smothered him. He had to get away from time to time, with or without Lila.

There was no clear path ahead. The creature - the man, whatever the hell he was - had been enormous, Lila tiny in his arms. It was unbelievable to Bud that he hadn't busted a visible swath through the trees as he ran. *How could any human run so fast?*

Judging that he was plenty far enough away from the house, he called out for Lila. He stood still for a moment, listening. The sound of a dog barking was all that came back to him.

It had been his idea to demand that the troopers get a K-9 unit onto the mountain to track Lila, but they hadn't jumped on it. What were they waiting for?

CHAPTER TWENTY-FIVE

TRIPP WOKE TO THE DRONE of an engine. A small plane? No, a deeper sound. A helicopter was crawling across the sky, above Devil's Oven. Where was it going? Sometimes he forgot there was a world beyond the mountain.

He opened his eyes.

He was stretched over the couch in his living room, the cashmere throw that Lila had bought to match the couch laid neatly over him. Remembering the woods and the bloody visions, he pushed off the throw and tried to get up. But the pain in his head was like a wall that kept him down, and he fell back with a groan.

"Don't."

Soft fingertips gently pressured his temples, and the sharpest edge of the pain melted away. Jolene. The girl in his dream. *Also Jolene.*

I remember the woman. The dead man's eyes. The taste of his hair on my tongue.

"I'm going to throw up," Tripp said.

Jolene quickly stepped away. The small plastic trashcan from the bathroom sat beside the couch as though she had known what was going to happen. He felt her watching as he leaned forward to hold on to the can's sides. He retched again and again, tasting bile, but nothing came. His body was in more chaos than it had been when he chugged a half-pint of tequila on a dare, back when he was training in the forestry program. He should have had his stomach pumped that night, but they had been forty miles from the nearest phone or hospital, and he'd just had to sweat it out.

When the heaving stopped and his breath returned, he sat back.

Jolene had retreated to the other side of the coffee table. *Wise move.* Whatever she had stirred up inside of him wasn't letting go easily.

It whispered inside his head: *Again. Kill her again.*

He shook his head, trying to dislodge the voice.

Now she came close and knelt in front of him just like she had at the cabin site, but this time her presence repelled him.

"Nobody knows when it takes hold of them. I promise you aren't the first," she said.

"Get out of my house," he said. "I don't know who or what you are, but you need to get the hell away from me."

"It has you," she said. "And the man who was dead. The man who killed Claude."

When he laughed, it sounded so natural, so *right* to his ears. She was batshit crazy, this girl. He had screwed her and she had done something to him. Maybe her crazy had rubbed off. Crazy people were poison. He knew that well enough from the reprobate behavior he saw when the tourists and the meth heads came around. No wonder Lila didn't like her.

"Come on," he said. "You're just screwing with me because you're jealous of Lila. You're just a piece of stripper ass from over the mountain looking to get some of what she's got."

He waited for her to answer and was satisfied when she didn't even bother to deny it. Was that some kind of pity in her eyes? Pity from some little girl who had drugged him, then tried to make it seem like *he* was the crazy one? Fat chance.

"Let me guess. You've been messing around with Bud," he said, talking faster and faster. "You think you're going to get him away from Lila and he'll buy you all the flashy shit you girls like? Playing the whore with him, hoping it'll turn into Christmas."

The pain in his head roared back, but he stood anyway. She looked small there on the floor below him. *Lying bitch.* She had made him unfaithful to Lila.

"He has Lila and she's going to die," she said. "Just like my brother. Just like my father."

"Shut up," he said. He wanted to kick her.

She wrapped a hand around his right leg as though she had read his mind. "Stop. Please," she said. "It's not you who wants to hurt me. Please, *please* listen."

CHAPTER TWENTY-SIX

A T THE SAME MOMENT that Tripp had opened his eyes, Lila opened hers. But she squeezed them shut again on seeing the man's face above her, his dead eyes reflecting the tease of sunlight leaking into the cave. In the next second, she felt the jab between her legs. She screamed loud and long, wanting to wrap herself safely in the sound. Maybe if she could make the sound last forever, time would disappear.

She would disappear.

CHAPTER TWENTY-SEVEN

"MY MOTHER CHANGED IN A DAY," Jolene said. "She became someone else. I saw it. My father saw it, too."

Tripp watched her face for signs of lies - the *tell,* they called it back in his law enforcement classes. She had told him she was born on Devil's Oven over a hundred years earlier. *Bullshit.* No one lived that long. There were rumors of white oaks on Devil's Oven that had been growing for twice that long, but he had never seen them, and he knew every inch of the mountain.

The screaming in his head had a voice now. *She lies,* it told him. *She thinks she's an angel. Does she look like an angel to you? Look at those tits. Pretending to be a little girl with tits like that. She's an abomination!*

Maybe he was as bullshit crazy as she was, but he kept himself present enough to listen to her. She'd said something had happened to Lila. It didn't matter to him if Lila was at home with Bud. He just wanted her to be *safe.* But he was having trouble focusing on Jolene's words because the voice was scratching at the back of his brain, like an animal trying to get to the other side of a closed door. How long would it be before it demanded to be let in? Would he have to let it in?

"She wouldn't nurse the baby for more than a couple minutes at a time," Jolene said. "He screamed and screamed and I had to take him from her because she would just stop talking, stop looking at him. Like he wasn't even there." Her voice was agitated. The face she showed him was that of the young girl he had seen fleeing through the woods, her hair flying behind her, threatening to tangle itself on the low-hanging branches she passed. Even from far above her, he had been able to smell her fear.

Far above her. He couldn't expel the images she had put in his mind. He didn't want them, damn it. He wanted to grab her and shake her and make her stop lying. He squeezed his fists tight, willing himself not to hurt her.

"Why are you telling me this? You're telling me I screwed a corpse? A corpse that comes back every so often to ruin people's lives?" he said. "I don't know what bullshit you pulled on me, but it stops now."

The voice had a sound like the hiss of burning coals: *The little slut drove her mother mad. Her own mother!*

"You saw," she said. "You saw what she did to them!"

"I saw what you wanted me to see," he said.

"Have you ever watched a child die?"

How many animals had Tripp seen, their lifeblood feeding the dirt? Injured bucks, fawns dying quietly from shock. Bodies from the last two plane crashes, dead already. Was Lila already dead? If he had to, he would kill this girl - *this liar* - to find out.

"I begged my father to dig up the money he kept buried in the woods, and go down and buy a milk cow so the baby could live." She looked down at the floor like she was ashamed. "At least for a while."

"You're screwing with me," he said. "Drugs. You gave me something. It was at the diner, wasn't it?"

"Believe whatever you want," she said, tears nearly choking her words. "What you saw was as real as you are. But there's something else here. It's kept me here, kept me safe.

It's not like the other. It's not like the thing that destroyed my mother, killed my family." She tried to touch him, but he jerked away as though she had burned him.

"Get away from me," he said.

Her voice dropped to a whisper. "I live. And then I don't," she said. "You saw it. You saw *me*."

"I had a goddamn *dream*," he said. "You drugged me and I had a goddamn dream." *Lila. Lila.* He had to stop being angry. He had to find out about Lila. He closed his eyes a moment to get a grip.

"Living it was like a dream," she said. "I could see it in her even before she did it. All around her was black. Black like *she* was already dead. As black as the stupid crow."

Here, she looked at him, accusing. So if she was any kind of angel - even he had thought she was, seeing her up on the stage, bathed in light - she wasn't a true one. She had no real compassion. But he wasn't going to let her know she was getting to him.

Ask the slut what she let her father do to her. Ask her who the baby really belonged to. Make her tell you how they shared a bed. All of them.

The voice was trying to distract him. He tried to focus on Lila, but he couldn't hold her face in his mind. It kept slipping away. "You know, it doesn't matter what you did to me, or anybody else," he said. "You know something about Lila, and I don't give a flying shit if a talking raccoon told you what's going on." He pushed his face into hers. "You're going to tell me."

If she felt threatened, she didn't show it.

Dead. Lila could be dead.

She's going to let your woman die, her eyes open to the snow and rain and my children, the insects. Just like her father. Just like her brother. Just like Ivy Luttrell's father. She did that. The slut did that!

Her shoulders dropped. She finally looked defeated. "I didn't stop my mother. And I didn't stop Ivy's father, either. I was a coward. I had two chances," she said. "Two chances to change things." Her voice trailed off.

She stared, taking all of him in. "All around you," she said.

The voice was louder now, and he could feel the scratching at the back of his brain intensifying.

"The darkness - it's all around you," she said. "You're going to let it in."

The answer screamed in his brain, but he wouldn't speak.

"You can kill me and bury me on the mountain. You can go on and kill your Lila - which you *will* do - if that creature doesn't kill her first. But I'll come back," she said. "I can't help it. I always do."

Tripp hit her across the cheek with the flat of his hand. She didn't flinch.

"You'll be gone, Tripp. You'll die. She'll die," she said. "Haven't you done enough to her already?"

The scratching quieted some. He'd seen how afraid Lila had been up on the mountain the morning he chased her through the woods. All he had wanted was to be with her the way they were meant to be. Was she really in danger from him?

He knew the answer

"We can help her," Jolene said. "We can help her and no one else has to die." Now she pressed his hand. Her palm and fingers were warm. Real. He felt the thing inside his brain jump, lunging one more time at the door of his resolve. He started to pull away from her again, and the thing seemed to get stronger, but Jolene held on tight.

Tripp squeezed his eyes shut, witnessing the battle inside. It wasn't the bird itself inside him. Whatever it was, it was putrid. Cruel. Desperate to live. The strength in Jolene's hand was overpowering it, driving it back. It snarled, clinging to him. He knew he had to make a choice. He thought of the blackness suffocating Lila. Tripp laid his other hand on top of

Jolene's. The scratching thing backed away, its oily protrusions retreating from the pathways it had made in his brain. The voice was quiet.

Tripp opened his eyes. Jolene's soft eyes looked back at him. They both knew the thing wasn't gone completely, but it was enough. For now.

Jolene looked tired, and so young. In that moment, he felt more sorry for her than he did for himself.

CHAPTER TWENTY-EIGHT

D WIGHT PRESSED THE ANSWER button on his phone earpiece, barely pausing as he stacked bar towels and aprons on a kitchen rack. "Twilight Club," he said.

"Hey there, buddy." The call disconnected, but he knew the voice well enough. A car door slammed out back.

Shit. He shoved a pile of aprons onto the shelf and hustled out of the kitchen.

His first thought was to grab the coach gun from behind the bar, but he hesitated, hoping he was mistaken about the call and who it might be. Maybe it was a wrong number. Maybe he was just jumpy, what with the cash in the supply closet and Claude Dixon's murder, and the two girls who had already called in sick for the night. He hadn't been able to reach Charity or Jolene to see if they could work, either. Charity almost always was willing to pitch in. She was the most professional dancer he had on the call sheet.

By the time the kitchen door buzzer rang, Dwight was tucking the 9mm from the office safe into the back waistband of his jeans. He shook out the hem of his loose Leon Redbone T-shirt to make sure it covered. The video screen monitoring the kitchen door showed a man there, his back to the camera.

But Dwight knew him by the hunch of his meaty shoulders and the way he dropped his spent cigarette, stubbed it out, and picked the burned end away before putting the used filter in his pocket.

Pat was always very tidy.

Dwight would've liked to relax, knowing that Pat had come all the way from up north to see him, but he knew this visit was nothing to relax about.

⋆ ⪡ ⪢ ⪡ ⋆

"I'm worried about you, D," Pat said. "When I see your brother at Knights meetings, I seem to know more about what's going on with you than he does."

"You're the one doesn't look too good," Dwight said, pouring daiquiri mix into a shaker filled with ice and two shots of rum. They didn't speak while he shook the drink and strained it into the glass.

"Since when do you drink at lunchtime?" Dwight tried to keep his real worry out of his voice.

"Same shit, different day," Pat said. "Only more of it than usual." He sipped the daiquiri and flicked his tongue over his lips, tasting. Then he drank it down.

Dwight watched, surprised he could see Pat's Adam's apple working in his fleshy neck.

"Nice," Pat said. "You always could make a decent drink."

Dwight waited while Pat dabbed at his mouth with the cocktail napkin, folded it, and put it in the empty glass.

"What I need to know is why you're doing me wrong, Dwight. Making my life hard." He sighed, as though emphasizing what a shame it was. "I've got a wife for that." He kept his voice friendly. They were indeed friends.

"How is Marie?" Dwight said. He had the money Pat was after. Most of it, anyway. If Bud showed up while they were negotiating, there might be a problem. But if he could keep Pat reminded of their friendship, Pat was likely to settle for the fifty grand. For now. It felt good to be shooting the shit with him, just like they did when they had worked together at the same bar before Pat met Marie.

"Expensive as ever," Pat said, smiling at the mention of her name. It touched Dwight's heart to see that true love could stay true.

"She did that teeth-whitening thing they do with lights at the dentist. Cost me three hundred bucks, but she looks like a movie star." He plucked a few nuts from a nearby bowl and popped them into his mouth. "You should try it."

"Yeah, probably," Dwight said. He didn't like people giving him shit about his teeth. Even Pat.

"So, where's your boss?" Pat said, looking around the empty bar. "Time for me to meet him. I didn't come here to this hell hole to bring you a box of Yummy pies."

"You always were a selfish bastard," Dwight said.

Pat followed him down the back hallway.

"So, this Bud didn't mention anything about someone coming down to see him a couple weeks ago? I've never met the Anthony guy, but I hear he's pretty hard to miss," Pat said.

"Bud usually tells me everything," Dwight said. "Must be the stress of the situation made him uptight. He's a good guy. An honorable man."

Behind him, Pat snorted. "Yeah, what a guy," he said. "Putting a friend like you in this kind of position. Messes with our relationship, you know? I hate that, man."

Pat's words touched Dwight. He stumbled in his response, tried to laugh it off.

"Yeah, I'm everybody's sweetheart," he said. "I got a whole harem of admirers here in Bugtussle. I'm a G.D. pushover."

"You're such a shit," Pat said. "I never should've let you

talk me into this deal. And I definitely should've asked them to send down someone else to follow up on this Anthony. They're looking for more than money, Dwight. You don't know how it is. Things are tight."

Dwight unlocked the supply closet door. He turned back to Pat. The dark circles beneath his friend's eyes were mushroom gray, and he had put on forty pounds since they had last seen each other. *Sad.* Pat looked seriously stressed. Maybe he should've made his daiquiri a double.

"You did me a solid," Dwight said. "We'll get this straightened out."

He gave Pat a smile of genuine gratitude. Maybe they weren't screwed after all. It meant a lot that Pat was on his side. When it was all over, he would have to tell Bud what a good guy Pat had been. He turned back to the closet to dig out the briefcase.

It was only dumb luck that made him stand up again so quickly that Pat's gun came down hard on his right shoulder rather than at the base of his skull. As he lost his footing, he got a look at Pat's face. It had transformed into something ugly and fierce.

"Shit a G.D. brick!" Dwight said. The 9mm cut into his back, reminding him he didn't have to go down helpless. He grabbed for the vacuum cleaner to right himself. But Pat's pearl-handled derringer - a prissy-ass piece for a gangster, Dwight had always thought - was pointed at his face.

"Why did you make me do this?" Pat's face was screaming red. Spittle flew from his mouth onto Dwight's cheek. "You're such an asshole!"

Dwight felt his bowels start to loosen, but he held on.

"It was a mistake, man," he said. "You're right. It was business."

"Even Marie," Pat said. "Even *she* thought it was a suck-ass idea and I didn't listen. She's smarter than you are. You had to go and screw me over."

Pat was genuinely upset. Dwight could see that now.

He regretted that part.

"I said, you're right."

The big advantage he had over Pat was Pat's own ungainliness. Dwight kicked the wheeled mop bucket into Pat's legs, causing Pat to stumble forward. He didn't fall, but dropped the gun onto Dwight's stomach as he tried to catch himself.

Dwight pushed up off the floor and launched himself at the larger man. When Pat went down, Dwight rolled on top of him. His shoulder hurt like hell, and he didn't like what he was doing. Pat was the innocent party here. Pat, who had only tried to help.

Pat grabbed hold of Dwight's hair with one hand and landed a wobbly punch in his side. But Dwight just took it as he worked to get at the 9mm. Getting his hand on the grip, he tried to pull away to get a shot at Pat, but Pat suddenly pulled him close, like a lover. Dwight could feel Pat's soggy breath, his lips on his ear. The warm tingle that spread through the bottom half of his body scared the hell out of him, and his mind answered it with a blank wall of rage. Then Pat had his ear between his teeth.

Dwight felt the cartilage tear as Pat worked to get the ear loose. He roared.

Riveted by the pain, Dwight pushed the 9mm between them and got off a shot into the left side of Pat's rib cage.

Pat's scream entered one side of Dwight's head and stayed there. He pushed off of his friend and onto the floor. Dwight lay there, breathing hard and staring up at the ceiling, not wanting to watch Pat die.

CHAPTER TWENTY-NINE

B UD WAS SWEATING LIKE A PIG, but there was no way in hell he was going to take off the leather jacket Lila had made him put on that morning. The jacket was the color of the dried leaves and pine needles carpeting the ground, and he was counting on it to camouflage him from the helicopter buzzing overhead. When he found a low place that looked like it recently had water running through it, he knelt and scraped some dirt into his hands. He hesitated only a second before smearing it over his head and nose and cheeks. At first, he had thought the people in the helicopter were looking for Lila, but now he understood they were after him.

As a kid, he had stayed out of trouble unless someone really provoked him. Because of his size, people assumed he played football, or was a natural bully. He *had* played football for a while, but he stopped after his first year on the varsity team, because he felt miserable every time the coach told them to go out and put the other team in a *world of hurt*. Bud started to think about the world of hurt as a real place, where the maimed and injured hid themselves and their pain behind fragile walls that would only stand until the next game, the next big competition where they would again get their asses handed to them. It shamed Bud to put people in that place. It had only recently occurred to him that not all coaches demanded that kind of thing from their players. Only coaches like the ones his old man was fond of.

The police obviously thought he had killed Danelle, and had done something with Lila. *Morons.* They probably saw it as a crime of opportunity. Everyone knew some creep was on the loose, so Bud had taken advantage of the situation by making it look like the creature had killed Danelle, then killed Lila. And done what with her, exactly?

He had no reason. No motive.

Lila was his treasure - his beautiful, lovable, funny, pain-in-the-ass treasure. And now some kind of beast had her.

Had the sonofabitch touched her? The coroner, who liked the occasional, discreet evening at the club, had let Bud slip into the morgue at the county hospital to take a look at Claude. It was the image of Claude's tortured body that propelled Bud forward, panting and desperate.

Finally, it got almost quiet. Bud could hear dogs in the far distance, but the helicopter had moved to the other side of Devil's Oven, or had gone off to refuel. He slackened his pace enough to catch his breath. When he put the back of his hand to his brow, it came back muddy brown and wet. Dirty sweat trickled around his thick brows and into the outer corners of his eyes. Lila would be embarrassed for him to be seen looking like this. And what about her? Naked, dragged up the hillside. What a joke on them both.

He unfastened several shirt buttons to cool off and sat down on a log. Now was the time to keep moving, he knew. If the dogs were off their leashes, he was screwed. But the adrenaline that had driven him up the mountain had abated and he was exhausted. Worse, his chest felt tight, like the breath was being squeezed out of him.

His mother's brother, Stephen, had died of an enlarged heart. They said it was as big as a grapefruit and had crowded the walls of his chest until it burst with the effort of keeping him alive. Bud didn't want to die out here, leaving Lila alone with the beast. Though maybe the police would actually start looking for her then.

When Bud heard the dogs again, closer, he knew it was time to move on. He wished for water. There had been no time, no thought of bringing anything with him except the gun.

CHAPTER THIRTY

IVY FORCED HERSELF TO WORK, putting the extra couple of inches into the pregnant bridesmaid's dress. She teased out the seams she had already made, not really minding that she was undoing her own stitches. It was the nature of her business, changing things, transforming things. Nothing was ever truly finished.

The house was quiet, except for the rainy patter of dead oak leaves that the afternoon wind brought to her window. For once, she had the door open to the hallway because there were no sounds to shut out, no grating snores from Anthony or the soap operas Thora had always watched at full volume. When had she last been alone in the house? Probably in early March, when one of the women from the church had picked up Thora for the monthly women's lunch because Ivy was too busy to drive her.

Ivy had never been a worrier, but she was worried now. Something was going to happen to Anthony, and it would be her fault because she hadn't paid attention, hadn't kept him occupied and happy.

What was happy to Anthony? Piles of food on the table. A passive hour in Thora's chair watching television game shows, his eyes blinking as slowly as a cat's.

She wondered what went through his mind when he watched people acting silly on those shows. Sometimes he smiled his hideous smile, or grunted his approval, but no matter how ridiculous the people were, she never heard him laugh. More than anything, she wanted to be able to see inside his mind, to learn how to please him, to keep him out of trouble. Be a friend - or more - to him. She had always suspected she was meant for someone besides the truck farmers, government drones, miners, and handymen who managed to eek out some kind of living from the region. For a long time, she had thought she would eventually have to leave Alta and Devil's Oven to find the man she was meant for. But Anthony had come to her.

When she finished the bridesmaid's dress, she hung it on the hook on the back of the door and steamed it so the few wrinkles she had put into it would fall out. The way she had fashioned it, working a barely noticeable dart into the seam where the skirt was attached, guaranteed that no one would know the girl was pregnant.

Was she carrying a baby girl or baby boy? Did the girl know, or even care? She had seemed pretty smart, but Ivy knew that having intelligence didn't provide immunity against making stupid decisions about boys.

Once upon a time it had mattered to her deeply to have a boyfriend or husband. Someone to make babies with. She had even secretly enjoyed it - just a little bit, hadn't it been thrilling? - when in sixth grade, Lila and one of her more obnoxious friends had "accidentally" locked her in the sports equipment shed behind the grandstand with Tripp Morgan and Sheryl Dixon's younger brother, Isaac. Isaac, two years her junior, had been the one to kiss her, his dry lips pressing against hers until she thought the edges of her front teeth would cut through and draw blood. Tripp was there to make sure they didn't chicken out. He had stared down at the dirt floor, where the lines of sunlight coming through the badly hung door made a kind of ladder near his feet.

"This is stupid," Tripp had said before Isaac could kiss her a second time.

His words made Ivy feel stupid, too. She had pushed Isaac away, suddenly ashamed, hating that she had told Lila about liking Isaac. Why had she let Lila talk her into doing it? She wondered if Tripp remembered that day. She saw him in Alta a few times a year, and still didn't feel completely comfortable looking him in the eye. She didn't know what had happened to Isaac. Now his brother-in-law was dead, murdered by Anthony.

Like a circle, it came back to her.

The pregnant bridesmaid would be back the next day. Had she told anyone about Anthony? Surely she hadn't, what with her own secret so precious to her. That secret wouldn't remain one for all that long, though. And what then? Ivy's secret would mean nothing. The girl could tell anyone she wanted about the naked man she had seen in Ivy's hallway.

They would come for Anthony, and there would be questions about Thora. Just the previous day, she had thought to fry up hamburgers with fresh-cut French fries for Anthony's lunch. But Thora was in the freezer, swathed in the same clear, thick plastic Ivy delivered her wedding dresses in. Thora's body was covered with paper-wrapped packages of meat, the remaining blueberries from last summer, and the two bags of ice they kept in case they had to fill a cooler for a shopping trip or church potluck. It had felt wrong to violate Thora's resting place for something as trivial as hamburger.

She hadn't loved Thora enough. She had been too selfish.

It wasn't Thora's fault that her own mother, the first

Mrs. Luttrell, had died so young, leaving Thora to the tender mercies of her barely interested father. Ivy's own mother had tried and tried to be a friend to Thora. Ivy wasn't sure how she knew this; she had been so young. She just remembered what her mother was like. Still, Thora had rejected her.

I needed you, Mama.

At night, when she was overcome with sadness about Thora and feeling afraid of Anthony, she talked quietly to her mother in the darkness of her room. Asked her what she should do. The only answer she got was more wind coming off the mountain, whispering things she couldn't understand.

Burying Thora was going to be like Anthony's resurrection, in reverse.

Ivy set up her *Sorry, I'm busy sewing* message on the an-swering machine, and went to change into a comfortable pair of corduroy pants and her soiled barn coat. When she opened the gardening cabinet in the carport to retrieve the shovel and spade, her eyes rested on the axe she often used for breaking up small tree limbs that came down near the house. A shud-der moved through her. Thora, lying bleeding on the floor, the flesh of her neck rent by the carving knife. *No, I'm not going to do to Thora what some monster had done to Anthony.*

When Thora had stopped bleeding, and Ivy had sopped up the pooling blood, she mended Thora's wound with the same thread with which she had repaired Anthony. Thora's skin was so fair that the color didn't quite match, but somehow it made Ivy feel better to see her half sister whole again.

As Ivy loaded the sled with the shovel and spade, she also tied on a couple lengths of burlap and some heavy twine. Last time she came out of the woods, Missy had been waiting for her. She wasn't expecting anyone, but it wouldn't hurt to show up with a small, wild rhododendron in tow. Just in case there were questions about why she had spent her afternoon digging up on Devil's Oven.

Sometimes Ivy wondered what else she might find up on the mountain. She had found Anthony, so anything was possible. Her mother's body had never been found on the mountain - or anywhere else, for that matter. Everyone in town, including the police, had just assumed she either ran away or was murdered by Ivy and Thora's father, who then hung himself out of guilt. What if she found her own mother's bones as she was burying Thora?

CHAPTER THIRTY-ONE

THE WOMAN WOULDN'T MOVE.
He kicked at her leg once, twice, with all the rancor his empty stomach engendered. She didn't cry out or try to roll away. The flesh on her thigh jiggled some, but that was all. Her eyes were open.

The cave was getting dark. There were noises - animal noises - from deep inside it that raised the hair on the back of his neck. It wasn't good to be there. He had to leave the cave.

He stood over the woman so he could see her face better. He liked her, liked the way his prick felt when it was inside her. When he was there, pictures of other women came into his mind. Women like her who screamed and tried to hurt him, but also many women who didn't scream, but gasped and cried out *Anthony! Ohmygodohmygod, Anthony!* They never wanted it to stop.

Moving closer to the front of the cave, he undid his pants and urinated against the wall, just as he had at Ivy's house. He thought of Ivy's face and her name together now. She had yelled at him, but she didn't always yell. She gave him food. A lot of it. When he was with her, his stomach never felt empty like this.

The air coming into the cave's entrance carried in the

scent of men, dogs. He didn't like dogs. But he could run from the men if he had to.

He looked back at the woman. Like Claude, she wasn't food. It was possible that whatever was living far back in the cave was food, but he wasn't certain enough to venture back there.

It was time to leave the cave and go back to the house where Ivy and her food lived.

CHAPTER THIRTY-TWO

BUD STEPPED OUT OF the derelict shack he had been searching, and held the dusty water jug he had found to his nose. It didn't smell of vinegar or piss, so he brought it to his lips and drank and drank until the stale water ran over his chin and he began to cough. When the fit subsided, he sank down onto the four-by-four stoop pressed into the dirt.

It was almost evening. The police hadn't found him, and he still hadn't found any sign of Lila or the creature. That's what it was - inhuman. Bud had seen it in the way it handled Lila, the way it was able to move away so quickly, like an animal with a prize.

He listened. No helicopter. No dogs.

About an hour earlier, the sound of barking dogs had stopped. He thought maybe he had been wrong, that they hadn't been police dogs after all. Just a feral pack, or someone's guard dogs. People were always getting busted for growing pot up here, and the woods were dense enough in some places that you could hide a still or a meth operation pretty easily.

Did the bastard still have Lila? Was she even alive? She had to be cold as hell. She was always complaining about being cold. Lila was the only woman he knew who could wear a mink coat all through a service in a steaming church while the other women shedded layers like molting snakes. He smiled to think that her body temperature probably wasn't the whole reason for the coat.

He liked that she enjoyed nice things. The women in his family - his mother and aunts - mocked people who took pleasure in their clothes and appearance. It was a prejudice that only the very wealthy could carry off convincingly, but it had always irritated the hell out of him. They seemed like hypocrites to Bud, in the way they amassed money but refused to enjoy it.

Setting off, he figured he would be at the top of Devil's Oven within half an hour. It was only about three miles square with a couple of tourist lookouts and a fire tower. No one lived up there that he knew. Would the creature know that and take Lila there? Or was he just running, even more blind than Bud himself was?

He hadn't been walking more than two minutes when he heard the sound of something moving quickly through the woods. He had been fooled by squirrels or deer or his imagination twenty times that day, but he pulled the 9mm from the waist of his pants anyway.

Whatever - or whoever - it was, was moving to the west of him. The sound of its progress was fast, assured. After hours of feeling drained by the climb, Bud was suddenly primed and ready. He moved at an angle so he would end up slightly above whoever it was. He knew it was the creature; he could feel it. He clenched his jaw to stop himself from calling out Lila's name so she would know he had come for her. Everything would be all right once he had her. When they were together again, there would be plenty of time to deal with the mess he had made of the businesses. Nothing was more important than to have her safe with him again. An inexplicable surge of happy anticipation flooded his chest.

Dusk was falling fast, but it wasn't dark enough to hide Lila's hair, which darted like flames between the thin trunks of the pines. Then he saw the rosy flesh of her back, which he knew far better than his own. He ran toward her, not caring what kind of noise he made.

When they were finally in full view just twenty feet below him, he ran the slide. The bastard had Lila draped across his shoulders as though she were a dead lamb or a calf he had killed.

Now he did scream Lila's name to get her attention, so that she might fight her way clear if the creature were distracted enough. Bud didn't have enough confidence in his aim to try to take out the son of a bitch with her right there.

The creature stopped and turned to look up at him, but Lila didn't move.

The blooming twilight hid the creature's expression, but Bud felt the menace of him, or rather, the absence of anything vital about him. The creature was like the opposite of a black hole - repelling every good or living thing.

Without any kind of warning or significant sound, a dog ran into the space between them and stopped. Turning toward Bud, it sent up a frantic series of barks. This was no feral stray, but a collared mastiff, glossy with health.

When the creature took a single step toward it, the dog stopped barking and turned its head to look. Still, Lila didn't move.

"Put her down!" Bud screamed.

But the dog and the creature were locked on one another and ignored him. The dog made a sound in its throat that Bud felt down in his gut.

Despite all the dog's training, it lunged at the creature and Lila instead of keeping Bud nailed to where he stood.

The creature brought his arm up to defend himself, and caught the dog in the throat. It fell on its hind end, but then quickly rolled on its side and struck again. Its teeth sank into the creature's arm, and now the creature howled.

The dog clawed frantically at both Lila and the creature. Bud realized it was only a matter of seconds before Lila was seriously hurt.

Knowing the risk he was about to take, Bud exhaled deeply and aimed for the base of the dog's skull.

Within a second of the shot, the dog's legs stopped moving, and he hung, suspended, from the creature's right arm. The creature flung it away, and the dog landed in the dirt not far from Bud's feet.

Bud glanced down at it. Its eyes were closed, but he couldn't tell if it was dead or alive. He felt like vomiting. He had never shot a dog in his life.

When he looked up again, Lila and the creature were almost out of sight.

"Lila!"

Knowing he couldn't chance another shot, he ran after them. Before he had gone a hundred feet, he heard shouting and glanced back to see a second dog, a German shepherd, chasing him. Their brief eye contact was enough to make the shepherd seem to double its speed.

"Tucker!"

Flashlight beams blurred the gray dusk behind the dog. "Police. Stop!"

Still running, Bud sought to distinguish Lila's precious skin from the trees and brush around her, but she had disappeared.

Which choice gave him a better chance of getting Lila back? The troopers or the creature?

No contest.

Let the troopers try to shoot him in the back. He quickened his pace, trying to ignore the pounding in his chest, in his head.

But he wasn't fast enough to outrun the shepherd.

One moment he could hear the dog's feet brushing the ground right behind him, then for a long, long second, there was no sound at all.

The shepherd hit him in the upper back with the full force of its body, knocking him off balance and onto the ground. Then the dog was on his chest, and Bud felt its teeth break through the fine calfskin of his jacket and into his shoulder.

CHAPTER THIRTY-THREE

*D*AMN YOU, PAT.

Dwight rolled the big man onto a blue plastic tarp. For a fat man with two bullets in him, Pat hadn't bled a whole lot. That was good news, and Dwight desperately needed some good news. Twice in the span of three weeks, he had killed someone. For five years he'd been able to avoid it. He had retired a week after he overheard someone refer to him as *Dwight, that butcher*. It wasn't his fault he was good at carving up people. With a father who had been a kosher butcher, he came by his skills honestly.

He hated that this time it was Pat who was dead. He had meant it when he told Pat he'd done him a solid, that he really owed him. But Pat had freaked out. Pat hadn't trusted him, and that really hurt his feelings. Everyone knew that if Dwight Yarbro was anything at all, he was trustworthy.

Should he empty Pat's pockets, take his ID? What the hell was he going to do with the body? His friend's body.

Who was he kidding? People you could trust didn't shoot you. Well, at least they didn't shoot you dead. Usually.

Another forty-five minutes and the girls and the bartenders would be showing up. He hadn't finished next week's schedule, and he still had this mess to clean up. Pat was going to be the kind of handful he couldn't deal with alone.

Bud's the only one who could help.

The thought of getting Bud involved made him feel worse than ever. This was all supposed to go away without Bud getting too messed up. What burned him was that all this bullshit had happened because of some money. It was just money! Now he knew his grandma had been right about money and greed being at the heart of everything that was wrong in the world. Bud was going to hate him after this. But he didn't know if Bud could hate him any worse than he hated himself at this moment.

Bud's cell phone rang five, six times. Dwight was about to hang up when a man - someone younger who wasn't Bud - answered.

"Who is this calling, please?"

Dwight checked the number he had dialed. It was definitely Bud's.

"Who wants to know?" Dwight said. "Let me talk to Bud. What the hell are you doing answering his phone?"

The man on the other end cleared his throat. "This is Officer Petrillo of the Eastern Quadrant Trooper Detachment. Who am I speaking with?"

Dwight swallowed. *Shit.* This was bad, really bad, on so many levels. *I have to keep it together.* He ran his hand down the chest of his bloodstained shirt as though he were trying to look respectable.

"I'm looking for my boss," he said. "I run The Twilight Club for Bud Tucker. Is there some kind of problem? Is Mr. Tucker okay?"

He was so freaked out about having Pat lying dead just a few yards away, it didn't occur to him that something might have happened to Bud until the words were out of his mouth.

"Mr. Tucker is in custody," the trooper said. "I need

your name, please."

Dwight told him what he wanted to know, and assured him that he would certainly make himself available if any questions came up.

"Wait," Dwight said when the officer started to hang up. "What's he been arrested for?"

"He hasn't been charged. Yet." The smug way the trooper said it implied the actual arrest was just a formality. "We're holding him for questioning about the murder of Danelle Pettit and…"

"Danelle?" Dwight said. "Danelle's dead?" He liked her. She was always nice to him, sending leftovers by way of Bud, and making sure he had plenty to eat and drink when Bud and Lila threw their company parties, with the truck business people mixed in with the dancers and bartenders from the club. Bud liked the mix, liked everyone in the same way. Dwight could tell Lila was never thrilled about it, but she smiled and threw the parties anyway. She was phony like that.

"I'm not at liberty to discuss the details of the case," the trooper said. "There's also the possible disappearance of his wife. You haven't heard from Mrs. Tucker, have you, sir?"

"I'm not understanding here," Dwight said. What in the hell was going on?

"Have you heard from Mrs. Tucker, or do you know her whereabouts?"

"I'm not exactly a close personal friend," Dwight said. "She takes off for the city every so often. Maybe she went shopping? She likes the stores."

The trooper's face remained impassive.

"I've got to get back to work," Dwight said. "Thanks for the info."

"We'll be in touch, Mr. - was it Yarbro?"

Bud, in custody? No one who knew Bud could think he would

actually kill someone. Bud just didn't have it in him. Dwight wanted to kick his own ass for thinking for a second that Bud could have stomached dealing with Pat's body.

Shit, again.

Thirty minutes. That was the most time he had left to do something about Pat. Less time if the police decided to come right over. After that? His money friends up in the city had already sent two people - Anthony and Pat - to talk to him and Bud. How many would there be next time?

He wasn't sure where Pat's car was parked, but there wasn't time to get him into its trunk so they could both be sunk in some local water. He unrolled the tarp and felt his way into the dead man's pockets, avoiding looking at Pat's flaccid, pained face. He apologized as he pulled out Pat's wallet, keys, loose change, and a box of those wintergreen breath mints Pat was so fond of.

"Sorry, man," Dwight said. "I know this really sucks."

"You're an asshole, Dwight. You always have been. But I had hopes for you."

Dwight fell back on his heels, stunned. But when he looked closely at Pat's face, he saw it hadn't changed.

"The hell you say?" Dwight said. "Don't talk to me, dead man. Quit messing with my head."

He put the breath mints, wallets, keys, and change in his own front pocket. Then he put the mints in a rear pocket.

"Maybe you did me a favor," Pat said. His mouth wasn't moving, but it was his voice all the same.

Dwight began to sweat profusely under his arms.

"Shut up!" he said. It wasn't right to scream at the dead, he knew. But it wasn't any more right that Pat was talking.

"I thought Marie might have been screwing around," Pat said. "Bugged the hell out of me the way she flirted with every dickbreath who came to the house to fix the toilet or whatever." He gave a sigh of regret.

Dwight glanced around, looking for some joker who

might be screwing with him. But the voice was definitely Pat's.

"I don't know what the hell is going on," Dwight said. "I'm sorry, man. You know I'm sorry. You shouldn't have pulled a gun on me."

"She never did, you know," Pat said. "My mother always told me that when you die, you know everything you ever wanted to know, ever wondered about, ever gave a shit about. Of course, she didn't use those words. She was a lady."

"I know she didn't like Marie."

Pat belched. Just a small one, like he'd had a few swallows of beer.

"Her loss," he said. "My mother had a hard life, you know? My granny tried to keep her from marrying my old man by locking her in a closet the night before they were supposed to get married. Tried to make my old man think she had run away. What a bitch."

Dwight knew he didn't have a hell of a lot of time to talk to a dead guy, but he and Pat hadn't had much chance to talk in the past two years. And they almost never got really personal.

"Marie never screwed around. She had to fight off a couple of assholes. Including you." Pat paused.

Dwight had been drinking back then, and had driven Marie home from a party once when Pat refused to leave. Even as he tried to kiss her, he knew he shouldn't have done it.

"I apologize for that," he said to Pat. "It was an asshole thing to do."

Dwight decided he was going crazy. All this shit with Bud, this killing people again - it was making him insane. The police would be there any minute and he would be screwed.

"Like *killing* me wasn't an asshole thing to do?" Pat said. "But I wasn't honest with you, was I? It ain't nice to mess with your friends that way, as you well know. We can call it even."

"I've got to get rid of you, man," Dwight said. "You wouldn't believe how sorry I am."

"Yeah," Pat said. "Doesn't matter. I'm not going any-where."

Dwight had to get Pat's body out of sight. Both the of-fice and the storage closet had doors that could be locked, but the police would want to see inside because of Lila. There was the kitchen's lock-in. No. Too much regular traffic.

Maybe under the stage. No one ever wanted to go under the stage. It spooked people. Dwight likened it to the underside of a bed. You never knew what might be hiding there.

"I'll be back in a minute," he told Pat.

After grabbing a flashlight from the storage room, Dwight squatted beside the stage and pushed aside the shim-mering polyester curtain that trimmed the apron. He flicked on the flashlight and duckwalked to the back. Bud had or-dered the stage lights a year earlier, and the crew that had delivered and unpacked the long black crates the lights came in had asked if they should be hauled away. Bud had said *sure*, but Dwight, who didn't like to throw away things that might be useful later, had convinced him to keep them. He hadn't been thinking at the time that they looked like coffins, but now he saw that they did.

Pat was so heavy - even heavier in death, it seemed - that Dwight had to position one of the smaller step stools beside the crate and raise one end of Pat's body onto it. It took several tries, and Pat rolled more than once off the stool, col-lapsing in an undignified heap.

When Pat's body was finally inside the box, Dwight stood up, almost breathless. Pat lay on his side, his face stuck into a corner like a kid being punished. The tarp had slid from around him and now Dwight laid it over him as a kind of blanket, covering him from his head to his feet. He apologized again, but Pat didn't answer.

As he pushed the box back underneath the stage, and into position beside the others, he tried to think how long he had before Pat started stinking up the place. Two, maybe three days? Everything depended on how serious the police were about going after Bud. It was possible they would tear up the place right away.

Would they bring in tools and lights and that glowing stuff to search for bloodstains? They were likely to find a hell of a lot of nastier fluids staining the floors and walls. People were pigs. There was nothing like working in a strip club to learn that, and fast.

But Dwight could deal with only one thing at a time. He needed to wash up the blood, get rid of the cash, put away the 9mm, take a quick shower in the girls' dressing room, and change into the extra set of clothes he kept in the office. And he only had about fifteen minutes to do it all.

CHAPTER THIRTY-FOUR

"ARE YOU ALL RIGHT?"

Tripp was clutching the steering wheel of his truck so hard that his knuckles had turned white. Jolene was worried for him. She didn't like the way his aura flickered, like the light from an ugly green bulb. He seemed to have lost all his inner strength, all the good and playfulness she had seen in him when she had first noticed him at the club. She hadn't told him she had been watching him ever since she started working there. He was already skeptical. And she had played a part in that. Showing him her life, her first life, had weakened and frightened him.

She didn't know everything. She didn't know why he was as vulnerable as he was. Was it from living on the mountain his whole life? The mountain had nurtured him, but now it was destroying him, just as it had her mother, and others she loved. There was no way to explain to him the dual nature of Devil's Oven. It was just something she understood. She had understood it the moment it saved her, enfolding her in its warmth, like the once-loving arms of her mother.

"There's no way they're here," he said. "Not Lila. Why would she be at Ivy's?" He looked at her like he was sure she was lying.

Jolene wanted to touch his face, to try to heal him. Sometimes she could heal spiritual brokenness the same way she could physical pain.

"Because he'll come back here. He has Lila Tucker. I can feel it," she said.

"I hope to God you're wrong," he said.

"Ivy knows," she said. "She began all this. She thinks she needs him."

"If this really is some kind of monster that Ivy made...shit, there's no way," he said. "You can't sew up people and bring them back to life. She's going to tell you you're crazy. You know that, don't you?"

Jolene shook her head.

"I told you the truth," she said.

"Bullshit."

"Ivy has a gift."

Tripp laughed. "Ivy can sew a seam straight. She has a gift for making pretty clothes."

Jolene wondered about her own nature. This part of her that lived now, that touched and tasted and sometimes felt happy, or ill, or deeply sad - this part of her needed someone, too. Their coupling in the woods had been necessary for Tripp, so he could be shown the truth. But it had felt necessary for her, too. She was sure she wouldn't be here long now. She could feel it.

But first, she had to heal Ivy and Thora. Lila and Bud, too. Tripp would be more difficult. She was sorry there were others, like Claude Dixon, who had just been in the way. She couldn't help them.

"I told you already that you scare the shit out of me," he said. "I'm here because of Lila. You need to get this thing moving, or I'm going to go look for her myself. And it's not going to be at that Ivy's place."

"I thought you'd believe me by now," Jolene said. "What more do I have to show you?"

"Stay the hell out of my head," Tripp said, stopping the

truck in Ivy's driveway. "Let's get this over with."

"He's been here," Jolene said. "Can't you smell it?"

"If there is a *him*," Tripp said.

They began to search the house.

"No one's here," Jolene said after they had combed the back bedrooms. Standing in the doorway of the guest room, Tripp covered his mouth with a sleeve to keep from gagging at the stench.

"Jesus," he said. "It's like a damn zoo in here."

They went to the kitchen.

"Wait," Jolene said. "Where's her sister?" *Where's Thora?*

She pushed past Tripp and hurried back to the living room. Thora's three-footed cane stood beside the empty chair, and the tissues and medicine bottles had been cleared from the table. Her stomach went cold.

I couldn't know everything.

"Maybe they went out to eat," Tripp said from down the hallway. "I sure as hell wouldn't eat here."

"The car's outside," she said. Her voice was low. Tripp didn't hear her.

"Or they're up at that trailer," he said.

Jolene closed her eyes. She couldn't feel Thora's presence, a presence she knew. Thora was need, wrapped in anger and pain. She regretted that she hadn't touched Thora when she saw her that day. She might have been able to give her some relief from the diabetes ravaging her body. She owed Thora so much. Thora had protected Ivy, maybe even loved her.

Tripp came back into the living room.

"Five minutes," he said. "And then I'm getting the hell out of here to find Lila. You can walk back to the trailer park."

Jolene barely heard the door slam. Her mind was seeking Thora.

Thora. Poor Thora.

Thora had been an awkward teenager, but she'd had a kind of stoic charm. Her shy smile as she unwrapped the Christmas robe with her name over the pocket. The beautiful pile of cookies she'd made for the church potluck. She had been so proud. But she had mixed baking soda instead of baking powder into the flour and salt, and they had tasted like medicine. It was a moment that even elicited a rare laugh from her father. There was a night, a few weeks after Ivy was born, when Thora had come to Jolene crying because a boy had kissed her, but then startled her by trying to put his hand up her shirt. She had run away from him, leaving her coat behind. As soon as she got inside the trailer, her usually composed face crumpled with tears. Her nose and cheeks were red, her fingers stiff from the frigid January night. Those thick, mannish fingers of hers. So cold.

Jolene opened her eyes. She could hear Tripp pacing the porch. He wouldn't wait.

She went to the kitchen. Ivy had kept it neat even in the midst of dealing with the chaos she had brought on. Ivy the calm. Ivy the obedient.

What Jolene sought wasn't in the kitchen. She slid open the door separating it from the laundry room.

The chest freezer sat against the back wall. It had a bolt to which a padlock could be attached, but there was none on it.

She had seen the faces of the dead: the peaceful, the questioning, the faces sculpted in fear or surprise. No one face was the same as another, as though Death required a unique reaction from each victim as payment or tribute.

Even through the stiff plastic, she saw that Thora's once-bitter face held equal measures of resignation and regret.

For the briefest of moments, Jolene's face transformed into the one Thora would know well, if she were to wake. *Poor Thora.* Jolene's heart welled with pity. She put out her hand, wanting to tear away the plastic and lay her hands on Thora, to bring her back, to purge her of every unhappy thing she had ever known or seen.

No. Not yet. Could I ever?

She gently replaced the packages and containers Ivy had arranged over Thora's body, and closed the freezer.

Ivy, what have you done?

CHAPTER THIRTY-FIVE

IVY DIDN'T MIND BEING UP on the mountain in the dark, but Thora's grave was only half dug and she was already exhausted. The joints of her hands ached, and the shovel's handle had given her blisters despite her work gloves. The early rains had soaked the ground, making the first few inches of soil thick and muddy. Worse, the deposits of red-orange clay beneath the soil clung stubbornly to her shovel. No wonder whoever had buried Anthony hadn't bothered to dig too deep.

Ivy guessed they hadn't known that the only things that could be hurried on the mountain were frightened animals or streams swollen with rain. To her, Devil's Oven was like time itself - a permanent mystery, but with rules you could spend a lifetime learning. Some days, she would think of her past - of hide-and-seek games with her mother, of her father's gruff voice, the arguments with Thora, the hours she spent teaching herself to sew on her mother's machine - and she was right there, so lost in the vision that she couldn't find her way out until the phone rang or Thora called for her. Now there was Anthony, and she was in a new time. One whose boundaries she couldn't see.

Maybe Anthony would live forever. It didn't seem fair

that she should eventually die and he might go on living. But after seeing what he had done to Thora, could she really expect to live that much longer?

She wished Anthony were here to help her. She hadn't asked him to do any kind of work thus far, and he was a big, strong man. Telling him it was his responsibility to bury Thora because he had killed her wouldn't work. Anthony had no concept of guilt or responsibility. If he even understood what she was asking, he would probably just smile and do nothing.

It's not too late.

Ivy's mother knelt beside her, fastening the layers of net around her waist. She had stitched the net into a white boll of a tutu, and glued flower buds shaped from ribbon all over it. The buds had long ribbon streamers that flew behind Ivy as she ran.

We can make the luncheon, her mother told her. It's not too late. Don't mind Daddy.

They walked the two miles to the state motor vehicle office, where her father worked, to get the car. Her father had told them he was sick of the fuss and the tinny music filling the trailer when they put on the practice record her mother had bought from the teacher. I never paid for Thora to do that foolishness, he had said. No, she can't go.

They snuck the car from its space behind the little shopping center the office was in, knowing her father wouldn't come outside again until five o'clock. They drove to the Legion Hall in the next town for the luncheon recital, and Ivy danced for the Legionnaires' wives, wearing one of the silk rose wreaths the teacher had made as a surprise for her and the other girls. The teacher took a photograph of each girl and put it into a cardboard frame as a keepsake.

Walking home later, Ivy giggled and held her mother's hand. She felt as though she were dancing on a cloud borne by fairies.

The whole adventure remained their secret for weeks, until Thora found the photograph in their room and asked Ivy about it at Sunday lunch. Ivy felt her father's eyes looking at her over the roast, and, even though she was only five, sensed a wave of grim pleasure from Thora. Ivy started to cry, and her mother squeezed her hand and calmly told her to leave the table. She ran to her corner in the barn's hayloft and stayed there until dark. It had been Thora's secret place when she was younger, and Ivy's mother had fixed it up for her, with gingham tacked to the walls and two big pillows for seats, and a plastic tea set she had bought at a garage sale.

Her parents fought for days. Her mother cried and told her not to worry. A week later, her mother was gone, and Thora found their father hanging in the woods.

It wasn't too late.

She could still go to the police and tell them about Anthony. She could lie and say he had forced his way into the house and killed Thora. She could say she had been too afraid of him to come forward, that he was the one who had put Thora in the freezer. They were already looking for him, or at least a person who looked like him. His DNA would be everywhere. Surely on Claude Dixon. Definitely in her house. There was no reason they wouldn't believe her.

Oh! The pregnant bridesmaid had seen him! The girl would be her proof.

Even though night had fallen around her, Ivy felt lighter than she had in weeks, or possibly years. If Anthony didn't come back - and she was certain now he wouldn't - the burden of Thora's death *God rest her soul* was suddenly lifted.

Is that what I want? Let that be what I want.

But if the answer wasn't fully *yes* at that second, she knew it was the right answer. Even though she ached for him, she thought that if she tried, she could bring herself around to turning him in.

She started to fill the hole back in with a new energy, pushing the huge chunks of clay into the hole with her shovel, and then her hands. She worked without stopping for about fifteen minutes before she realized it didn't matter if she refilled the hole or not. There were no laws against digging holes. Or maybe there were rules about doing it in the state forest. But who would know or care? Packing up, she forgot all about tying a wild rhododendron to the sled.

It was dark enough that she needed the electric lantern she had brought to see her way back to the house. Had she left any lights on? She couldn't remember.

Would Anthony be there, waiting, wondering where she was? The thought brought on a wave of melancholy. Was it going to be like this? Was she going to change her mind from one minute to the next?

Anthony was cold-hearted. He had no conscience. But he hadn't hurt *her*; he was gentle with her. And he might come back, after all.

It's not too late.

Ivy turned at a sound coming from behind her. The reality of being alone on Devil's Oven in the dark hit her. She had no gun, only the shovel and a pitiful light. *Foolish* didn't begin to describe how she felt.

Grabbing the shovel and the rope of the sled, she left the spade and her water behind. Almost immediately, she regretted bringing the sled. Twice it banged into her ankles, nearly knocking her down. She was thinking of the coyote that Anthony had killed the previous night, but whatever was out there could just as easily be a wolf. A lot of people in the area who kept livestock complained about the wolves.

Desperate to know what it was, she stopped to look over her shoulder. Holding up the lantern, she saw Anthony, his teeth gleaming. He had that look of blank, humorless joy on his face. When he saw her, he slowed to a fast walk. He wore pants, but his shirt was gone, and his skin was filthy with dirt. The skin of the woman he carried reflected the lantern's light more brightly. Her skin was white, her buttocks two half moons in the dark.

Anthony stopped when he reached Ivy. He was panting like a dog.

Ivy couldn't speak.

Anthony slid the naked woman off his shoulder, dumping her on the ground at Ivy's feet, her red hair spilling over them like blood.

CHAPTER THIRTY-SIX

"**Y**OUR CHOICE TO USE A FIREARM while being pursued by peace officers almost got you killed, Mr. Tucker. That happens too often in these situations."

The search team had brought Bud in handcuffs to where Detective Burns and the EMTs waited at the forest's main gate. The dog bite wasn't deep enough to require stitches, but Bud flinched as the EMTs irrigated it with antiseptic. He had told them they could skip the hospital, that they needed to be focusing on finding Lila, not dicking around with the stupid idea that he had harmed her and killed Danelle Pettit.

"The bastard had my wife. *Has* my wife, damn it," Bud said, trying not to lose his temper the way he had up in the woods. The frustration was killing him. They hadn't seen the son of a bitch because they had been so focused on capturing *him*. The first dog had seen the monster, and had even gotten his teeth into him, all in defiance of his mission to stop Bud. But no one would listen.

What if I hadn't shot the dog? What if I had just waited a few more seconds? Lila might have been injured, but they would have seen the creature, would have seen Lila. If they never found her, it would be my fault.

The realization made him feel guilty. Sick inside.

"Just see what you get off the teeth of the dog I shot," he said. "Please."

The reminder of what he had done got him a sharp twist of the handcuffs from the officer who was putting them back on after the EMT finished. Bud gritted his teeth. He wasn't going to let them change his focus.

"We'll be sure to take care of that right after he gets out of surgery," Burns said. "Though I have to say, I'm glad you were such a piss-poor shot. May keep you out of prison." He gave Bud a grim smile. "For that, anyway."

He nodded to the officer standing behind Bud. "We'll catch up with you boys later at County," he said.

Bud stumbled as the officer pushed him toward the waiting patrol car. They passed the second dog, the shepherd called Lord, who was standing affectionately close to his handler as though waiting for a scratch behind the ears. When the shepherd didn't move or even look in Bud's direction, Bud was hit with the realization that he was just another criminal to the dog and to the men and women around him. They had already decided he was guilty, and they were ready to move on.

CHAPTER THIRTY-SEVEN

ANTHONY STOPPED MORE than once on their way down the hillside, wanting to put Lila down on the ground again. Each time, Ivy begged him to *please, please* hold on to her until they got back to the trailer. Each time he indicated he was hungry.

"At the house, Anthony," she said. "As soon as I get to the house. Just the minute we get there. *Please.*"

She couldn't even think. Where in the world had he found Lila Tucker? Why hadn't he killed her like he had killed Claude Dixon and Thora?

She did her best not to notice the way Lila's head bobbed against Anthony's back, and she prayed Lila wouldn't die. Or would death be a sign of God's mercy? Only He knew what Anthony had done to her. The lantern light had revealed ragged, bloody scrapes on her back, and bite marks on her shoulders and breasts and neck. Her eyes were open, but focused on some unseen thing in the distance. They blinked only every once in a while.

Poor Lila. Ivy didn't care about her the way she had cared for Thora, but Lila didn't deserve the attack any more than Thora did.

When the house and trailer came into view, Ivy gath-

ered her strength and rushed to overtake Anthony. Taking Lila
to the house was way too dangerous, and there was no way to
keep an eye on her at the trailer because Ivy had to be down
at the house most of the time. *Am I already thinking that Lila's
presence has to remain a secret?* Lila was surely almost dead from
exposure and fright and - dear God - abuse. The rational place
for her to be was in a hospital.

Once again, Ivy had had a choice to make, and without thinking about it, she had chosen Anthony.

She had seen him standing there in the dark: belligerent, evil *yes she saw that now*, a bringer of death. She finally understood that she wasn't going to change him or teach him or
save him. He was like a child who would never grow up. But
she had made him, and it was up to her to take care of him.

*We should have left Lila to die in the woods, but now it's
too late.*

"No, we can't have her here," Ivy said. "She has to go
somewhere else."

But Anthony strode around her and onto the trailer's
back porch, ignoring her pleas. He laid Lila down in the
rusting chaise beneath the kitchen window, then went inside
without looking back.

Ivy hurried to Lila, who lay staring up into the star-
filled sky, and covered her with her own jacket. Lila's entire
body trembled with cold. Her eyes looked glassy and unreal in
her head, like she was a broken doll.

"Wait here," Ivy told her, as though Lila were capable
of running away. "Just wait."

Ivy went inside the trailer. Glancing down the hallway,
she could see Anthony in the kitchen, looking for food. In the
master bedroom, she pulled the worn quilt from the bed and
shook it out to dislodge many months of dust. Taking it outside, she covered Lila all the way up to her neck, tucking the
blanket around her legs and arms to give her some warmth.
Lila's body didn't relax or change position, but Ivy knew she
had to be close to freezing to death.

"You're safe now," Ivy said. "I'll take care of you. Everything's going to be all right." She wasn't sure why she felt compelled to try to comfort Lila. She didn't even know if Lila could hear her.

She ran inside again and turned on the thermostat. This time of year they kept it turned off because the air inside the trailer wouldn't get quite cold enough to freeze the pipes. She heard the propane gas jets in the furnace *tickticktick* to life.

"Anthony."

The floor creaked beneath Anthony's feet as he came into the living room, a handful of cereal in one hand and the cereal box in the other. He stuffed some cereal in his mouth.

"I need you to bring her inside the trailer," she said. "Put her on the couch for now."

When he didn't move but continued just to watch her, she said, "I'm not going to make your supper until you do what I ask."

He stared at her. She watched for any sign of decision in his eyes, but there was none. He tossed the cereal box on the floor behind him and went outside to get Lila.

CHAPTER THIRTY-EIGHT

WORD HAD GOTTEN AROUND about the viciousness of Danelle Pettit's murder, and Lila's disappearance, so the club was busy as soon as the doors opened at eight. Dwight kept his head down and backed up the bartender as unobtrusively as possible. Charity had phoned to say she would cover for the girl who had called in sick, and would bring in Jolene if she could find her. All the activity put a balm of normalcy on the evening for Dwight. So far, the police hadn't shown up to ask any questions or to check out Bud's office, which was fine with him.

It had been Dwight's good luck that the bartender was late. Dwight had given him a small amount of shit, just to make it look good, but he didn't go overboard. That the guy had shown up every Monday through Saturday night for the past two months was a miracle. When the bartender put his key in the back door about two hours earlier, Dwight was combing his hair into shape with hair gel belonging to one of the girls, and had just popped one of Pat's wintergreen breath mints into his mouth. He didn't usually go for them, but the smell of blood hung in his nostrils and he couldn't blow it out no matter how hard he tried.

Maybe it was some sort of haunting, and he would be

smelling Pat's blood for years. It wasn't a thought that made him happy.

Usually on a Friday night, he would start out the music easy and kind of fun, but tonight he went straight to a hard rock loop because he was in the mood. Too bad if it pissed off the girls and wore them out early. He was past caring. There was a dead guy beneath their feet, and their boss was in jail. They might all be out of a job in a matter of days. The music kept him going.

What a G.D. mess.

Maybe Pat was down there mumbling to himself, listening to the girls stomp all over his head. Pat talked more dead than he did alive. The whole thing made Dwight want to take a seat on the other side of the bar with his own personal bottle of Wild Turkey for company. But if he didn't keep his shit together, there was nobody to keep it together for him.

Charity showed up about eight forty-five, just fifteen minutes before the stage shows would start, her blonde hair in a messy pile on her head and her face bare of makeup. She looked like she had been out running. When she spotted Dwight behind the bar, she headed straight for him. He liked Charity, but didn't need any of her bossy bullshit right then.

"You going to tell me what really happened to Bud?" she said. Several customers turned on their stools to stare at her.

Dwight swept the pieces of lime he was slicing into their bin and wiped his hands on a towel. He jerked his head to indicate she should follow him to the office.

"What in the hell are you doing coming in the front door like that?" he said.

"I want to know what you know about Bud," she said. "*Our* Bud. I heard on the radio that somebody got killed at his house and he's in jail."

"Yeah, well, you know as much as I do," he said. "You need to get back there and get your butt onstage. Where's Jolene? Is she with you?"

She shook her head. "Bud hasn't called you?" she said. "How come?"

"I hope to hell he called a lawyer instead," Dwight said. It did irk him that Bud hadn't called, but what could he do for him, anyway? He had enough going on. Everything was going to shit.

"Jolene's pretty shook up," she said. "She wanted to take a quick shower. She spent the day with that Tripp guy, the mountain cop. You know the one."

Tripp Morgan was not even close to being on Dwight's radar screen, and he only cared about that freak show Jolene to the extent that it affected the club.

"What's Jolene shook up for? Does she have a thing for Bud or something?" he said. He licked his lips. His mouth had been dry for the last few hours. He reached into his pocket to take out another mint. That something might be up between Bud and Jolene had occurred to him, but he also knew Bud was stupidly loyal to his undeserving wife.

"Be serious. Jolene's not the type," she said. "Jolene is - I don't think she thinks like that. And I'm not saying that just because she's my friend. There's good and there's *good*, you know? Freaks me out the way she is. Like she knows every- thing and nothing at the same time."

Dwight shrugged. "She's nothing special."

"Just don't be a jerk to her," Charity said. "She's a good kid, and she didn't do anything to Bud or with Bud, no matter if he wanted her to or not."

"*You* need to get to work," Dwight said. "If that's what you think about Bud and her, make sure you tell it to the cops if they ask, okay? Bud didn't do anything to anybody."

"Of course Bud didn't," she said. "But somebody did."

Pat's mournful voice came to him over the music, whispered in his ear. *Now, who could that somebody be, I won-*

der? You really screwed up this time, my friend.

What in the hell does that mean? Dwight wanted to scream. It pissed him off that his dead friend knew things he didn't.

CHAPTER THIRTY-NINE

DAMN IT. Tripp couldn't help himself.
He approached the entrance to Bud and Lila's driveway slowly, wanting to get a look at what was going on. There were messages on his phone from his boss, Denise; Keith; and Detective Johnson; all wanting to know where he was, wanting to get a little piece of him. In the second message from Denise, her voice had an edge to it, like she was angry or worried. Whatever they wanted from him didn't matter. He turned off the phone. He had heard everything he needed to hear on the radio and his police scanner about Lila being missing and Bud being arrested.

A state trooper sat in his cruiser at the head of Lila's drive. Because of the darkness, Tripp wasn't sure if he knew the trooper or not, so he looked carefully ahead as he passed the driveway. But as the truck climbed the hillside, Tripp felt the draw of the place. If only he could be around her things, get the scent of her, then maybe he could find her.

Jolene had been hiding something. She knew more and he could feel it. All her mystical bullshit made him want to squeeze the life out of her slutty little body.

He turned the truck around in the middle of the road and went back.

Outside the kitchen windows, the somber patio lights revealed that things had changed some since he had been a guest at a big summer party the Tuckers threw over a year earlier. The sheltered arbor in which he had cornered Lila - trying quietly to convince her to come up to see his place in the woods, where they could talk - had been moved, replaced by an outdoor kitchen with a massive stainless steel grill, a sink, and a small refrigerator. Lila wasn't much of a cook, but she didn't need to be, did she? The lights also illuminated the hot tub where Lila was supposedly last seen.

Detective Johnson stood beside him, acting like he owned the place.

"So, you believe Bud?" Tripp said.

"Is there a reason I shouldn't believe him?" Johnson said. "Or a reason why I should?"

"Why would he kill the housekeeper?" Tripp said, turning to the detective.

Johnson had shown him the hallway with its blood-sprayed walls. Bud wasn't capable of that kind of violence. Tripp suspected even the sight of that scene would wreck Bud. Anyone who had ever met him would know better.

Tripp felt bad about the Pettit woman. He had only seen her once, but Lila had spoken of her frequently. Mostly complaints, but then Lila was particular about her house, and she had paid the Pettit woman well.

"I'm interested in why you would track me down here," Johnson said.

"Your message said you wanted to see me, and I was in the neighborhood," Tripp said. It was enough of the truth. "No sign at all of Lila - Mrs. Tucker?"

Lila was all around him: her white jacket hanging over the back of the chair in the breakfast nook, the box of peppermint herbal tea sitting on the counter. A box just like it sat beside the stove in his own kitchen. There was a framed pen-

and-ink drawing of some flowering herb above the kitchen desk. He had recognized Lila's fine hand and the decorative "L" down in the right-hand corner. She'd had her drawings in art shows in high school, but she had never taken lessons or pursued it further. He had meant to ask her why.

He wanted to go upstairs to her bedroom and touch her clothes, hold them against his face. They might hold some clue, tell him where to find her. When they were freshmen, she had once left a sweater on the school bus, not long before she started dating only boys who could drive her to and from school. He had quickly stuffed the sweater in his backpack and later hidden it in the bottom drawer of his dresser. Months later, it still smelled like her lemony perfume. But then it disappeared, and he knew his mother had found the sweater and taken it away. They never spoke of it.

"How long have you known Mrs. Tucker?" Johnson said. He wasn't writing anything down, but Tripp suspected he didn't need to. He didn't seem like the kind of man to forget things.

"Seems to me you guys are wasting a bunch of time not looking for her," Tripp said. "If the son of a bitch who killed Claude Dixon has got her like Bud Tucker says he does, then she's probably dead already. Just like the housekeeper."

Johnson picked up a paper coffee cup that Tripp recognized as being from Lori Ann's and took a drink from it. He made a face.

"Coffee's not so good cold," he said. He put the cup down beside a clear plastic carryout box that contained the remains of a sandwich. It bugged Tripp that the guy was insensitive enough to eat with Danelle Pettit's blood on the other side of the wall.

"Why are you hanging around here? Looks like the crime scene folks got done a long time ago," Tripp said.

"Good question," Johnson said. "I've got an hour's drive home, and I've got Mr. Tucker at County. My partner's taking care of him."

"Yeah, well, if that's all," Tripp said. "I'll let you get back to whatever you think you're doing here."

When Johnson cleared his throat, Tripp knew he was screwed. Johnson wasn't going to let him leave without trying to get information from him.

"How long have you been sleeping with Lila Tucker? You understand why we need to know. Might help us find her."

"Understand? Hell," Tripp said. "What I understand is that you're not out beating brush looking for her. You think that guy's not on the move in the dark?"

"You admit you're sleeping with her?"

Tripp's mind worked fast. There weren't any real secrets in Monroe County because at least one person knew everything about everybody: Sheryl Dixon.

"I don't have to answer your bullshit questions," Tripp said.

"How does Mr. Tucker feel about your friendship with his wife?"

Tripp felt the blood rush to his face. It took every bit of restraint he had not to knock the smug look off the detective's face with his fist. He pointed a trembling finger at Johnson.

"You better make sure you send an official invitation to my lawyer the next time you want to talk to me. You need to demonstrate a very good reason why I would touch a hair on either Danelle Pettit's or Lila Tucker's head."

Lila/Jolene lying on the path like white, bloodless death. The man, Jolene's father, his still eyes open and glistening, so tempting, like they were waiting, begging him to pluck at them.

He couldn't trust himself to continue. He turned to leave by the patio door. No way did he want to pass through the front hall again.

"Hey, before you go, Mr. Morgan, I should ask you where you were earlier today. You weren't at your cabin and nobody seemed to know where you were. Not even your co-workers."

Tripp hesitated, his hand on the door handle.

"You don't need a lawyer to answer that, do you?" the detective said. "Unless, of course, you do."

Tripp turned around. The detective's presence in Lila's kitchen was a kind of blasphemy. He didn't belong there, and Tripp wanted to drag him outside and beat the shit out of him for being where Lila should have been at that moment - safe and warm in her own house. Better yet, safe and warm with *him*. Far, far away from here.

"I went for a walk with a friend," Tripp said. "My supervisor told me to take some time off. Not that it's any of your fucking business."

The detective shrugged. "Works for me," he said. "Thanks for your help. You have a nice evening, Officer Morgan."

Tripp slammed the door behind him, leaving the detective alone in Lila's dark and empty house.

CHAPTER FORTY

JOLENE BLEW OUT HER HAIR with Charity's dryer so that it hung straight and glossy down her back. She had memories of her earliest life, before electricity, before deodorant, days when being able to find food in the forest or build a crude shelter meant the difference between living and dying. In those days, work made her tired in a way it didn't now. Milking a cow or carrying buckets of water or washing clothes in a stream were all a lot more difficult than dancing on a stage for money. It didn't bother her that she was nearly naked when she did it. Such an idea would've been inconceivable in that other life. Now, she understood her body was a transitory thing, useful in the temporal world, but otherwise inconsequential. That men got pleasure from watching her didn't matter to her at all.

The women at the club were mostly nice to her, and she had some kind of talent for dancing, which was a blessing. Bud wanted her to work in his trucking office, but she didn't see the use of encouraging him. She wasn't even sure where she might be in the next hour, let alone the next day.

When she finished drying her hair, she turned off the light. The mountainside was a shapeless blot outside the window of the bathroom. Lila was somewhere out there, and the evil that had roused itself from its mountain slumber was embracing Lila even in that moment. Jolene leaned against the bathroom wall and closed her eyes.

Had the mountain - the same mountain that was bringing Lila such pain - really saved her the morning her father and brother were murdered? Maybe it had only been another kind of death. Something had heard her prayer, her wish to be hidden. The God of her father's Bible had never given any kind of sign that He was listening; each of her lives was more full of pain than the last.

Sounds came to her through the open window. Neighbors laughing, a car starting, a cat crying for food. She heard the whispered play of water running in the storm drain at the back of the trailer park, too, as her soul drifted out the window and into the night. Curling around an upper branch of a nearby tree, she gave her attention to the shadowy hills.

Should she call out to Lila with the strength she had left?

If she did, others might hear. The creature. Maybe Ivy. No. Once abandoned by her mother, Ivy had taught herself to ignore the part of her that was attuned to such things.

I didn't leave you because I wanted to, Ivy.

Lila had to be somewhere near Ivy. It was the only thing that made sense. The creature - what was he like? She couldn't fix a picture of him. Sheryl Dixon had described a cartoon kind of monster. More like one of the costumed wrestlers Byron had liked to watch on television than a man. But the creature was no cartoon. He was walking death.

Unfurling from the tree, she rose into the night. Below, the trailers disappeared, revealing the colorful auras of their inhabitants like Christmas lights shining through the fog. Up, and up, over Alta, into the dark, cold sky. Devil's Oven ahead of her, a black wall, with just a few spots of faint light, the homes of the people it hadn't yet driven away. People like Tripp, who were of the mountain, or those who had found it kindred.

She could feel their presence, their tenacity. She was one of them, but up here her connection to the mountain was weak. What if she just kept going, toward the larger lights in the sky? Maybe there was a place there where she could forget the pain of being earthbound. She could be Mary, the child, again. She could feel pure again. She could rest.

Lila Tucker would die. Tripp would be destroyed by what was already inside him. Ivy would be betrayed. Again. But I would be free.

"Jolene! You here?"

Eli's voice was clear. Distant. Regretfully, she let go of the night and, with the suddenness of a rogue, chill wind, shifted back into herself. She took two long, deep breaths, filling her lungs.

"Here I am, Eli," she said. She wrapped the towel loosely around her chest, turned on the light, and opened the door.

Eli, with his mellow, yellow-green aura, was trustworthy and kind. He was almost always calm, at least when Charity wasn't yelling at him. He was good to Charity, and good *for* her. He stayed away from the club, but was proud of how professional Charity was about her job. Jolene could see he would always be faithful. If she saw Charity again, she would tell her to hang on to him.

Seeing her in the towel, Eli turned away quickly.

"Shit. I wish you wouldn't do that, Jolene," he said, blushing.

"I'm sorry," she said. "Let me grab my clothes." She hurried to the living room, where she grabbed her jeans and sweatshirt from the chair and went back into the bathroom. She never reminded him that he had seen her walk naked down off the mountain.

"Guess you heard about Bud," Eli said through the door. "I only found out when I dropped Charity off."

She pulled on the sweatshirt.

"What?" she said. "Did you say something about

Bud?" When Eli didn't answer right away, she put on the jeans as fast as she could and came out of the bathroom still fastening them. She found him in the living room.

"Do you know where they've got him?" she said.

"At the jail in the new courthouse," Eli said. He popped the top of a Mountain Dew that he must have brought with him; Charity wouldn't keep the stuff in the trailer. "Poor guy. I don't believe anything they're saying about him. No way Bud could kill anybody, you know?"

It was wrong. All wrong.

Jolene sank down on the threadbare arm of the couch. She had been so worried about Ivy, and about finding Lila, that she hadn't thought fully about what was happening to Bud. He didn't belong in jail. He needed to be out looking for Lila.

"They took him in to ask him questions, but I don't know if he's arrested or not." He looked at his watch. "Hey, you ready to go? Charity said you needed to get there just as soon as you got cleaned up. She's all stressed out because she thinks the club's gonna shut down."

As weak as she felt, Jolene knew she had to do something. It occurred to her that Eli might understand, that he could help her, but she didn't want to bring Charity and him any more trouble than she already had.

"I just need ten minutes," she said. She stood and touched his shoulder. "I couldn't ask for better friends than you and Charity. I'll be right back."

❧

Eli pulled the truck up to the club's stage door, which opened onto a hall of dressing rooms.

Jolene gave him an encouraging smile. "Don't work too hard," she said, getting out.

"Not me," he said. "Hey, remind Charity to call me when she gets off." He put the truck in gear as soon as she had closed the door behind her.

At the stage door, she put her finger on the button that would buzz inside the dressing rooms, and pretended to press it. She turned back to wave, but Eli was already gone.

Digging Charity's extra set of car keys from her pocket, she hurried to the side lot where Charity always parked.

CHAPTER FORTY-ONE

"HE SAID HIS LAWYER'S COMING from out of town. That's all I know." Jim Fowler, the sergeant on the third-shift duty desk leaned closer to Dwight. "Dumb mistake, if you ask me," he said. "One of the lawyers next door would've had him out of here by now, or at least first thing in the morning."

The brand new Monroe County Jail and Courthouse complex wasn't really a complex at all, but a single, fifty-foot-high monolith covered in iron gray concrete. A pair of bronze-washed eagles as tall as two men stood guard on either side of its entrance. *Lord save us from ourselves* was Dwight's thought when he saw it for the first time. The faded storefronts and lawyers' offices crowding around it looked like movie set miniatures in comparison. The place didn't even look like it was built for humans. Maybe some kind of uptight, giant aliens, but not flesh-and-blood people. The thought of Bud being swallowed by this place - by the system - really burned him up.

"So this is why you haven't been to the club lately?" Dwight said. He squinted against the jail's garishly bright interior lights, which were so intense he thought his corneas would probably melt if he looked directly into them. All that brightness had to have been intended as some symbol of truth and its revelation in the light. Another government idea, no doubt.

"Yeah, I'm four days on, three days off," Jim said. "Screws with my digestion. Drinking's out of the question. Sucks to be me."

Dwight shook his head. "Too bad. We've got a couple new girls. Real dancers," he said. "They're all effing gymnasts now. Some of them even come in with resumes like they think they'll be filing and shit." He paused while Jim scanned the bank of eight monitors to his left.

"No matter how old they are, these guys in here are little kids," Jim said. "You gotta watch them every minute. Doesn't matter what they're here for. It's all suicide watch."

Dwight couldn't see the screens from where he stood. Bud was surely on one of them, his every move recorded by a camera mounted securely in the ceiling. But there was no way Bud would ever commit suicide, right? He'd been charged with shooting a dog, a charge that sounded dumb as hell to Dwight. It wasn't like they had charged him with murder or kidnapping. The irony was that a murder had happened at his house.

The fact that *he* was the one who had actually committed murder that day wasn't lost on Dwight, either.

"So, you get why I can't let you see him tonight."

"Sure," Dwight said. "I get it. I wouldn't want you to jeopardize your job, man."

"It's just that it's not visiting hours, and he *has* been charged with a felony," Jim said. "Everything will happen in the morning."

"Funny how you and me always do our business at night," Dwight said. "Sometimes I feel like an effing vampire, you know?"

Jim held up a finger to have him wait while he answered the radio. The other deputy was going on a break. "Ten-four," Jim said. "Let me know when you're back." He put the radio down.

"I should probably go, man," Dwight said. "The club

won't run itself."

Right before he left for the courthouse, a lone deputy had shown up at the club and had a cursory look around, as though Lila might have been shackled to the walk-in or tied up beneath the sink in the women's bathroom. The deputy was a good-looking kid who had hauled some troublemakers off the premises in the past, and his firm ass and blue eyes gave the girls backstage a little thrill. Dwight had taken a risk leaving the club in the hands of Charity and the bartender. A small risk, but still a risk. He hated the thought of waiting until the morning to see Bud. The cops would probably be all over the club by then, and he had Pat's body to get rid of in the meantime.

Pat's body. Shit.

Jim nodded, then put up his hands in a gesture of self-defeat. "I didn't get my stripes being anyone's girlfriend," he said. "Screw the regs. I need to stretch some, anyway."

He stood, pressed a button near the video screens, and motioned for Dwight to follow him down the stairs.

"He's in a basement holding cell. There's an empty room a couple doors down. You can talk, but he's got to keep the cuffs and shackles on."

"I owe you, man," Dwight said.

They stopped outside a gray door with a coded lock.

"Oscar likes to take himself an extra long break about now, but this can't take all night. Five minutes?"

"No problem."

"Wait," he said. "Come over here."

In less than a minute, Jim patted him down and had him empty his pockets of everything, including his wallet, phone, handkerchief, and a substantial Gerber knife he hadn't carried with him in years.

"Just in case," Dwight said, when Jim held it up to inspect it.

"I bet," he said. He put everything in a shallow tray and locked it in a cabinet behind a nearby desk. "By the way, what the hell happened to your ear, man? Things getting rough at the club these days? I'm not sure I want to mess with those girls if that's how they leave you looking."

Dwight raised his hand to lightly touch the bandage on the side of his head. "It was my own fault," he said. "A misunderstanding."

≺≼ ✦ ≽≻

"You've got to find Lila," Bud said. "I can't do anything from here."

Bud was sitting down, but Dwight had a sense of the violent internal battle he was fighting. The bags beneath his eyes were gray and pronounced, though Dwight didn't think for a second that Bud had been weeping.

"You're absolutely sure she didn't take off somewhere?" Dwight said. "You know how she is sometimes."

"Of all the people who've asked me questions today, I thought you'd be the first one to believe me," Bud said. The note of scorn in his voice stung Dwight. "The same sonofa-bitch who killed Claude ran off with her. And nobody's listen-ing!" He banged the table with the flat of his hand.

Dwight had never seen Bud so angry. Below the anger, there was an unmistakable current of fear that shook Dwight.

"If you say that's what happened, then that's what happened," he said. "Just calm down. We'll figure it out." He didn't really know what there was to figure out. The story about the big man who had run off with Claude had sounded like a fairytale, something that loon Sheryl Dixon had made up. She was a freak, and it didn't surprise him that she would claim a freak had run off with her husband.

"Didn't you see the poster they did of the guy who got Claude? It's the same guy. That's who we need to find if we're going to find Lila."

Dwight shook his head. He had heard one of the girls say that the guy on the poster was kind of cute in a scary way, but things like posters never got his attention because he never had the chance to see them. If it wasn't front and center at the club or on his bedroom wall, it didn't exist. That's how his life was.

Bud closed his eyes. The tension folding his brow told Dwight he was picturing Lila.

Opening his eyes, he whispered, "She was naked, Dwight. She had no defense. No protection from the cold, the ground - nothing. She hates to be cold. Hates it. Starting in November, she even puts socks on when she goes to bed."

Dwight wanted to reach over and put his hands over Bud's to comfort him, but he didn't do it. Bud was suffering. Bad. But Dwight couldn't help this time.

Or wouldn't.

"They can't be serious, not looking for her," Dwight said. "They're not stupid."

"They're hinting around that maybe I did something to her," Bud said. He looked in Dwight's eyes as though waiting for some kind of response. "Maybe you already know why."

"I don't get it," Dwight said, puzzled.

"They said they heard she was sleeping with that Tripp Morgan guy. The DNR officer that's at the club sometimes."

Ah, so it was true. Dwight knew he should've been paying better attention.

"They said it was common knowledge. Common enough for Sheryl Dixon to bring it up when they asked her about Claude working in my office."

"Bullshit," Dwight said. "Sheryl Dixon's a crazy bitch who doesn't know her ass from a hole in the ground. Nobody listens to her."

Even as the words came out of his mouth, he knew he was wrong. Not about Sheryl Dixon being crazy - that was true enough - but about her knowing about the affair. Tripp Morgan had been coming around the club more and more, but he never messed with any of the girls or brought one in with him. Rarely even talked about them. But Dwight had seen him following Lila around at some party at the house, and Morgan had mentioned that he'd gone to school with Lila and Sheryl Dixon and any number of other locals.

Tripp Morgan. Too bad. And too bad it was messing with Bud's head. Why hadn't any of the girls at the club mentioned the affair to him? The girls knew everything about everybody, and they disliked Lila Tucker to a person.

He glanced at the door. Jim looked back at him through the window and held up two fingers. Dwight nodded. Jim was a good guy. He would have to arrange something special for him with one or two of the girls.

"They think you found out about it and Danelle Pettit got in the way?" Dwight said. "You know Lila better than that. She wouldn't do that to you, man."

"I thought I did. But they made me doubt her, you know?" Bud said. "What would she want with a guy like that? What would she want with *any* other guy? I mean, not that I'm such a catch or anything. I'm over six feet tall of ugly. But we have a life. Lila loves me. Tells me every day."

"Exactly," Dwight said.

Some of the tension left Bud's face.

"So you don't think it's true?" he said. "You think they're just trying to get me worked up?"

"That's what I think," Dwight said, hoping he sounded convincing.

"Thanks, man," Bud said.

"We've got to get you out of this shithole," Dwight said. He looked around. "As shitholes go, it's not too bad, though. I've seen worse."

Bud seemed not to hear him.

"I told them his name," he said.

"Whose?"

"The creep who has Lila," he said. "His name was written across his back. You know, a tattoo. A big one."

"No shit," Dwight said.

One of his hands stiffened reflexively into a fist.

Almost everybody had tattoos these days, but hadn't he seen one recently that had been pasted like that across someone's back? He didn't see that many guys without their shirts. In the dead of summer, the occasional biker would try to get in the club wearing an open leather vest, both his arms sleeved in tattoos. The area had its share of bare-chested guys in pickups, but Dwight tried to keep himself from looking in case they thought he was staring.

"It was blue and gold and white," Bud said. "*Saint Anthony*. Who in the hell would have the balls to call himself a saint?"

Dwight didn't have to think about it. He knew exactly who'd have the balls to do so. *Impossible*. If it had been any other day, he might have doubted himself, but he'd been listening to a dead guy bitch all afternoon.

"Goddamn, Bud," he said. "Goddamn it to hell."

"What?"

Jim stuck his head in the door. "You need to get along," he said. "Time's up."

"Three more minutes. That's all I need, Jim," Dwight said, pleading. Jim *had* to give him the extra time.

"I can't do you any more than that," Jim said. "You owe me. Big time, buddy."

Dwight nodded, wanting to scream for him to get out of the room again. Jim let the door close.

Dwight grabbed Bud's forearm and squeezed it so hard that Bud winced. "I need you to hear this," he said. "And you're not going to believe me."

CHAPTER FORTY-TWO

LILA HAD BEEN FLOATING without any sense of time passing. Not on a cloud, or anything so magical or comfortable, but she had seen her body beneath her and didn't want to recognize herself.

She wasn't floating anymore.

She kicked at Ivy from the bathtub, landing her foot solidly on Ivy's bony chest. Ivy let go of Lila's soap-covered leg and flew backward onto the floor, her mouth gaping.

Lila's scream was a siren of rage, barely human, bursting with every drop of pain she had suffered since that animal first touched her. Ivy kept scrambling away, driven by the sound, but the wet floor was treacherous and she slid into the hollow door, banging her head. But Lila couldn't hear her whimper of pain over the sound of her own voice. Like an inconsolable child, she kept on.

Ivy felt her way up the wall from the floor and grabbed on to the doorknob, poised to run away. She shouted for Lila to *stop!* but Lila might have been blind and deaf in that moment.

When Lila's screams finally subsided, she collapsed back into the water, exhausted with fear.

"Shhhhhh," Ivy said, crawling back over to the tub.

"Shhhhhh. It's all right, Lila. Everything's going to be all right."

Who was this woman coming toward her? Lila had a sense that she knew her, but couldn't be sure. She shrank away. She was freezing. The water she was sitting in was ice cold. Had it ever been warm? Where the hell was she?

"Lila, Lila. It's all right, I promise."

The strange mouth. The white hair. It had always been white, hadn't it? This woman didn't seem safe to her. *God. I just want to be home with Bud!* The thought of her husband elicited a soft cry from her lips.

Bud. A man. My husband. My help. He's not the other man, the one with the weird stitches on his neck, his wrists. The man who couldn't be real.

"Lila," Ivy whispered.

"Go away," Lila screamed. "Get away from me. Get away from me now!"

This woman, this *Ivy* - that was her name - wanted to hurt her. She had been with the other man. It came to Lila now, their talking in front of her. Ivy talking to him, telling him what to do. *Ivy knew.* But *he* hadn't talked at all, had he? Because he *couldn't* talk. He could only grunt.

His breath was foul on her face, in her nostrils and mouth. His hand had gripped her hair so hard that she couldn't turn away. She grabbed the edge of the bathtub and hung her head over it to vomit on the floor. It splashed on Ivy, marking her clothes. But Ivy didn't move away.

She put her hand out to touch Lila's water-soaked curls.

"You're going to hurt yourself," Ivy said. "You need to let me help you. Please."

She was begging now. Lila had heard her beg before. Was it yesterday? Some faraway time? Maybe she was wrong about everything. Time had collapsed in on her and she suddenly couldn't imagine existing in any other time, in any other place. It was just her, here with Ivy.

She pulled back and wiped at her mouth with the back of her hand. She looked at Ivy.

"I'm cold," she said. Her entire body was shivering.

"Of course," Ivy said, sounding relieved. She got up to grab a threadbare towel from its place on the rack.

Lila stood. She didn't want to look down at her own body. She never wanted to see her body again. She moved slowly, careful to avoid the pool of vomit on the floor, but lost her balance stepping over the tub's edge. Ivy caught her, and they were suspended for just that second, the two of them touching, almost embracing.

CHAPTER FORTY-THREE

A S IVY TRIED TO HELP LILA stand, she told herself that what Anthony had done to Lila couldn't be her fault. She had done nothing to encourage him. Like a spoiled child, he reached out for whatever might please him, and struck down whatever - whoever - displeased him. Despite Lila's connection to Claude Dixon, Anthony's finding her had to have been chance and nothing else. But feeling the weight of Lila's misery in her arms, Ivy was suddenly certain that she was indeed guilty.

When Lila was steady, Ivy draped the towel around her shoulders, and lifted her hair so it wouldn't be caught underneath. She averted her eyes from Lila's bruised and bitten torso and instead concentrated on Lila's grubby feet, with their once-shiny, manicured toenails.

Ivy would never let some stranger touch the ticklish parts of her feet, or hold her hand in theirs. A sloe-eyed woman with thick white streaks in her black hair had set up a fancy table to do fake nails and manicures at Sassy Scissors, where she and Thora got their hair cut. Ivy didn't like the way the woman looked at her when she came in; her smile was too automatic, too forced. But someone like Lila would find that appealing, wouldn't she? She liked to be flattered. Catered to.

Ivy was nothing like Lila. Who would care what her toes looked like? No one had ever cared what her face looked like.

An excuse, Thora was always saying. *You use that lip as an excuse.*

Lila dabbed at her skin with the towel in a slow, absent motion. Ivy wondered if she was even aware of what she was doing. Ivy had made the bathwater plenty warm, but not hot enough to bother the sores on Lila's body.

She had seen the purple and black striations between Lila's legs and the way the flesh around her groin was swollen and red. Anthony had done this, and he had brought Lila back to the trailer because he wasn't finished with her. What would he do now? What should *Ivy* do now?

"I have some things you can put on," she said, reaching for the clothes she had set on the back of the toilet. Unfolding them, she realized she didn't have any underwear in the pile, only socks and pants and a sweater. Lila wasn't nearly as large as Thora, but Ivy had found an old pair of sweatpants in the trailer's rag bag that she thought might fit, as well as a soft cotton fisherman's pullover she had bought for Thora a decade earlier. The sweater had shrunk several sizes in the dryer, but Thora had still kept it. The idea that Thora might have kept it for sentimental reasons bothered her. That wasn't the Thora she had known her whole life. Or thought she'd known. She pushed the thought away.

She held Lila's shoulder as she bent to put the sweatpants on and noticed Lila looking away, not focusing on her own body. Lila winced as she pulled the sweatpants over her hips, but didn't cry out.

When Lila was dressed, Ivy positioned her on the edge of the tub so she could towel dry her hair. She tried to be gentle as she worked the bathwater out of the curls. Lila's hair was matted in places, and really needed to be shampooed, but she knew Lila was too fragile right then. Anything might set her off screaming, panicked liked an animal, and Ivy needed time to think.

⋆ ⊰ ✦ ⊱ ⋆

Lila sat propped up in the bed, her head tilted back against the warped headboard. She breathed evenly, but stared forward, still and silent.

"Let's try to eat this soup."

Ivy cradled the back of Lila's head with one hand to keep her upright, and held the spoon to Lila's lips with the other. It was only chicken broth, her mother's prescription for hurting tummies and bad colds.

Lila responded by pursing her lips at the edge of the spoon. She sipped, still staring forward at the drawn curtains.

"Are you warmer?"

Lila didn't answer, but accepted another spoonful of broth.

It was strange to have Lila back in the trailer. She had been there as a client several times, always in the front room, where Ivy had set up a screen for clients to change behind. They hadn't been close enough friends when they were younger for Ivy to bring her home. By junior high, Lila had made it clear that she was beyond people like Ivy, people who were obviously never going to leave the mountains. But she had been kind sometimes. Particularly when she wanted something from Ivy. And she had come back to Alta, hadn't she?

Can I let you walk away from here to tell everyone, Lila?

When the broth was down to a scant spoonful, Lila slumped against the headboard and closed her eyes. Ivy put aside the bowl and adjusted the pillows so that they were beneath Lila's head. She reached over and turned off the lamp. Almost immediately, Lila's breath deepened and Ivy knew she would sleep for hours.

Distorted shadows covered the bed and walls, making the room seem empty and lonesome. It had once been her parents' bedroom. Thora had taken down the bright, inexpen-

sive pictures and cheerful curtains that Ivy's mother had put
up, and replaced them with dull things: brown curtains like
burlap, and generic, black-framed photos of buildings from
the thrift store. "Better for renters," she had said. It was not a
happy room.

Ivy stood over Lila, wondering what all those boys
had seen in her. As a teenager, Lila'd had corkscrew curls and
a mouth that was too wide for her face. Freckles, too. She had
never been hesitant or shy, and had tormented the teachers
with her willingness to do things like climb out of second-
story windows for a joke, or make cookies in the shape of a
penis and testicles in Home Ec class. Then she would pull off
a tear-jerking performance in a school play. It wasn't just boys
who wanted to be near her. Girls did, too.

"Sleep is good," Ivy said, tucking a curl away off Lila's
forehead. *How much do I owe you? Is this enough?* "Sleep. Then
we'll know what to do."

Down the hill, the only light coming from the house was the
television's chalky glow from behind the living room curtains.
Ivy let herself in and turned on the overhead light. The television was blaring, but Anthony wasn't in the room. The floor
was littered with cupcake wrappers, an empty potato chip bag,
and peanut shells that had first been crushed in his careless
hands and then ground into the carpet. She had discovered
he liked to shell peanuts when she pulled a bag of them out
of the cabinet to put some on an ice cream sundae. He had
shelled fifty or sixty in one sitting, not even bothering to eat
half of them, but sprinkling them on the floor as though that
was what the floor was made for. Seeing the mess, she recalled
that she had thought they were out of peanuts. Where had he
even found them? She was too tired to think about it. At least
he had fed himself, and not forced her to come down to the
house to make him a meal.

Ivy took a quick shower, and changed into dry corduroys and a violet cotton sweater whose wide portrait collar made her feel more civilized, as though she hadn't been half-covered in vomit and mud and Lila's blood only an hour earlier.

Back in the living room, she swept the wrappers into one hand and dropped the remotes into the pockets of the denim caddy hanging over the arm of the recliner. Each of the caddy's three pockets had an initial embroidered on it - Thora's initials. Ivy had made it for Thora the previous Christmas after seeing one in a magazine, and laid it on Thora's chair for her to find Christmas morning. Thora was everywhere in the house, as much of a presence as when she had been alive. She felt Thora's vexation as she used a whisk broom and dustpan to clean up the peanut shells so she wouldn't wake Anthony with a noisy vacuum. Eventually the room was clean, but Thora wasn't exorcised. She had just become invisible.

Ivy dumped the debris in the kitchen trashcan and went to wipe down the sink. Movement in the window caught her eye, and she looked up to see her own reflection. The light shining behind her made her features look blurred and flat in the glass. Her face had been transformed into a narrow oval with shadowed indentations for eyes, a faint triangle of a nose, and a thin line where her lips should be. No lashes. No scars. No hollows beneath her cheekbones. But the light had also transformed her hair into an aura of yellow gold.

She reached out, and the fingers of the woman in the glass met hers in cold union.

Ivy woke to the sound of the front door slamming.

She scrambled to kneel in the recliner so she could push back the curtain and look out the window. Outside, the sky was clear, the moonlight stronger.

Anthony's long shadow led him up the driveway, toward the darkened trailer.

She opened her mouth to call him back, and her breath made a small wreath of fog on the glass. All she had to do was open the front door and shout after him. But nauseating fear kept her where she was until he disappeared behind the trailer. She sank back down into the chair, and turned off the lamp.

She couldn't move. Closing her eyes, she tried to will herself to get up out of the chair. To go up to the trailer. To do anything but sit there.

CHAPTER FORTY-FOUR

JOLENE PULLED CHARITY'S beat-up car into a parking space around the corner from the courthouse. It stalled out before she could put it into park. The last time she had driven a car had been over thirty years ago. Working a clutch properly seemed to her like one of those things she shouldn't forget, but it hadn't happened that way.

The concrete and marble courthouse was a tomb whose thick walls couldn't keep the silent pain of the men and women inside from reaching her. Hospitals, nursing homes, prisons - they were all islands of misery, and she stayed away from them if she could. Up on the mountain, she could hardly feel anything at all. She had strength, there. But being around all this humanity was draining her body of its usefulness. Her time was coming, and she hadn't even gotten close to what she was supposed to do.

Lila was out there, holding the hand of hell itself. Ivy - her dear, sweet Ivy of the serious questions and snowy hair - was lost. And Thora. At least someone had closed her eyes. Ivy? It had to have been Ivy.

She had to do something right this time. She couldn't bear to be born again. To suffer life again.

⸎

"You mean I can't see my own father?" There was a particular little-girl tone of voice that some of the other dancers at the club used when they wanted something from the men. It made Jolene laugh when she heard it - baby talk from cotton-candy pink or red-painted, pillowy lips. But that didn't mean she couldn't imitate it. The advantage she had over those girls was her ability to maintain innocence in her eyes. She had changed from the sweatshirt into one of Charity's fluffy, V-neck sweaters, and had left her jacket open so the man at the jail's front desk could get a good look at what was inside.

"I understand your concern, miss, but the visiting schedule is posted right on the front door."

The gleaming gold tag over his left breast pocket read FOWLER, and his aura was a putrid, muddy orange. He seemed lonely in his defenses, like he had been loved once but had forgotten what it was like. His brusqueness was part of an act that wouldn't be difficult for her to break.

"But I came all the way here from school, Officer Fowler," she said. "I came as soon as I heard from the police, and now you tell me I can't see him?"

"Really wish I could help you." He shook his head with exaggerated regret.

Jolene nodded, playing along. "Please."

"Sorry," he said. "You'll have to wait until tomorrow to talk to *Da-dee*."

Ah, there was the sarcasm. He must have recognized her from the club. It still surprised her to realize the low esteem in which the dancers were held. Most of them were young mothers, or girls who had wanted to dance all their lives but didn't have much training. A very few were addicts and even fewer had sex for money, but they were all the same to the public. It had been foolish of her to imagine that she could sail into the courthouse, ask to see Bud, and be taken to him immediately.

The prospect of the next hour - of having to persuade this man the way he wanted to be persuaded - filled her with visceral dread. It had been different with Tripp. Even though he was touching evil in the worst way, she had found a kind of solace in his arms. She had forgotten what it was like to be touched with tenderness. And Tripp *had* been tender - for a while, anyway. She had let herself feel human, almost vulnerable, in the same way she allowed herself to feel when she danced at the club.

"I know he's upset." This was not a lie. She could feel Bud's rage around them. He was afraid for Lila. Desperate. "Where's his lawyer?" She looked around the lobby as though a lawyer might suddenly appear.

"Said I can't help you."

Fowler moved some papers around on his desk and put a bright green apple on top of them. The apple was obviously a nod to a doctor-ordered *healthy lifestyle*, because sickness - physical as well as moral - was consuming his body.

"But how come you don't have a line on what's up with the lawyer, seeing as you're his daughter and all?" He gave her an insincere little smile. "You don't seem too worried about Mrs. Tucker - your mama."

"She's my stepmother," Jolene said. "We don't get along, you know?"

"No. I can see that you wouldn't," he said. The gray around him intensified.

"What if I just sat over there in a chair and waited until the morning visiting hours?"

"I think that would be a waste of your time, but go ahead and do that if you want," he said. "Free country, public place."

"Okay," she said, returning his smile. "Works for me." She knew he would watch her walk away.

The "L" of chairs in the waiting area sat beneath a bank of bright but indirect lights. A wall-mounted television tuned to a twenty-four-hour news channel yammered at her from above. She was weary enough to close her eyes and sleep for hours, but knew she had to stay alert if she was going to

see Bud. She sat paging idly through a fishing magazine, four
years old but its content still brand new to her. Every so often
Fowler would look up from his desk, staring at her without
apology or acknowledgment.

Fifteen minutes and two dull stories about fishing
equipment passed before he spoke again. This time into the
radio.

"Kenny, what's your ten-twenty?"

"Second floor down," Kenny replied. "One of the boys
had him a bad dream. Raised all kinds of hell. Need me to
come up?"

Fowler cleared his throat. She glanced over at him to
see that his cheeks and ears were lightly flushed.

"Nah. I'm going to take a break, though," he said. "If
anybody shows up, they can wait outside for five."

"Ten-four," Kenny said.

Fowler took his time making a show of setting up the
space for his absence, and then ambled to the waiting area, absently tucking in his shirt and adjusting his belt. Jolene looked
up and gave him a hopeful, innocent smile. He wasn't looking
for real innocence. That was the last thing he wanted.

"So you want to see your daddy in a bad way?" he said.
What he was really asking her was in the flush of his skin and
the way his voice had dropped a throaty octave.

She nodded. "You just tell me what to do," she said.

"Let's go," he said.

The storage room was larger and neater than the one Dwight
maintained at the club, with the labels of the cleaning supplies
carefully facing out of their shelves, and boxes of paper towels
and toilet paper stacked so that their corners met in perfect
lines. She had a moment to look around while Fowler shifted
a stack of boxes to reveal a folding chair and a stained, square
pillow.

"No reason we shouldn't be comfortable," he said.

She tried to pretend surprise at his preparations; this was obviously something he did all the time. Or did he usually just come back here to nap?

He held a stainless steel flask, engraved with some kind of lodge insignia, out to her. "You like sloe gin?" he said.

Staying in character, she let herself look surprised, and waited until he gestured with the flask a second time before taking it. The gin passed over her lips and coated her tongue with sweetness. She took several sips before passing it back to him.

"I like that," she said. She ran the tip of her tongue over her lips, making him smile.

"Bet you were expecting 'shine." He shook his head. "That stuff will mess you up. There are plenty of sloeberry bushes around here if you know where to look. Every one of the berries that went into this was pricked with the bush's own thorns." He held up the flask. "Never metal. That'll sour the batch before it's even started."

She smiled.

By the time he was settled on the chair, with Jolene standing close enough to look down on the freckled skin between the gelled clumps of his salt-and-pepper hair, they had passed the flask back and forth three or four times. She was careful to let the syrupy liquid press against her tongue for just a second at each turn.

He set the flask on a nearby shelf, all the while staring at her chest.

"Why don't you take off that jacket?" he said.

She shrugged off the jacket, letting it drop to the floor. He grabbed her sleeve to pull her closer and slid a damp hand beneath her sweater. When he pushed her bra up over her breasts, the underwire pinched as it caught on his wedding ring, but he didn't pause and his wheezing breath didn't change. Closing his eyes, he began kneading her breasts. His jowls slackened with perverse serenity.

"Sweet amen," he said. Now he shoved the entire sweater up to her neck and filled his mouth with her.

His gray viscous aura enveloped her, and the tang of his sweat invaded her nostrils and lungs. But she let it pass through her - away, away - so that she could barely feel his beard against her skin.

When he seemed to have had enough of both breasts, he fell back onto the chair, fumbling at his fly.

"Why, lookee here," he said. "Treat time." His voice was breathless as he revealed himself.

Jolene unhooked her bra and slipped it off with her sweater. She pulled them over her head, glad to be able to hide her revulsion for those few seconds.

"Oh, you better start now," he said, gripping his penis in one hand. "Daddy's not going to make it."

"Sure you will," she said, straddling his lap and pressing close so he could feel her skin and hair against his face, her breasts against his chest.

"It would mean so much if you would kiss me first," Jolene said, close to his ear.

When she leaned back, he looked in her eyes. She thought he might demur - then what would she do? Kill him? No. She could hurt him, and she *was* going to hurt him. Murder had never been in her nature. God knew if it had, she wouldn't be here in this closet. She wouldn't be anywhere at all. She would have lived out her natural life decades and decades earlier. She might even have married back then and had children, sweet children. Her descendants, and those of her brother, would have covered Devil's Oven with goodness. But she hadn't been brave enough to kill back then.

Was she brave enough now to kill the creature who had Ivy in his grip? She told herself that killing the already dead wasn't killing at all.

Fowler's eyes shone with a brief spark of compassion, but it disappeared as quickly as it had appeared. When he crushed his mouth against hers, she tasted ash and coffee and damnation.

Reaching deep inside him, she opened the gate that held back the darkness every human tries to keep hidden. Fowler's darkness flowed with a ferocity that washed over them both. He struggled, trying to pull away from her. But she held him fast, held their kiss until she felt him weaken then stop struggling altogether. Between her legs, his member melted back into its cotton/poly hiding place, and the flood of darkness revealed his soul - a crusted, barely-breathing thing that cowered in a corner of his mind. She showed him how close it was to death, how his every vile thought killed it a little more.

Was this what her own soul had become? Did she even have one anymore?

Fowler jerked once in her embrace. His tongue went rigid in her mouth.

She let him go.

Bud stood up quickly from the lower bunk, almost banging his head on the steel frame of the one above him.

"Jolene!"

"Here are your shoes and stuff," Jolene said, whispering. She was weak, though not as weak as the man who stood in the doorway behind her. Fowler faced the hallway, unwilling - or unable - to look at either of them.

"We have to go," she said. "We have to go right away."

Bud's aura was a confusion of blue and yellow. He tried to ask her questions, but didn't seem to know where to start. He finally gave up and slipped on his shoes, put his wallet into his pocket without looking into it, and threaded his belt onto his pants.

She hated to see how much pain he was in. Lila didn't deserve all the love he felt for her.

How much does any of us deserve?

"Don't look at him as we go out," she whispered. Bud's

face held no understanding, but he nodded.

She touched Fowler's arm so he would move out of the doorway.

Staring down at the floor, he took a single plodding step sideways. His aura was translucent, gaining slow strength to a peaceful, healing green.

"You need to drive," she said, opening the passenger door of Charity's car. "We have to hurry."

Bud cast a doubtful glance at the tiny car, but hardly hesitated before folding into the driver's seat. His head only cleared the interior roof by an inch or two. He grunted as he felt for the seat adjustment lever, and there was the *prrrong* of a spring breaking as the seat jerked backward.

"Holy hell," he said. "This your car?"

"No," Jolene said. "It's Charity's. Come on, we have to go."

But he just sat there. Confused.

"Bud," she said. His aura surged a passionate red through all the murk that had collected around him. He was ready, she knew, if he would just let himself act instead of think.

"What if Lila's dead?" he said. "What Dwight told me...I think he's lost it. None of it makes any sense." His face sagged with helplessness.

She touched his hand. Her strength was fading, but she closed her eyes to try to pass some of what she had left to him. She felt his sadness. His fear.

"Not dead," she whispered. "Not yet."

CHAPTER FORTY-FIVE

TRIPP SAT IN THE TRUCK watching the drunks go in and out of The Twilight Club. Trouble always seemed to come back around to this place. No one had wanted the club here when he was a kid. The Cornerstone Baptist Church had organized a letter-writing campaign to the county supervisors and the big state newspaper to stop it from being opened. They had even bought space on a billboard out on the highway and put up a picture of a sweet little girl with an unshaven man looming behind her. The sign asked what kind of life would she have when her daddy started to "drink himself to death and fall at the door to hell."

But the land had been unincorporated, the club builder's brother-in-law on the supervisor's board, so nobody could stop it. Tripp's own father had never gone inside. In fact, his parents hadn't been back to Alta in twenty years, preferring to stick close to the tiny condo they had bought on a southern beach. But there were plenty of other men who made the club their home.

Jolene had almost talked him into trusting her, but now just picturing her face caused a slicing pain deep inside his head. She was poison. But she was also the key to finding Lila, and she would lead him to her if he had to break her head off her skinny shoulders to look inside it to see what she knew. If Lila was dead - and he was truly afraid that she was by now - Jolene was responsible, no matter if the creature had killed her with his own hands. But all would come full circle when Tripp gave Jolene what she deserved. She had some kind of kinship with the creature. He had felt it on the mountain.

Jesus Christ, what's wrong with me?

He took a long drink from the liter bottle of water he had picked up at the Git 'n' Go, and unzipped his coat. He had begun to sweat, his body burning with energy. The mountains were barely visible against the black sky, but he felt like he could get out of the truck and run the miles between him and them without tiring.

It was *her*. Jolene had done this.

There'd always been talk of witchery on Devil's Oven, and now he felt it inside his body, like death itself had taken up residence there. He rubbed the heels of his hands against his eyes to relieve the sting they had developed staring at the club's entrance. He was falling apart.

He came back to himself when something smacked against his window. Dwight's sickly white face looked back at him, his eyes bloodshot behind the thick lenses of his glasses. An awkward white bandage covered one of his ears.

It's got him, too.

"Open the G.D. window!"

The glass between them muffled Dwight's voice, but Tripp heard him clearly enough.

"What the hell?" Tripp said. Dwight was a particular flavor of crazy, and he wasn't in the mood.

Dwight hit the window again with the side of his fist and bounced away on his toes like a deranged bantamweight.

Tripp shut off the truck and took a good look at Dwight before getting out. For a second, the malaise that had gripped him for hours lifted, and he thought he might laugh. Dwight looked the fool - so like Dwight, but funnier. Tripp opened the door.

Dwight rushed at him, his greasy head bent, ready to butt his chest. Tripp responded automatically, turning sideways to aim a kick at Dwight's oncoming shoulder. When it landed, Dwight fell, skidding backward onto his ass and ending up on his side, curled up like a baby.

Damn, it feels good.

Tripp dragged the stunned man to his feet by the front of his windbreaker.

"You really don't want to mess with me tonight, buddy," Tripp said. "Let's keep this friendly."

Dwight's glasses balanced awkwardly on his nose and a thick bubble of blood hung on his mustache. "You screwed her," he said. "You screwed Bud's wife, you hillbilly sonofa-bitch. I saved him and you screwed everything up."

Tripp shoved Dwight away, causing him to stumble again on the asphalt.

"Get away from me, douchebag," he said. "You don't know what you're talking about." *Sheryl Dixon and her big-ass mouth.*

A man and a woman on their way into the club stopped a few yards away.

"Bud knows, you asshole," Dwight said.

"What's your point?" Tripp said.

"They've got him locked up."

"Not my problem," Tripp said.

"You know he didn't do anything to Lila."

Tripp, breathing hard, addressed the couple staring at them. The woman - a girl, really; he would have bet a hundred bucks she had a fake ID on her - was leaning forward, obviously more interested than the guy, who had a forefinger in his mouth, digging something out of his teeth.

"Law enforcement," Tripp said, letting his wallet drop open to expose his badge. "Just go on in." The girl seemed reluctant, but the man nodded, unperturbed, and started for the entrance. Tripp was pretty certain the girl winked at him before she turned around.

"You owe him," Dwight said. "You owe *me!*"

"Right now, I'm just looking for Jolene," Tripp said. "I don't have any business with you." The guy was out of his mind. Tripp started to walk around him to get to the club.

"You're screwing the kid, too?" Dwight said. He spat blood onto the asphalt. "Figures."

"I swear to God, Dwight. Shut the hell up! You don't know what you're talking about."

How is it possible that it's suddenly all about Jolene?

"I thought you were a human being, not just another randy asshole." A chunk of gelled hair fell down into Dwight's eyes.

"Get out of my way," Tripp said.

"Jolene's not here."

"Bullshit," Tripp said. "She said she was coming in with Charity." But the words sounded false in his ears. She had lied to him. Everything she had said about wanting to help him, about how she actually cared about Lila, was total bullshit. He had been fooled once, and now she was playing him all over again.

Watching Dwight rub his shoulder where his kick had landed gave Tripp a faint twinge of regret.

"Stay the hell out of my club," Dwight said. "I don't want to see your sorry ass here again."

"Yeah, well, I don't think it's going to matter much what I do," Tripp said. Over Dwight's shoulder, he saw three cruisers come around the highway curve and slow to enter the club's parking lot, their lights strobing against the mist-laden clouds that had begun to slide off the hills and into the valley. "You've got company."

CHAPTER FORTY-SIX

EY, YOU THINK THEY'LL FIND ME? Pat sounded like he was playing hide-and-seek and it was all a great joke. *I don't think they'll find me. I think I'm going to rot in this plywood piece of crap you've got me in, buddy.*

Dwight stood with his back to the stage, wishing Pat would shut the hell up so he could concentrate on the conversation with the cop who was standing way too close to his face.

The customers had all been shepherded out to the parking lot, and the dancers, except for Charity, were back in the dressing room packing up their gear. Charity and the two waitresses stood at the bar looking pissed off.

So the cop wanted to get cozy? Dwight got right back in his face.

"What *you* don't understand is that you scared the shit out of all my customers when I already told you Bud didn't come by here today. Not at any time. Why don't you people listen to me?" he said.

The detective nodded. "We appreciate your cooperation, Mr. Yarbro."

"So why the G.D. rush, then? Couldn't this wait until morning?"

"That's the thing about warrants, Mr. Yarbro. They're

like money to us, burning a hole in our pockets. Especially when someone's dead, like Danelle Pettit, or missing, like Mrs. Tucker. We like to use them when they're fresh."

Pat snorted. *Fresh, he says. Wait until they get a whiff of my tighty-whities. It's a damn shame what a man who's about to die does to his undershorts. I'd be embarrassed if it had been anybody else but you. A man can relax around his friends, if you know what I mean.*

Inside his head, Dwight screamed for Pat to shut up, but he tried to keep his face neutral for the cop.

"Well, good luck with that," he said, stepping back. "I don't know what you think you'll find lying around here."

Good one, man! 'Lying around'!

"So you haven't seen Mr. Tucker at all today?"

How was he supposed to answer that? Jim Fowler would be up shit creek if he told the truth. Then again, there were video cameras all over the courts building. They would know sooner or later.

"I might have seen him for a few minutes tonight over at the jail. We just talked about the club. Business."

The things you do for that Bud guy, Pat said. *What's up with that? When did you get to be Mr. Sweetness and Light?*

"Business?"

Business about how he had cut up and buried the guy who'd come to collect on Bud's debt, and how that dead guy, Anthony, had managed to kill several people, up to and probably including Bud's own wife. It was a bad business. Business that made him feel like he was losing his shit.

"This is part of the man's livelihood," Dwight said. "A lot of other people's, too. A fact about which you people don't seem to care."

The overhead lights came on, causing the waitresses to make complaining noises, and at least one of the cops to shade his startled eyes. With the lights on, the club looked naked and vulnerable, like a classy woman without her makeup. Despite the chaos in his head, Dwight felt bad that so many outsiders were there to see the faded carpet and gash marks on the long, varnished bar. The catwalk needed polishing and the ceiling tiles were dingy with antique smoke.

And me the untidiest of all, Pat said. *How long do you think this stupid tarp is going to keep my juices in?*

"Hey, sir?" One of the uniforms was shouting across the room. "There's a locked storeroom back here. Can we get a key?"

The detective looked at Dwight.

"Screw me," Dwight said under his breath. He dug his keys out of his pocket. With the detective and officer follow-ing behind him, he tried to think of what all he had done after he killed Pat. His hand tightened around the key ring until it hurt.

Forgot about the cash, huh, buddy?

❧

They were back in the office, Dwight sitting on a chair be-tween the two detectives. All they needed was a bare bulb swinging from the ceiling to make the picture complete. They were even letting him smoke a cigarette. He noticed that the older detective, Burns, kept glancing up at the Pole Danc-ers' Association calendar tacked on the wall. A brunette Miss March was in full splits, hanging from a silk scarf tied around one ankle, her breasts and ass snuggled into a tiny pink athletic bra top and boyfriend shorts.

Time to give him up. Maybe you can get out of Podun-kville before they find me under here. You owe that guy nothing.

"So far as I know, there's nothing illegal about keeping money in a closet," Dwight said.

"That would depend on where that money came from," Detective Johnson said. He had loosened his tie and unbuttoned the top button of his shirt. It was, after all, close to one in the morning. Dwight guessed the detectives weren't used to working so late. Unless, of course, Detective Johnson had scheduled this visit for the benefit of the girls in the club. Dwight could see that his face was carefully shaved, like he had done a midnight touch-up before stopping in. "I'd say a hundred and fifty thousand bucks is a pretty large amount of cash to keep in a briefcase in a storage room."

"Did you witness Mr. Tucker putting the cash in the storage room? Did he tell you what it was for?" said Detective Burns.

"He didn't need to tell me because it's my cash," Dwight said.

"Bullshit," Johnson said.

"That's enough," Burns said, nodding the Johnson guy off. He leaned forward in his chair. "But I tend to agree with my colleague."

"That's your problem, then," Dwight said. "It's my money. Legal. Prove that it's not."

Burns sat back. "Given that the building is owned by Mr. Tucker, and his initials are on the briefcase, I would have to conclude the cash belongs to Mr. Tucker. And that much money - well, a person would want that kind of cash if they were, say, thinking of getting out of town for a while."

Or saving his own ass. Which it certainly didn't.

Dwight mashed out his cigarette. Smoking didn't calm him like it calmed other people. It stressed him out even more. There was so much he could tell these assholes, like the name of the ghoul - wasn't that the old-fashioned name for zombies? - who was doing all the killing. And had Lila Tucker.

"What I don't get is why you're not out looking for the sonofabitch who snatched Lila. Bud saw him, and Bud wouldn't lie to me. She's probably dead out there already."

"You know this?" Burns said.

"You people are so fixated on Bud, you don't see what's going on around you. That thing's out there now, probably killing someone else, and all you want to do is ask me stupid questions about my play money."

Johnson barked a laugh.

"You're wasting our time, Mr. Yarbro. When did Bud Tucker bring that money here?"

"Am I arrested or something? I can stop answering questions anytime, right?" It was a rhetorical question. He knew what his rights were.

"Of course," Burns said. "But we're going to have to take that briefcase in for evidence."

Now you're screwed. Pat, who had been quiet, was back.

The office door opened.

"Detective Burns?"

"Yeah."

"I got a call from Kenny at the jail. Bud Tucker walked out of there about half an hour ago."

CHAPTER FORTY-SEVEN

LILA WOKE TO A DRAFT cooling her face, opened her eyes to the same tenebrous quiet in which she had fallen asleep. As the horror of the past day flooded over her, she felt herself slipping back into that empty place where she was safe, that place where nothing could touch her. But the sound of heavy footsteps in the next room broke the silence and she lifted her head from the pillow, alert.

He's going to kill me this time.

She knew this room. When Ivy was still working from the trailer, she'd had her change in here sometimes. There were two small windows in the wall, but being in the front of the trailer, they opened onto nothing but air. It was easily fifteen feet to the ground.

Wouldn't it be better to die that way? If she doesn't die, what then?

Pushing the quilt away, she tried to get out of the creaking bed without making too much noise. Despite the adrenaline rush in her veins, it wasn't easy to get her arms and legs to respond. The unfamiliar clothes aggravated her wounds, her tender, bruised breasts. She lodged a thumb sideways in her mouth and bit down to keep from screaming aloud.

Ivy. Why is Ivy doing this to me?

She didn't have any more time to think. She had to get out. She could hear him lumbering around in another part of the trailer. Ignoring the raging pain, and her subconscious, which begged her to let herself come away into that sweet, empty place, she made it to the door of the bedroom and peeked out.

Outside the door, the air smelled foul, like rotting meat and urine. She saw him in the light from the kitchen - the first good look she had gotten of him since he took her from her backyard. Instead of being half-naked, he now wore khaki pants and a pale blue sport shirt that made him look like an over-muscled golfer. Still, he was barefoot. He stood in profile, upending a peanut can, trying to shake something out of it but it wasn't making any sound. Frustrated, he hissed and tossed it into the sink. It clanged around several times before it came to rest.

She felt a flush of satisfaction when she saw that the right side of his face was rent with four deep scratches. But there was no sign of blood, only grotesque, plum-colored flesh that looked like rotten meat. He went to the counter and picked up an open bag of pretzels, scattering several on the floor as he poured some into his hand. He turned around. Seeing her, he dropped the pretzel bag.

He rushed toward her, his feet pounding on the trailer's shaking floors, but she was able to slam and lock the flimsy bedroom door before he reached her.

She pressed her back against the door and looked around for somewhere to hide. She couldn't let him touch her again, couldn't survive those brutal hands. *His neck also has the stitches.* She couldn't bring herself to think about what that meant. Even if he didn't kill her physically, her mind, her soul couldn't survive much longer. There were things worse than death. Things that had already touched her.

Out in the living room, he was trying to work the handle out of the door, whining like a frustrated dog.

If she dropped the fifteen feet to the ground, there

would be more pain - a lot of it - and her body and mind resisted the thought. She made herself run to the window and push aside the blind. The glass was filthy, but she could see down the hill to a car passing on the highway. She pounded at the glass, screaming, and fumbled at the lock. Its lip was jammed tight, rusted to its bed. Down in the house, she saw movement at a window, a flicker of light, shining white hair. She screamed for Ivy. Ivy couldn't let her die.

No!

Now the figure moved away from the window. Toward the door, maybe?

Please, please, please, Ivy!

The light down in the house went off.

A thought flashed through her head: If she survived this, she would make sure Ivy Luttrell paid for what she had done to her. Bud wouldn't hesitate to kill Ivy if Lila told him.

The doorframe split, knocking the door - hinges attached - into the room so that it lay like a ramp onto the bed. He stood in the doorway, still smiling, obviously pleased with himself.

It was too late to get out.

His arms spread wide as though he would embrace her. He ran up the door, stooping so his head wouldn't scrape against the ceiling.

Lila dove for the floor, trying to get underneath the bed. If she could make it to the other side of it, she might get out the door before he caught her. But she wasn't fast enough, and he was on her. He grabbed her legs with a sound that might have been laughter and tried to pull her back. He mostly got hold of the too-large sweatpants and they began to slide down her legs. She dug her nails into the carpet to hold on, and felt the pants begin to peel off as he got a better grip on her.

She kicked and closed her eyes and screamed, loud and long. Surely Ivy would hear her. Ivy would take pity on her. How could one woman let something like this happen to another woman? What had she ever done to Ivy Luttrell? Dull, sad Ivy Luttrell, who'd had such tragedy in her own life. It was inconceivable.

When she opened her eyes, she found herself facing the back wall behind the bed. In the space between the night-stand and the bed, she saw the pointed tip of the walking stick she had seen, but not registered, when Ivy brought her into the room. She kicked at the man that much harder and gained an inch or so of ground. When she grabbed for the stick, it fell over. Her mouth was full of dust from underneath the bed, but she ignored it, and enjoyed the brief surge of hope she felt as her hand wrapped around the solid shaft of wood.

She didn't struggle when he grabbed her again, but held firmly on to the stick.

As a child, Lila had spent all the time she could in the woods, and had often gone camping with the scout troop run by her third-grade teacher, Mrs. Jarvis. She had loved riding along the mountain's muddy tracks in the Jeeps and pickup trucks be-longing to boys in her circle of friends, sneaking beer from the refrigerator in her grandfather's basement and drinking it be-side one of the rocky streams far off the road. They sat on the rocks, scaring the crap out of each other at dusk with stories about the murders on the mountain, the people who had gone hunting or walking in the deepest part of the forest, never to be seen again. One of her favorite stories was of the man who had married and killed six different wives. He just dug the first grave wider each time he put a body in, so that the women all lay in a companionable row.

And Tripp. She had made love to Tripp on a blanket in his backyard beneath the pine trees, with the stars peeking through the distant branches.

The mountain is all wrong now.

As she stood on the back deck of the trailer, looking

up the trail that led into the trees, she knew she would never go onto the mountain again if she could help it. Tripp had taken most of her love for it the moment he had looked at her like he didn't know her, when he had seen that girl's face in hers. That animal, the one who had tried to kill both her body and soul, had destroyed the rest. Both had come from the mountain. What kind of place was Devil's Oven that it could bring both happiness and terror into her life? Into the lives of everyone around her? She had been born so close to it and yet she hadn't known.

Ivy has known.

She knew she couldn't stay at the trailer. The man lay stunned in the bedroom, the walking stick jabbed into his throat, but he was still moving. He would be looking for her again.

Turning her back on the woods, she began to run down the hill toward the house.

Ivy! She would kill Ivy with her own hands.

When she was almost to the porch, she slowed and stopped. There was no way she could face Ivy alone. She was too weak. There would be time later. Lila Tucker had it all over pathetic Ivy Luttrell. Always had. Always would.

She pulled the sweater more closely around her and began to run again, past the darkened house and toward the highway.

CHAPTER FORTY-EIGHT

"A GUN'S NOT GOING TO HELP US," Jolene said. She couldn't make Bud understand. "He's not alive. Not like you are." *I'm not even alive, not really.*

"Bullshit," Bud said. He pulled the little car as far as he could into the gravel edging the driveway. He cut the lights, hoping they wouldn't be seen by anyone who might be watching the house. "Dwight said he killed him once. So he can be killed again. Right?" He paused. "Jesus, that sounds insane."

Getting Bud out of jail had left her drained. Even if she had the chance to confront the creature, she didn't know if she could do anything to stop him. Bud had told her what Dwight had said, that Anthony had come to confront Bud about the money he owed, and Dwight had killed him, cut him into pieces, and buried him on the mountain. What neither Bud nor Dwight knew, or could ever know, was that it had been Ivy's fault, Ivy's passion, Ivy's *need* that had resurrected him. Now this Anthony's resurrected self was carrying out whatever plan had been in his brain when Dwight had first killed him. His rage was focused on Bud and anyone close to Bud - Claude, Danelle, Lila. Surely Bud was next.

Had Thora just gotten in the way? Jolene refused to believe Ivy killed her. Thora had probably done something to make Anthony angry. Willful Thora, who always had to be right. Just like her father, Byron.

"I don't want you to wait here by yourself," Bud said.

Jolene saw the compassion in Bud's eyes. It didn't matter that he had been grievously hurt by Lila, or that he was willing to kill to get her back. Nothing would change that part of him.

"I'll be okay here," she said. "You just have to hurry. If he has her…"

"No. Come with me," he said.

◂◂♦▸▸

No one was watching Bud and Lila's house, but the police had left most of the interior doors ajar, and drawers and cabinets standing open, their contents ravaged. Bud didn't stop to look or comment, but motioned for Jolene to follow him up the back stairs. The house itself didn't have an aura, but the fog of death hung about it, a cloying sadness through which Jolene found it hard to move. When they reached the upper hallway, she felt it streaming over her, welling up from downstairs, where Danelle had died.

"Let me check my closet," Bud whispered. "I've got a flashlight in there, and the safe. I'll get us coats, too."

Jolene nodded. She waited in the doorway of the bedroom, but found herself standing on tiptoe, trying to look - not too closely - over the railing.

"This is where they found her," she whispered.

Bud didn't answer. He had disappeared into his bedroom.

Jolene walked to the railing. She had never been in a house like this. It was like a palace in a storybook. The carpet beneath her feet was thick, a luminescent shade of pearl. Large paintings framed in textured gilt covered the expanse of the opposite wall, which rose to the second floor. It was too dark to see their details, but she had an impression of thick forests, idyllic blue skies, and richly dressed women. Near the bottom, a single, upturned light shone on a portrait of Lila herself, her hair tamed into a loose chignon at the back of her head, with just a few teasing curls hinting at the richness of her hair. Around her neck was a necklace of dark stones and diamonds. She held an emerald green drape to her chest, and one alabaster leg peeked from beneath it. From where she stood, Jolene couldn't get a good look at Lila's expression, but she knew her face well enough. It would be a smug, teasing look, because this was Lila's fantasy.

Jolene tried not to hate Lila for what she had done to Bud by making a fool of him with Tripp. She tried not to hate anyone, but it was hard to avoid with Lila. Lila had wasted herself. She had wasted Bud.

Still, she didn't deserve to die.

The moonlight from the massive window above the front door, along with the small amount of light from the bulb below the painting, was enough to illuminate the shadows on the checkered marble floor. Some of the white squares near the center bore amorphous stains punctuated by pieces of reflective tape, no doubt put there by the police. But one white square showed a perfect handprint.

Danelle's handprint. The woman Bud had always mentioned so casually, the woman who made his food and did his laundry and kept Lila from feeling too much like a housewife. Poor Danelle. It was Danelle's pain that filled the house and made Jolene's throat feel tight.

She started to call out to Bud, to ask him to hurry. Then she saw movement on the floor.

Jolene watched in silence as the handprint lifted, detaching itself from the marble. The thumb and C-shape of the palm and the splotches made by the fingertips thickened and joined together, becoming a solid, breathing blackness. It was a hand, flexing and turning itself. The surrounding stains pulsed with life, and slipped across the floor to join the hand, knitting together faster and faster until they made a definable shape:

the featureless body of a woman, shining and liquid black, like
oil. Earth's blood. Jolene took a step backward, but found she
couldn't look away. The figure pushed itself up onto its knees
and looked from side to side like a ponderous animal unsure of
its surroundings. Then it raised what might have been its face
to Jolene.

She felt its pleading. Its pain.

It stretched out a lumpish hand to Jolene, just as Jolene
had reached out to be free of the earth that was swallowing her
so many years ago. The earth offered her shelter and safety, a
safety she now knew was more of a hell. Now *she* was the witness, just as the crow had been hers.

"I can't help you," she whispered. "I can't."

The figure's need pierced her. It crawled across the
floor, making tortuous progress toward the stairs. Jolene
couldn't help but be drawn to it. She knew that she and the
thing reaching out to her weren't so different. But she couldn't
give it what life she had left. She had to save it for Ivy.

Jolene understood this was all her doing. She was the
one who had run. She was the one who had seen the colors
of death around her mother, and she had done nothing. Her
father, her baby brother - innocents - had died because she
hadn't warned them. She hadn't acknowledged or fought the
evil that had consumed them. Evil that had lived beneath their
feet, even in the roots of the trees. Only she had been given the
gift of seeing it, but she had done nothing.

She'd been given a second chance, with Thora and Ivy.
But she had run again, when the evil consumed Byron, Thora
and Ivy's father. She had abandoned them, too.

It happened so fast. I was afraid.

She stepped down a single stair. The wraith's hand
reached for her.

If she couldn't save Lila or Ivy, maybe it was right for
her to give what she had left to the fearsome thing at her feet.
If she gave herself willingly, without running away, without
hiding, she might be absolved. Released.

Doing well by doing good. Something Byron had liked to say.

True death. It has to be better than the endless dark, the absence of time and touch. Waiting. Over thirty years had passed since she had come down off Devil's Oven the first time. The wait had seemed momentary and eternal all at once. But she hadn't been able to breathe inside the mountain. She couldn't go back to that purgatory, that gritty nothingness. She couldn't do it a third time.

"They drilled into my safe, but I've got another..." Bud was behind her. "My god, get back!"

He grabbed her around the waist and dragged her away from the top of the stairs. The thing below let out a mournful cry that sank into her skin, tore at her heart. She tried to fight Bud off, but he just kept repeating her name, over and over again, trying to get her away.

Bud managed to get her down the back stairs. She had stopped struggling, and he half-carried her into his study and pushed her into a chair. He was out of breath, his forehead covered in perspiration.

"Stop," he said. "Just stop."

Jolene's head dropped forward, her hair falling into her face. *I'm so tired.* The weight of her failure settled over her, crushing her.

Bud lifted her chin with one of his enormous hands. He bent down to look closely at her.

"Jolene," he said. "I don't know what's happening here, but you can't give up. You have to help me find Lila. You're the only one who can help me."

"I can't," she said. "Just leave me here. I can't do anything."

"I gave you a chance," he said. "I trusted you. I don't know what you can do, but whatever it is, you have to do it. Don't let Lila die. *I'm begging you.*"

He didn't wait for her answer, but crawled beneath his desk. After a few seconds, he backed out again.

"We're good to go," he said, showing her the gun he had taken from underneath the desk. Then he pushed aside the front of the sheepskin jacket he had changed into and secured the gun in the rear waistband of his pants. "They drilled out my safe and took every other gun I own like I'm some kind of criminal. Bastards."

He picked up the matching woman's coat he had brought downstairs, and pulled Jolene to her feet. "This'll be a little big on you, but it'll keep you warm." He helped her into it, and she didn't resist. They went back to Charity's car.

"We need to get to Ivy's." Jolene's voice was weak.

She leaned back in the passenger seat and closed her eyes. "They'll be looking for you," she said. She had drunk the can of energy drink he pulled from the fridge, but it had only wet her mouth and made her shiver.

"Can't help that," he said.

She felt the car speed up. "I need you to pray or find us some good luck or something right away," Bud said.

She opened her eyes. They were approaching the club, its parking lot blazing with police lights. Small groups of men and women huddled near the entrance. A cop in full uniform stood rigidly in front of the door.

"Do you think they're looking for you?" she said. "What are they doing?"

"Don't stare," he said. "Just look forward."

No one looked at them or followed.

They didn't speak again until they got near the town proper, where Bud took the old county road that rose up behind the town so they wouldn't pass the courthouse building. It was only two miles around, past some of the town's older houses and a couple of churches. She stared out the window, fogging it some with her breath.

Breath I don't deserve.

"Just a few minutes to go," Bud said. "Hang in there."

She had no idea what they would find when they got to Ivy's place. When she had been there with Tripp earlier in the day, there'd been no sign of Lila. *She has to be somewhere.* Besides the trailer, there were the other outbuildings. She had never been allowed in the tiny smokehouse - Byron's private domain. It didn't seem big enough to hide someone in for very long. The barn was barely standing. They hadn't used it for much, only for storing hay to sell. Thora and her mother had kept two horses for riding, but that was long before she'd arrived. But the creature - he wasn't a secretive being. He wouldn't care if someone knew where he was. He wasn't afraid of people, of Bud, of Ivy, of being seen at the Git 'n' Go or anywhere else. He didn't need to hide in the smokehouse or the barn.

To the left of the car, she could see the lights of the trailer park - the orderly rows of trailers and the nine or ten streetlamps, a car driving slowly down the main road to the highway beyond. Most everyone there would be asleep.

When Ivy was four, she never wanted to go to sleep in her bed. She had wanted to lie with her head in her mother's lap - *her* lap - and have her silky head stroked. She had lain there, sucking her thumb, sometimes humming tunelessly. Or she would play with her mother's hair, twisting it in her fingers until she got sleepy and her hand slipped onto her mother's breast, resting there.

She wondered if Charity had discovered that her car was gone. She hated to hurt Charity, who had taken her in without question or regret. Charity would try to hide the hurt, make some smart remark to Eli about Jolene going back to wherever she came from. Eli would know, though. He always knew what Charity was feeling.

The road met the highway just west of the fuzzy bright lights of the Git 'n' Go.

"I wonder if Lila's had anything to eat today," Bud said, as though to himself. He turned onto the highway.

His aura was subdued, and it seemed that when he turned to Jolene a moment later to ask if she was doing okay, his eyes had lost some of their softness.

It amazed her that he still loved Lila even though he knew about Tripp. It amazed her that anyone could be loved that way, and not feel like the most blessed person on earth.

CHAPTER FORTY-NINE

"I DON'T THINK JOLENE CAN EVEN DRIVE," Charity said. "Shit. Did she even think for a minute about how I'm supposed to get home?"

Nervous energy had Dwight working, and Charity had started helping without being asked. He could tell she was trying not to be pissed off at Jolene. No one liked to be angry with Jolene. Being mad at her was like being mad at a little kid.

Still, there was something about Jolene that bugged Dwight. She seemed *too* sweet, too defenseless.

You always were a crappy judge of character. I tried to tell you, man. Pat's voice sounded strained and hollow. *Listen, I feel like six kinds of hell. I don't know how much longer I can handle this box.*

"Yours is not an opinion I need at this moment," Dwight said. He shoved a chair so hard onto a table that the other two on it bounced to the floor.

"So, I'm supposed to walk?" Charity said. "Are you kidding?"

"Wasn't talking to you," Dwight said.

She shook her head and moved on to the next table.

He was tired of being afraid and worried. People like

Charity, men like him, they always just got on with the business of living. It was what they knew how to do. People like Bud and Jolene were the feeling kind. The prey of the world, thinking everyone could just get along if people kept smiling.

Why was he such a sucker for people like them?

Because you know most people are sheep, Pat said. He coughed several times. *Hey, you remember that lady you did when you were broke?*

Back in the city, maybe a decade earlier, Pat had gotten an out-of-town job he didn't want, and passed it on to Dwight. If he hadn't needed the money so badly, he never would've taken it. The only woman he had ever killed.

Ha! That bitch bit you on the ankle. Knew she would be a pain in the ass.

"Do me a favor and go make sure the lights are out in the dressing rooms, okay?"

"I guess you're taking me home, then?" Charity said.

"No. We'll see if one of the cabs is available. I'll pay," he said. There was no reason to keep Charity around. He needed to think, and she didn't need to be involved in what was going down. She had only brought Jolene to the club out of kindness.

"You sure?" she said. "What's up?"

"Nothing. Go on and call."

When she disappeared into the back hallway, Dwight walked over to the stage and squatted down to pull the curtain aside.

"It should never have happened like this, man," he said, feeling only a little stupid talking to a dead man in a box twenty-five feet away. "I'll let Marie know there was an accident. She won't know it's me, but I'll make sure she gets the message. You have any cash put away or anything? Anything you want me to tell her?"

You're not going to get a chance to tell my wife shit, Pat said. His voice was a fading echo. *This is going to go bad from here on out, my friend.*

Dwight snorted. "Like it's been going so well up to now. Peaches and cream." He waited for Pat's next smartass remark, but there was only silence from beneath the stage.

CHAPTER FIFTY

TRIPP DROVE INTO THE TRAILER park, keeping an eye out for potholes and taking the speed bumps as slowly as he could bear. He passed two teenage boys drinking beer in the weak glow of a porch light.

"Not my problem," Tripp said under his breath. He gave them a cursory wave. They didn't bother to hide the beer or wave back. One of them lit a cigarette. As long as they kept their business in town and off the mountain, he didn't care what they did.

Charity's trailer was dark, its parking space empty. He parked and watched for signs of life inside. He had the police scanner turned down low, but loud enough to catch whatever came over it.

The scanner already told him that Bud had walked out of the jail in the company of a dark-haired woman, and Tripp knew it had to have been Jolene. The good news was that Bud's guilty behavior meant the state police would stop bothering *him*. That he knew they were wrong about Bud only worked in Tripp's favor. When he found Lila, he would make things right with her. She would feel some loyalty to Bud because of what they had accused him of, but Tripp would be the one to help her heal.

The most important thing was to get her away from that animal. Letting Jolene out of his sight had been a mistake.

Where the hell was Jolene, and where would she take Bud? She had no friends he knew of except Charity and that loser boyfriend of hers. Hell, she wasn't even human - if he could believe that.

I do believe. I don't want to, but I do.

As he saw it, there were two things he could do: look for Jolene, starting at Ivy Luttrell's (Bud would be with her, but Tripp would have to deal with him sooner or later, anyway); or head back up to the mountain and keep searching for Lila on his own. Something that was not only impractical this time of night, but borderline insane.

What's all this if not insane?

The radio crackled, and the dispatcher came on. He heard clearly the only words he needed to hear: "caller says the woman identifies herself as Lila Tucker," and "Git 'n' Go."

His heart soared. Lila was less than two minutes away.

Lila sat huddled in a blanket on the curb of the Git 'n' Go's front walk. The store was closed, its interior lights off, but the security lights gave Tripp a good look at Lila's battered face. Cautious of the man standing protectively over her - the concerned citizen who had called in to report he had found the missing Lila Tucker - Tripp choked back the rush of emotion that seeing her brought on. Lila stared up at him, recognizing him, but didn't react. It hurt him that she didn't run to him. She was obviously too damaged to be thinking clearly.

"Where'd you find Mrs. Tucker?" he said to the man.

"Who are you?" the man said. He was keyed up, his eyes wide behind his heavy-framed eyeglasses. A middle-age paunch lopped over his blue jeans, straining his leather bomber jacket. Crewcut, ex-military maybe, or just an enthusiast.

Tripp flashed his badge and looked the man straight in

the eye. This had to happen quickly, and he wanted the man to know who was in charge.

The man's obvious anxiety dropped a notch, but he was still wary.

"They're sending an ambulance," he said. "You can see she's hurt."

Tripp dropped down on one knee in front of Lila. "I need to ask you if this man had anything to do with what happened to you, Mrs. Tucker."

"You know he didn't," she said, her voice quiet and strained. "I want to go home."

"Good," he said. "Everything's going to be all right."

He stood up. "Did you give your name to 911? Do they know how to reach you? I'm sure Mr. Tucker will want to show his appreciation for everything you've done. I don't know any details, but I would think there's a reward involved."

As he spoke, he helped Lila to her feet. She moved cautiously, like an old woman. It would take a long time to get her back to her old self. They might even have to go away - far away - for her to recover properly.

"Wait a minute." The man followed them to the idling truck. "Where are you taking her? Where are the other cops? You need to wait for the ambulance."

Tripp opened the door to the truck's extended cab.

"We'll find Bud?" she said. "Please?"

The monster had stolen the life from her eyes. Tripp would help her get it back.

He nodded and put an arm around her shoulders to help her into the backseat of the truck where the prisoners usually rode. "Go on, lie down," he said. "Everything's going to be just fine, Mrs. Tucker."

She gathered the blanket closer and lay down on the seat. He shut the door, feeling relieved.

"This is out of your hands, sir," Tripp said. "The ambulance service is twenty minutes away from here. She could have internal injuries." He reached for the driver's door handle. The man stepped closer.

"I don't think you should take her," he said. He was strident, but his voice wavered with the knowledge that Tripp was the one with a gun strapped to his side.

"You're interfering with official business," Tripp said. This overstuffed rodent of a man wasn't going to ruin his chance to be with Lila. "Please step away from the vehicle." He rested his hand on his sidearm, flicked open the release on the holster.

The man took a step back, but they both looked toward the road when they heard the siren. It was faint, but definitely heading in their direction.

"I say we wait," the man said.

"You don't want to get involved in this, sir," Tripp said. "You've done what you needed to do. I don't want to have to take you into custody." Now he was starting to get pissed off.

The man gave a short, nervous laugh that puffed out his fleshy cheeks. "Yeah? I don't think so," he said. "What if I told you I think you're full of shit?"

Tripp took out the .44. Before the man, whose face was now stiff with alarm, could duck away, Tripp smashed the gun into his right temple.

The man fell to the asphalt, an arm across his face in belated defense. Tripp kicked him in the ribs once, twice, three times, and the man curled in on himself. His weakness made Tripp even angrier, and he kicked the man in the head.

Time to go. They're coming.

Tripp holstered his service piece, got in the truck, and slammed it into gear. Lila was silent in the back. He hoped she'd gone to sleep. Driving to the lip of the parking lot, he didn't bother to look back at the man who was lying still on the ground.

The safest way for them to get to the cabin would be to drive west, away from the sirens. But it would take half an hour and he would have to unlock two fire road gates. He needed more ammunition before he could take Lila to a truly safe place. Food, as well. The fastest way to his place was through the state forest's main entrance. The Good Samaritan was sure to be out for a while, so he would have some time before the state boys started looking for him and his work truck. Tripp turned left and drove in the direction of the oncoming police cars.

CHAPTER FIFTY-ONE

RUNNING. FOLLOWING THE SCENT of the woman. The woman who was not soft. The woman who tore at him and screamed. The woman who woke something inside of him.

He stayed far from the edge of the road, avoiding the few cars speeding past. The bottoms of his feet were hard now, better than the shoes. The hole in his throat where the stick had pierced him let in a ragged stream of air, but he felt no pain. There was no pain anymore, no anger. Only desire, a hunger in his gut that had nothing to do with food.

Lights rose ahead of him. Lights that brought the image of Claude Who Was Not Food to his mind.

Through the trees, he saw two men standing in front of the store where he had found Claude. The woman was nearby, but he couldn't see her. He watched as one of the men hit the other, and a few seconds later he smelled the blood. After the man who had done the hitting drove away, the scent of the woman was not so strong.

He ran after the truck, not bothering to investigate the man lying bleeding on the ground. He ran across the parking lot and up onto the sloping hillside, breaking through the bare, whiplike bracken without feeling it, trying to keep the truck in sight. For a long moment, he was able to keep up with the truck, but then the air filled with a piercing sound and he stumbled. The sound came toward him, bringing with it white, red, and blue lights that bounced off the tree trunks. Instinct drove him onto the leafy ground. He covered his ears with his hands.

The cars whined to a stop somewhere behind him, and the night reasserted itself. He took his hands from his ears and stood. The truck was gone and, with it, the scent. It was immediately replaced by the compulsion to finish what he had started when he first came to this place.

He ran.

CHAPTER FIFTY-TWO

THERE HAD BEEN A TIME when Ivy thought of leaving Alta. It was after high school, and Thora was gone every day to her job at the Department of Motor Vehicles, leaving Ivy alone in the trailer. Thora had tried to talk her into applying for cashier work at the feed and supply store on the other side of town, but the idea of it terrified her only slightly less than moving to the city to look for a job. Sewing was what she loved to do, nothing else. Sewing was something she could do alone, without anyone watching. She hardly had to speak to anyone when she was sewing. Even when she had helped Mrs. Young, the Home Ec teacher, do the costuming for the high school's production of the musical *Angel Time* during her senior year, she had been allowed to do most of the work at home, on her own machine. On quiet days, walking up on the mountain with Suki, the retriever mix that had adopted them for a year and then disappeared, she had thought about what it might be like to work in a real theater, making all sorts of costumes for plays.

When there were costume dramas on television, she would record them, hiding the discs from Thora. It wasn't that Thora wouldn't have liked them or would've made fun of her for watching them. Ivy just wanted to keep them for herself.

She liked the Elizabethan films best, with their sumptuous velvets and jeweled brocades. Seeing her own plain face in the mirror, she knew she would never be suited to wear such things, no matter what century it was. But she could make them, nourishing each garment with just a little bit of herself. She would live through them.

Then Thora had started getting sick all the time. Her government job meant she couldn't be fired easily, but Ivy felt obligated to take care of her. In her heart she knew it was a grudging obligation. In those days, she sometimes thought she didn't love Thora at all. But whatever she felt for Thora, she knew she couldn't abandon her.

One of the social workers who had shown up at the trailer door twice a year until Ivy turned eighteen asked her once if Thora acted more like a parent or a sister to her. Ivy's sincere response was that she owed Thora her life. When she looked back, she knew she had probably sounded melodramatic, the way young girls do. But it was the truth. The love part wasn't important.

Ivy lay on the guest bed, Anthony's bed, in the dark. She was finally accustomed to the rancid smell lingering over everything he touched.

At the foot of the bed, in a soiled pile, lay the contents of the hope chest that Ivy's mother had started for Thora: a pair of linen pillow cases, handkerchiefs with Thora's initials, a thick wedding-ring quilt that Ivy vaguely remembered her mother working on at night, candles, a glass pitcher, a delicate linen nightgown, and a Bible. Anthony had finally broken the chest open. Had she really thought he wouldn't bother it? Thora had come to see the thing as a joke, but she had never taken it out of the house or even suggested getting rid of it. Now everything was ruined - the pages ripped from the Bible, the nightgown ripped at the throat and shoulder seams as though Anthony had tried to put it on his own body.

This was what she had brought on them.

Lila had run away. Ivy had seen her run onto the highway, then veer back onto the shoulder, weaving like a drunk. Maybe she'd been hit by a car. That would be a good thing, wouldn't it? Then no one would know where she had been.

What kind of person have I become that I'm hoping a woman I've known all my life is dead?

Without Thora, Anthony was all she had left. Now she was afraid of the one person she had left in the world.

She closed her eyes. She would eventually have to go up to the trailer. He was up there. Alone. He might be hurt. Or suffering.

She was in a twilight sleep when she heard the gravel crunching out in the drive. Jumping from the bed, she put her face close to the cold glass of the window. Whoever it was had already reached the trailer, and was turning the vehicle around so that the headlights swept the thinning dark. The car looked small. Not a police car or any kind of ambulance or truck. Maybe the driver was lost. She thought of the girl, the pregnant one who was expected the next afternoon to pick up her dress. Whoever it was shut off the car, then the lights.

The motion detector light at the corner of the trailer came on, illuminating a man - large, and moving quickly toward the trailer's back entrance - and a small woman with dark hair. Or was it a girl? She couldn't see well, but they seemed to be wearing matching coats, a fact that was odd and not at all reassuring.

⋆ ◄ ✦ ► ⋆

Ivy opened the trailer's back door and leveled the shotgun at the girl standing in the middle of the living room.

"Ivy," the girl said, reaching out her hand to her. She didn't look at all afraid of the gun. She was the same girl Thora had wanted to rent the trailer to. What was her name? The same glow surrounded her, so Ivy couldn't get a good look at her face. Despite the obscurity of her features, Ivy wasn't afraid.

Behind the girl, Bud Tucker came out of the master bedroom, stepping over what was left of the door. His forehead was creased with worry, his eyes intent on the shotgun. Ivy had always liked Bud. Lila was lucky to have him. She had never heard a mean or unpleasant word said about him, not even from Lila, who had something critical to say about everyone. It had never been Ivy's desire to cause people like Lila and Bud pain. She knew that about herself, didn't she? Still, she kept the shotgun where it was. She didn't know what else to do. Lila was obviously gone, but so was Anthony.

"I'll let you leave if you go now," she said. "The front door is down that hallway." Her voice shook, but she couldn't do anything about it.

"You're not even going to ask why we're here?" Bud said. "What did we ever do to you? What do you have to do with all this?" He stepped to stand directly behind the girl.

Ivy looked at her. Why had she said her name like that? Ivy. Like she knew her. Like she was her friend. Something about the sound of the girl's voice calmed her, made her feel less like the world was collapsing. She felt stronger.

"There's no one for you to see here," she said. "Just get out and I won't call the police."

"*You* won't call the police?" Bud said. He lunged toward her and the girl put her arm out to stop him. Ivy backed up a step, aiming the shotgun directly at his chest.

"Shhhhh," the girl said. "You can put the gun down, Ivy. Nobody's going to hurt you. Nobody's going to bring the police. You don't have to be afraid."

Why was the girl talking to her like she was a child?

"There's blood and dirt all over the bathroom," Bud said. "Still wet."

"My bathroom isn't any of your business," she said. But she knew it was lost.

"Her hair," Bud said. He could barely get the words out. "It's all over the place."

Ivy lowered the barrel of the gun.

They stood, silent, as if Lila's body had suddenly appeared in the midst of them.

The girl walked over to Ivy, holding her hands out in front of her. As she got closer, Ivy could see how young she was. *So pure.* And all was ugliness around them. Ivy felt corroded in comparison. Vile to her core. She had touched evil, felt possessive of it like it was some treasured charm. She almost cried out when the girl rested her fingers on her cheek.

"You don't know where they are," the girl said. "Do you?"

Ivy could see the girl's eyes now. Kind. Comforting in their familiarity. She shook her head.

Bud picked up a piece of splintered wood from the floor. "If he took her, she didn't go without a fight."

CHAPTER FIFTY-THREE

WHEN THEY REACHED THE ROAD leading to the state forest, Tripp almost didn't take the turn. The clear part of his head, the part that had slipped further and further away as the day progressed, was telling him to just take Lila and run without stopping. Run to the nearest airport, or drive as fast as he dared to the interstate exchange fifteen miles away. They could drive south to his folks' place. His dad wasn't the kind of man to ask a lot of questions, and they could rest there for a day or two before leaving the country. Money might get to be an issue, but if he dealt with it right away, he might be able to get his money out before anyone realized he was leaving town.

But he couldn't make himself drive away. *Here* was the only place he truly felt safe, the only place he really knew. There were things they needed, whether they ended up on one of the mountains an hour or two north, stayed on Devil's Oven, or managed to get out of the area completely. Money, supplies, and a little time for Lila to get rested up and with the program. She wasn't in the best shape for travel.

Tripp figured they would have an hour at most. The guy he had cold-cocked wouldn't be out long, but it would take some time for them to figure out that Tripp hadn't taken her to the hospital or even to the troopers' station. The rank-and-file troopers like his friend, Keith, knew him as a good guy, with a string of drug, bootlegging, and arson arrests to his credit. He felt a little bad that he was putting Keith on the spot. Keith really was a good guy.

Tripp stood in front of the bedroom closet, a duffel bag sitting open on the bed behind him. Lila didn't have much at the cabin: a pair of jeans, a couple of sweaters, the bra she had left hanging in his living room. It pleased him that when they were together, she liked to roam the house naked, maybe putting on the robe she had bought him or tossing a throw around her shoulders when she got cold. She looked so vulnerable when she was naked. Soft.

A sound from the living room made him jump and he reached for his sidearm, but remembered he had laid it on the front table out of habit. He told himself there couldn't be anything to be worried about yet.

"Lila?" he said, coming slowly out of the bedroom.

The single desk lamp he had turned on didn't quite chase the shadows from Lila's tired face. She stood near the door, the grubby blanket still wrapped around her. How strange for her - a woman who was so beautiful, so careful about her appearance, so attached to jewelry and other precious things - to be dragged down into filth and violence. It was more than her injuries, her sleep-teased hair, or the fact that the blanket looked like it had been driven over a hundred times. She looked broken to him.

"Baby, I thought you were still asleep," he said. "Let's get you warm and out of those clothes." He turned aside to adjust the thermostat beside the bedroom door.

She was so quiet that it made him worry she couldn't speak. But she *had* spoken down at the convenience store. She had asked for his help.

"You've got some clothes in the bedroom," he said. "Want a quick shower?" As soon as the words were out of his mouth, he wanted to kick himself for pressuring her. She had been through - he didn't know exactly what, but he had seen what the creature did to Claude Dixon and Danelle Pettit. Lila had been left alive. He'd seen enough victims of violence to know that whatever had been done to her had affected her in ways he could never completely understand.

When she spoke, her voice was subdued. Rocky.

"Take me home."

"It's all over, and you're safe now," he said. "You need to get as much rest as you can. We're going to get you somewhere you can recover."

"I didn't get it before," she said. "What you were doing."

"I have a clean blanket here, too," he said. "You know how you were bugging me to get the wool one dry-cleaned? I meant to tell you I bought a new one."

"You're not..." Her voice faltered. "Something's happened to you."

He laughed. "Do you know how beautiful you are? Even now?"

"Not since that night," she said. "Maybe before. I can't remember."

"You can't remember because that sonofabitch almost killed you."

She was more damaged than he had thought. Delusional. Once he took her in his arms, once he held her, she would relax. She was so different from that bitch, Jolene. He couldn't tell Lila the truth about Jolene, that he had gone and had sex with her, just like she had suspected him of doing. What they had was too fragile right now, but he wouldn't tell her even if she were stronger. She could never know how close Jolene had come to driving him out of his mind.

"Don't touch me," she said. "You're not going to touch me again."

"Baby, I know," he said. "I know when you've been traumatized like this, you might not want anyone, you know, you might not want a man to touch you. We'll handle it. Together. And I won't touch you if you don't want. Not until you say it's time."

"I want the keys to one of your trucks," she said.

"Honey, we're out of here, don't worry. I've got our stuff in a bag. I packed up a cooler, too."

She let the blanket fall to the floor. Her hand was unsteady, but she was aiming the .44 at him. It was his service piece, the same gun he'd had her shooting in the backyard the past summer. She had joked about it, but he had seen how natural she was with it. She'd said that Bud had taken her shooting once or twice. Tripp suspected it had been more than twice. Right now, though, she wasn't in any kind of shape to be handling a gun.

"You don't need that," he said. "They aren't coming for us. Not yet. We'll be out of here before they think of it." Holding his hands out in front of him to show he wasn't going to hurt her, he took a step forward.

"Stop!" she said. "Just stop!"

He knew she wouldn't shoot him. If only she would let him hold her.

"That's not the kind of person you are," he said. He kept his voice low. Calm. "If you want me to die, I'll kill myself for you, baby. Is that what you want? I'll give you my life if it's what you want. You know I will."

Her eyes welled up. She would be crying in a minute. It was all too much for her. She needed to be held. Protected from herself.

He was close now.

It was only dumb luck and his own clumsiness that saved him from the burst from the gun. Lunging for her, he tripped over the footstool Jolene had been sitting on hours earlier. He fell just a foot or so from Lila, surprising them both. But he was the first to recover and, still on the floor, he wrapped an arm around her legs.

How can she try to kill me, the man who completes her?
He needed to keep her near him, even if it killed them both.

Tripp jerked her off her feet - one foot in a filthy gray
sock, the other bare, red and swollen. Falling, she dropped the
gun and tried to catch herself. Her cry broke his heart. Even
worse was the muted *thud* of her head hitting the table beside
the door.

CHAPTER FIFTY-FOUR

"**I** CAN'T STAY HERE," Bud said.

Every nerve in his body told him to head up into the woods to look for Lila. The bastard had her somewhere out there, if he hadn't already killed her. As nightmarish as that thought was, there was another one that ran a close second. The image of Lila with Tripp Morgan sat in the back of his head like an unwanted photograph, or a piece of porn like what he'd found on the office computer of the guy Claude had replaced: pictures of women having sex with animals; louche, grandfatherly men committing unspeakable acts with prepubescent girls. Morgan had to have done something to Lila, blackmailed or tricked her in some way into being with him. Because to think of it any other way made Bud feel sucker punched.

"You won't find anything," Jolene said. "Not when it's still dark. If you go, you should wait."

She was looking better than she had when they first got to the trailer. She was calm, as always, but there was something else. She seemed to know her way around. It was almost as though she belonged there.

Ivy was the one they should be worried about. If Jolene hadn't been there when Ivy showed up with the shotgun, he would've taken the thing from her and, God help them both, probably beaten her with it. His frustration, his hatred for what she had allowed to happen to Lila, was that great.

Does she really deserve that kind of punishment? Aren't I the one who borrowed the money, who attracted an animal like Anthony in the first place?

Ivy's eyes were empty and her face was a sickly beige, as though her life's blood had been drained away. She sat stiffly on the stained living room couch, her body inclined slightly toward Jolene's. God only knew what the creature had done to *her*.

"What if he didn't take her?" Jolene said, looking up at him.

Ivy sat forward, waking to her words.

"Ivy said the trailer didn't look like this when she left, that the bedroom door was open. What if Lila got away from him?"

"Wouldn't she have gone down to the house for help?" Bud looked at Ivy, who looked away. *Bitch. What have you done?* "What is it? What the hell do you know?" he shouted.

Jolene put a hand out to keep him away.

"I won't," Ivy said, narrowing her eyes. She curled her feet beneath her and shrank back into a corner of the couch. "You're not going to hurt him."

Bud had plenty of experience with obstinate people, but he had always been kind and forgiving. Life was just too damn short to be an asshole, was what he had always told himself. He left it to greedy people like his old man to rule the world through meanness. But now he couldn't hold himself back. He lunged for Ivy.

"Tell me, you bitch!" He shook her by the shoulders so that her head bobbed back and forth like a toy, her white, doll-like hair whipping her face.

"Stop it!" Jolene screamed. She tried to pry his hands away, but he paid no attention. Both she and Ivy were small. "She can't tell you anything if you kill her!"

He let Ivy go, pushing her against the couch so hard that she bounced forward again. She would've hit the table if Jolene hadn't caught her and held her still.

"You saw her, didn't you?" He could barely get the words out, he was so angry. "Did he have her?" He bent down to her face. "Tell me!"

Ivy bit her lip.

"Ivy," Jolene said. "Please."

"She ran out to the road. Toward town," she whispered.

"And your *Saint* Anthony?"

Ivy shook her head.

"I didn't see him go after her," she said. "I don't know where he is."

⋆ ◄ ✦ ◄ ⋆

Down at the house, Bud opened the coat closet where Ivy had told him he would find the keys to the Buick. He didn't want to chance driving Charity's car. The club had been closed for an hour, and she was certain to have realized it was missing. She might have even reported it to the police. He took the keys from their hook, but also grabbed a knitted black cap from the closet's shelf. He wasn't the kind of man who blended in easily, and having his head shaved bald didn't make him any less noticeable.

Jolene had promised to call the hospital and check with the police - anonymously, if she could - to see if anyone had brought Lila in. She had tried to encourage him, but he could see she was doubtful. Maybe she knew Lila was dead. Maybe she just didn't want to tell him the truth.

He wondered who the hell she really was, how she knew the things she did. She didn't seem inclined to tell him anything, and at this point, he had to be satisfied with the fact she'd helped him at all. His first concern was to find Lila. Nothing else mattered.

The cell phone Ivy had come up with sat on the Buick's passenger seat, silent. As hard as he was praying for it to ring, he
was certain Jolene wouldn't learn that Lila was at the hospital
or the police station. They weren't going to be that lucky.

There wasn't much between the Luttrells' place and the
start of town near the Git 'n' Go. A few county roads, including the one that ran above the town, and two private ones that
didn't reach very far. Besides an expanse of rocky land, they led
to little: an abandoned school, a dairy operation, a junkyard
that specialized in useless construction equipment. One circle
of half-built houses whose contractor had run out of money
a decade earlier. It took him only a few minutes to check out
everything he could. In the hours before dawn, traffic was
scarce and he was able to turn around in the middle of any
road without a problem.

He was sure Lila would've continued east, toward
town, or maybe flagged a passing car or truck. She was hurt.
How hurt, he didn't want to consider.

Did he dare take the highway right through Alta? It was
bullshit that he couldn't let himself be seen near the town
in which he owned two businesses, and paid more than his
fair share of taxes. But getting locked up again wouldn't help
anyone.

When he passed the Git 'n' Go, its parking lot was
filled with police cars, their lights flashing. Just like at the club.
What the hell was going on? He couldn't risk taking a long
look, but when he saw the ambulance, his heart beat faster.
He didn't dare slow the Buick, but he was certain it had to be
about Lila. Within a couple seconds, he was turning into the
trailer park's entrance so he could double back. It didn't matter
if they captured him. He had to know.

The phone beside him rang and he fumbled for it.

"I think they found her," Bud said. He felt such a wave of joy that he wanted to laugh.

"No, no, no," Jolene said. "No one found Lila. I talked to Charity and she said they know you're out of jail. You should come back here. You should come back here now, Bud."

"The police are at the Git 'n' Go," he said. "There's an ambulance. They've got to have her."

Jolene was silent.

"What?" he said.

"You should come back to Ivy's," she said. "It's not right."

"What? You know by magic or something?" he said. "She's there. I know she's there."

"Did you see her? If I told you I *did* know, would you believe me?"

"Look, Jolene. I've gone along with this so far, and I know there's a lot going on that I don't understand," he said. "But *this* I do understand: If they found her, she can tell them I didn't have anything to do with what happened."

"I won't be there to help you," Jolene said. She sounded defeated.

"I've got to go," he said. "With any luck I'll call you back in an hour." He closed the phone, ending the call before she could respond.

Lila was so close! But Jolene's voice was still in his head. *If I told you I did know, would you believe me?*

Damn. What if she was right?

Driving past the store as slowly as he dared, he saw that all the same vehicles were still there. The ambulance sat with its lights flashing, its back doors open.

A hundred yards on, he shut off the headlights and eased the Buick onto the highway's shoulder.

So close.

◦ ◂ ◂ ⁂ ◂ ▸ ◦

It wasn't Lila lying on the gurney about to be loaded into the ambulance. The man was conscious and seemed to be trying to get up, but the EMTs eased him back down. Bud recognized Detective Johnson. Detectives didn't hang around random accidents or crime scenes. Lila had to be nearby or they had some idea that this guy was connected. Bud strained at the naked tangle of blackberry branches, desperate to hear what was going on down in the parking lot, but he couldn't risk getting closer. When Johnson nodded to the EMTs, they fastened the straps around the gurney and started loading the finally calm - or at least sedated - man into the ambulance.

Johnson waved over the two uniformed troopers. When they finished talking, the troopers moved quickly to their cars, and Johnson headed for his. They were leaving in a hurry, which meant something was happening.

The blackberry branches tore at Bud's coat and hands as he tried to get back to his own car. But their thorns held him fast. He cursed. Behind him, he heard one of the police cars start. Finally, with a groan of frustration, he pulled out of the coat and let the greedy branches embrace it.

He ran.

CHAPTER FIFTY-FIVE

IVY STOOD AT THE WINDOW, her fingertips arched, tense, on the sill. The thinning night had turned the sky the color of tarnished silver.

"I'll make you some tea," Jolene said. "Maybe something to eat?"

"He's not coming back, is he?" Ivy said.

Jolene knew she could tell Ivy what she wanted to hear - that Anthony would probably return. She also knew if he didn't return, they would have to go out and find him to end it all.

What's going to happen to me when it's over?

"What you did wasn't wrong," Jolene said. "It's not a crime to want to be loved."

Ivy turned away from the window. Seeing the confusion and depth of emotion in her face, and the fading violet-gray of her aura, Jolene wanted to wrap her arms around Ivy. To heal her.

Wisps of Ivy's fine hair had escaped the old-fashioned blue bow clipping it back from her face. Somewhere behind Ivy's eyes, Jolene could see the child she had loved. But that child was disappearing even as they stood facing one another. The Ivy she'd known was almost lost to them both.

"Who are you?" Ivy said. There was fear in her voice. Jolene hated that she sounded so afraid.

"I won't hurt you," Jolene said.

"They're going to punish me," Ivy said. "And I don't care."

"Please, Ivy. Let me help you."

"I-I can't even…" Ivy stared at her for a moment, then pushed past her. When she found a safe distance, she turned back to Jolene. "You don't know anything about me," she said. "You come in here with Bud Tucker like you have a right to, and then tell me you'll make me some tea?"

So much suspicion in her voice.

"You're like him, aren't you?" Ivy said. "You're like Anthony."

Like Anthony? She was nothing like Anthony. They had come from the same place, but she could never be like him. He was darkness.

"Did you know I can barely see your face?" Ivy said. "That first day you came here, I couldn't see it. Thora didn't understand. She couldn't understand."

"See what?" Jolene put her hands to her face.

"The light," Ivy said. "You're covered in light."

Jolene had never been able to see her own aura. Her father had had a single, pitted shard for a shaving mirror. He sold the ornate hand mirror her mother had brought in her trousseau. Years and years later, when Ivy was small, Jolene had tried to catch her aura in different qualities of light, but she still could never see it. Ivy could. Her daughter…

The thought that Ivy was her flesh and blood - not of the lithe shell in which she had come down from the mountain this time, but the flesh of her spirit - humbled her. That she was in this place with her child again. A child who could see what she was.

"I don't want to know what you are, or who you are," Ivy said. "Please go away. When Anthony comes back, he won't like you being here."

"What do you see when you look at Anthony?" Jolene said, dreading the answer. Maybe what she believed about where she had come from was a lie she told herself. Maybe she had come from the mountain's darkness as well. Maybe there was only darkness. "Tell me."

"It doesn't matter," Ivy said. "Anthony doesn't ask anything from me. He's just mine."

"If Anthony's yours, why do you let him do these terrible things? People are dying."

"It's not his fault. He can't help what he is." Ivy seemed to take strength from the sudden declaration. Jolene hadn't realized that Ivy was almost two inches taller than she was. The angry set to Ivy's mouth made her look even more intimidating.

"He's nothing," Jolene said. "He's not even real."

Ivy laughed.

"I've touched him," she said. "I *made* him. It's not something you could understand."

"You're wrong," Jolene said. "God, you're so wrong."

"Wrong?" Ivy raised her hands to the air, a convicted evangelist. "I *made* him. My hands may be weak, but they gave him life!"

Jolene took hold of Ivy by the forearms. Her daughter was now a woman whose mouth was drawn with suffering, who looked twenty years older than Jolene.

"What did he take from you, Ivy? What about Thora? What did he do to Thora?"

Ivy froze, her eyes shifting automatically to the kitchen.

"Did Thora do something to him?" Jolene said. "I'm sure it wasn't your fault."

Ivy pulled out of her grasp. They stood staring at each other for a moment, then Ivy looked away, her face burning with heat and shame.

CHAPTER FIFTY-SIX

DEAR GOD, WHY WON'T SHE WAKE UP?
Tripp cradled Lila's head in his lap. Her eyes were closed and she was still breathing, but her breath was shallow. He could barely feel it when he put his face close to hers. She couldn't die. People didn't die from hitting their heads on tables. That only happened on television or in books. *But if she does?* Then he would have to follow her. There wasn't any kind of life for him without Lila. Even the room around them felt strange and foreign without her smiles or her laughter or even her anger.

"Lila," he whispered. "Lila, baby."

He had seen her fall from a cheerleading pyramid during a football game, and had needed to stop himself from running out of the bleachers to be the one to help her up. He remembered that second of holding his breath as he saw the girl beneath her begin to wobble, trying to push away the hair that had suddenly fallen in front of her eyes. Time seemed to stop for him as Lila fell, her mouth open, mid-cheer, her arms flailing. When she hit the ground, she seemed to bounce an inch or two on the rubberized track before lying still. The game continued on the field. The crowd around him caught on slowly to what had happened, but the announcers never took notice, the bastards. Her teammates crowded around her, and he *waited waited waited*. Finally, the girls surrounding her melted away like water repelled by a stone, and Lila stood, unsteady yet smiling, to a smatter of applause from the crowd.

How he wanted to see that smile again!

All of his emergency training told him not to move her, but when he shifted his hand from under her hair, he found it was streaked with blood. *What have I done to her?* He shouldn't have tested her, not in the terrified, fragile state she was in.

Sliding from beneath her, Tripp rested her head gently on the carpet. He couldn't stop staring at the blood on his hand. Lila's blood. Now her wound was bleeding into the carpet, the floor, the ground. Now a part of her would always be a part of his home, his bit of earth. His bit of mountain.

Somehow, that feels right.

He touched his hand to his face, smearing the blood over his cheek, and down to the edge of his mouth and lips until his hand was dry.

"Lila."

The blood felt warm on his lips and he touched it with his tongue. It tasted of metal. Not so different from his own. They were alike, the two of them.

Should he leave her there, bleeding? Part of him wanted to lie down beside her and put the barrel of the .44 into his mouth and pull the trigger. *The metal barrel, the taste of blood. So alike.*

But he couldn't do it. He wasn't ready to give it all up. Not just yet. There was still a chance they could get away together and start a new life. Their new life didn't have to be in death. *No.*

"Come on, baby," he said, gathering her into his arms. She was so light, as though her body had already cast off everything that weighed it down. Was that dawn breaking through the front windows? It couldn't be. If they were going to get away, they needed the darkness.

The sunlight breaking through the forest to touch her face.
That day, it had been Jolene's face he saw instead of Lila's. But
he'd broken the enchantment that bitch had cast over him.
This is Lila's face. It would always be Lila's face.

He laid her on the sofa and tucked a blanket around
her. Again, he tried to wake her, thinking that his voice should
be enough to call her back. But she just lay still, like a princess
needing to be awakened. He bent to kiss her lips, and felt her
breath. *Thank God you're still alive.*

If it hadn't been so quiet, if they had still been arguing
or hurrying to pack up, he wouldn't have heard the cars in the
driveway. Tripp dropped to the floor and crawled to the desk.
Keeping his eyes on the door, he felt for the switch on the desk
lamp and turned it off. He went to the window.

It hadn't taken the cops long to find them. He
should've killed the creep in the Git 'n' Go lot. What would
they have thought, then? That the creature had found Lila
again, and killed the bastard who thought he was her hero.
Then no one would know that he and Lila were together; they
would be free by now. It was all so clear. So obvious. He had
screwed it up, and now it was too late.

⋆ ⋆ ✦ ⋆ ⋆

"Not such a great time for a visit, Detective," Tripp shouted
from the porch.

Burns kept walking up toward the cabin. The cars
behind him had turned on their headlights so he appeared in
dull silhouette. The porch was flooded with light.

"I'm not here to make nice with you, Officer Morgan," Burns said. "I'm here to make sure Lila Tucker gets the
medical help she needs."

Tripp knew he was supposed to find the headlights
intimidating, but instead he felt liberated, like everything was
unfolding just as it should.

"Probably you know you shouldn't get any closer." He

turned slightly so that Burns and whoever else was watching could see the gun he held. It would have been so satisfying to take Burns out right then, but it wasn't time for that. "And don't give me any of that bullshit about how you just want to talk."

Burns stopped, his hands stuck deep in his coat pocket. "I hate this back and forth crap. You're law enforcement. You know how this is going to go."

"It goes however I want it to for the next hour - maybe two."

"I don't have that kind of patience, and Mrs. Tucker may not have that kind of time."

Behind Burns, behind the cars, there were shouts, warnings to *stop!*

"Bring her out here, you bastard, or I'll kill you myself."

Bud Tucker's immense form broke out of the miasmal light and ran, hell-bent, for the cabin. Before two equally large uniforms tackled him, Tripp saw that Bud's normally placid, friendly face was a caricature of rage.

Too bad. Lila is mine.

CHAPTER FIFTY-SEVEN

CRAZY-ASS, BULLSHIT HILLBILLIES *and their lame-ass mountains. Bud Tucker, the weakest son of a bitch I've ever known. A big, dumb kid of a man who thinks he can take care of everybody.*

For the first time in eighteen years, Dwight opened up a bottle of Black Label, poured three fingers of it into a glass, and raised it to his lips. *Bud Tucker.* He closed his eyes, inhaling the perfect scent of the whiskey. He liked the sweet, sweet nose of it, the way its subtle charcoal burn seeped into his brain. *Bud Tucker.* He was going to die because of Bud Tucker. As the whiskey spread over his tongue and down the back of his throat, he was able to ignore, for just those few seconds, the steady pounding on the club's kitchen door.

There had been only three people in his life he had given a shit about: his mother, his niece Angela, and poor, stupid Bud. His mother was dead, Angela had run away at the age of sixteen from her too-strict father - such an asshole; Dwight had warned him not to be so hard on her - and disappeared into the churning maw of the country's largest city, and Bud was as good as dead. Just like he was.

Bud Tucker. Dwight knew if he ever told anyone how he felt about Bud, they would probably call him a fag because they wouldn't understand. Love wasn't always about sex. Sex wasn't something that plagued him like it did some people. It entailed way too much personal involvement and exchange of bodily fluids. He'd had sex a few times with an ugly girl - Rowena something - who had begged him to take her to dances in high school. She had been good about regular blow jobs, too, but after a while, he began to think too much about being in her mouth, worrying that she could bite him and cripple him at any time. Plus, she always begged him to return the favor. It was one thing to launch his prick into the cavernous slop that was her pussy, but no way, no sir would he have put his face in there. He thought about her sometimes, wondered if she was still as ugly and if she had found someone to make ugly children with.

Bud Tucker. He just liked to be around Bud. Bud made you feel like everything was going to be all right. Forever. Bud was the guy you wanted to please because nothing truly bad could happen in the world if a guy like Bud was around. He liked the way Bud depended on him, counted on him to keep the girls and bartenders honest, to make sure he had cash when he needed it. It embarrassed the shit out of Dwight when he thought about it, but he lived for those days when Bud would ask him to drop by the trucking company or call him into the club's office, saying, *Dwight, buddy, I've got a hell of a mess. What do you think?*

Bud Tucker had needed him.

Dwight poured another two fingers of whiskey. The pounding had stopped, but he knew it was just some kind of trick to make him think he was safe. Nobody was safe in this place anymore. And it was his fault. He had brought this on Bud; he had brought it on that silly cunt, Lila; on Claude Dixon; and God knew who else; because, like Bud, he had wanted to help.

He drained the glass of the whiskey, not noticing the burn so much now. He had heard that the longer you were away from the stuff, the quicker the buzz would be. He was like a whiskey virgin. The thought brought a wry smile to his lips.

At the back door, there was a new sound. Dwight didn't have to be standing outside to know that the doorknob was being hacked off, courtesy of something large and very sturdy. Those violent blows were about to come his way. It didn't matter that there was also a deadbolt on the door. As he liked to say to Bud, *No worries.*

The Anthony guy they had sent down to collect from Bud was as dumb a dago as Dwight had ever met. Anthony had been told to find Dwight first, and he did, walking into the club like he owned the place, even though with his tailored lambskin jacket and gold pinky ring, he might as well have been from Mars. He didn't even have to ask for Dwight because Dwight knew right away who he was and why he was there.

He had introduced himself as Anthony, his voice higher and softer than his size indicated. Even though Dwight himself wasn't very tall, he wouldn't have described the guy as a giant, though he was big enough, with hands that were easily twice the size of Dwight's. Dwight had made sure to smile a lot, and asked if he wanted to have a seat and check out the girls for a while. When the guy gave the girls a tired glance, Dwight understood they weren't the class of girls he was used to, and suggested that they go into his office.

Anthony told him he would be hanging around for a few days to see how business was going. There was an investment to protect, he said, and he would be visiting Bud's trucking company as well.

There was something in Anthony's eyes that Dwight didn't trust. Big surprise there. Dwight trusted no one. No. One. Despite Anthony's subtle manicure, Dwight instinctively knew he was into wet work and had been sent to get Bud's attention.

Understood, Dwight told him. He even went so far as to dial a bogus phone number and pretend to leave a message for Bud to come straight to the club as soon as he got the message. Dwight made it clear he wanted to be helpful. When Anthony got settled in the overstuffed leather chair and sat turning the pages of an old rock and roll magazine, Dwight even offered him some blow. Anthony refused with a surly *I don't do that shit*, but he didn't turn down the drink that Dwight said he could get him from the bar.

The back door thudded open against the wall. No, the dead-bolt hadn't been any kind of deterrent.

Anthony's imported sedan took the mountain curves with real assurance, though Dwight got concerned when he turned off onto the fire road, thinking it might get too rough. Anthony slumped sideways, resting his drugged-out head on Dwight's shoulder until they completed the turn and Dwight could push him away. The guy's hair had smelled like flowers from some kind of hair product or girly shampoo. He had been a pain in the ass to get into the car, far heavier than Dwight had imagined. But they were almost there.

What made me decide to kill the sonofabitch? Hell, what makes anyone decide to do anything?

Then there was the big question: What had made him want to strip the guy naked and cut him up into parts like he was a side of beef or some kind of sacrificial ox out of the Bible? The answer was *habit*. Funny how an old habit came back when you needed it.

He had grabbed the fire ax and shovel out of the club's storage closet, and shoved them, along with the big-ass hunting knife a local beer distributor had given him that Christmas, into the sedan's backseat before dragging Anthony on a tarp from the club to the car.

Sticking the guy had been easy, almost too easy, like shooting a running man in the back. It wasn't game, he knew, to stab a guy in the neck when he was passed out so that he only jerked and groaned for a half-minute before sighing and falling back, as into sleep. But he more than made up for it with the work he did after the guy was dead: dragging the tarp-wrapped body through the scary-as-hell moonlit forest, where wolves could've pounced on him in a minute. Or a mountain lion. It was a good thing he had the body as barter if he needed it. No self-respecting mountain lion would turn down fresh kill.

Dwight wasn't sure how far into the woods he actually got. Anthony's size and the rough terrain meant he could drag him only twenty or thirty feet at a time. The sweat pouring off Dwight soaked his shirt and groin, so that he could only think of being back at his clean, warm apartment, standing beneath a full-blast shower.

Did he not bury the guy deep enough? No, that wasn't the answer. Nothing should have found him up there on that mountain in the middle of nowhere.

That mountain.

He wasn't a superstitious man. He never worried about ladders or black cats or spilling salt or opening umbrellas indoors. But now he realized he should have been. He should have been a lot of things.

Bud fucking Tucker.

Dwight looked down to see that both the whiskey bottle and the glass were empty. Warmth filled his stomach and his head felt blessedly light. The swinging door that led to the kitchen moved in the dim glow from the wall sconces.

Dwight reached beneath the bar and felt for the coach gun. No one at the bar had ever had to fire it, but he checked it regularly to make sure it was loaded and ready. He liked an orderly workplace.

Anthony - or what had once been Anthony - was crossing the room slowly enough that Dwight could get a good look at him. Oddly enough, he was dressed like Bud, in a polo shirt and khakis as though he were off to the country club for eighteen holes. The look didn't really suit him. In life, he had probably never picked up a golf club except to beat someone with it. But he was a handsome guy, even dead. Even with a ragged hole in his throat.

What Dwight had never seen before, though, was Anthony's smile. This smile was hideous, devoid of pleasure. It was simply teeth, exposed.

"Get the hell away from me, you G.D. freak," Dwight said, pointing the shotgun at Anthony's chest.

Anthony kept coming, as Dwight had known he would, his smile unchanged.

Dwight pulled the trigger. The report filled the air, momentarily deafening him. A hole erupted in Anthony's sport shirt and Dwight saw - or imagined he saw - a spray of flesh erupt from behind.

Anthony hesitated a step, but then kept walking forward.

So long, Bud Tucker.

Dwight put the barrel of the shotgun against the stubbled underside of his own chin and pulled the trigger again.

CHAPTER FIFTY-EIGHT

HE LEFT THE BUILDING through the broken kitchen door, carrying a bottle of something he had found behind the bar. He'd had to step over the man whose insides dripped from the mirror above the bottles. Another Claude Who Wasn't Food. He had come to do to him what he had done to Claude, but the man had cheated him.

Squatting in the parking lot, he drank from the bottle, letting some of the sticky fluid run over his chin and onto the ground. It was sweet and coated his mouth and throat. It filled his stomach.

He waited.

The lot was dark. After a few minutes, a single crow, drawn by the liquor pooling on the asphalt, lifted from the rooftop and glided down to land beside him. When he didn't move, the crow took a few careful steps toward the puddle of liquid.

The moon was gone, reminding him of the night he had spent in the woods, in the hole beneath the tree. Nothing as strong as desire piqued him, but the image of the house came to him, of the room with the soft floor. Comfort.

The crow finished drinking and backed away. It squatted, shook its feathers, and defecated. When it finished, it stared up at him.

He looked down at the bird's opaque eyes, and if he could have formed the thought, the words, he would have said it seemed he was looking into his own eyes.

The bird hopped toward the hillside and raised its wings to fly to the top of the concrete retaining wall. It landed, then looked back at Anthony as though it wanted his attention. After a moment, it took off up the hill.

He followed.

CHAPTER FIFTY-NINE

"THEY'RE COMING," Jolene said. "We have to go."

She had gotten Ivy calm enough to drink some tea and eat a few bites of a shortbread cookie. The items in the kitchen cabinets were arranged in much the same way she had arranged them herself, up in the trailer thirty years earlier. Despite Anthony, and the urgency Jolene felt about keeping Ivy safe, she clung to the sense of familiarity it gave her.

"I should wait for him," Ivy said.

Jolene went to the closet and started pulling out jackets. "Which one is yours?" She pushed a warm-looking barn coat at Ivy. "Put this on," she said. *How easily I've slipped into taking care of her.*

"He's going to come back for me," Ivy said. "I'm waiting. You can go. You should've gone before, when I asked you. You don't belong here." Her mouth was set, the scar on her lip now a slash of red that had deepened in color as she became more agitated.

"They're going to find Thora. You can't be here."

If they stayed at the house any longer, Jolene would have no chance to find Anthony. If he returned while the police were there, they were all lost. The police couldn't help

Anthony. They couldn't even kill him. She was the only one. She and Ivy had to find him.

"I don't care."

"You'll care a lot when you're sitting in jail for Thora's murder."

Oh, she hated to be so cruel. She hated to see the alarm in Ivy's eyes. Worse was the thought of Ivy being with Anthony again. He would kill her eventually; she no longer had anything for him. Surely it was Lila he wanted now. Lila with her glittering sexuality. Lila with her hearty, haughty air. There was something about Lila that reminded Jolene of her own mother, of the woman her mother had been before the mountain had changed her. The woman who danced. Who laughed. Lila's life force shone through Anthony's darkness, appealing to what he had once been.

"Thora was taunting him. Thora hated him."

"Of course she hated him, Ivy. He's evil. He's not a man anymore. He's..." What was he? *An expression of hell.* The brutal half of the dual nature of life. Death itself. Greedy death, the same that had gripped her mother and Byron, Ivy's father. The greedy death that had taken her own father and baby brother, Samuel. The same greedy death she had denied by hiding herself away in the mountain's flesh.

Jolene watched as an unfamiliar shadow of cunning crossed Ivy's face. In that moment, she looked most like her father. It chilled Jolene.

"I won't go unless you help me find him," Ivy said.

"What if we do find him?" Jolene said. "Do you think he's going to take you away with him? Do you think there's going to be some kind of happily-ever-after with him?"

From the moment Bud left, she had known she'd have to keep Ivy with her in order to keep her out of the hands of the police. Ivy didn't need to know that the bigger reason they had to go was because they had to find Anthony. She felt as though she were cheating by fooling Ivy.

"It doesn't matter," Ivy said. "I just want to be with him."

As soon as they stepped onto the trail, Jolene felt a change in the wind. It was fragrant and warm, like early summer. It told her where they would find Anthony. She reached for Ivy's hand.

"Please, Ivy," she said. "Please trust me."

She knew Ivy had lived a lifetime of mistrust because of her. But she needed Ivy's strength, Ivy's connection to the mountain - the best part of the mountain - if she was going to save her daughter. Could she save herself? She didn't know.

She stood waiting, as though there weren't police coming for Ivy, as though a dead man wasn't terrorizing people she cared about, as though their world wasn't about to end.

CHAPTER SIXTY

HE FOLLOWED THE CROW FOR A WHILE. Every so often, it would swoop down, flapping madly to stay in front of him, close to the ground. If he stopped, it lighted in a nearby tree, waiting. If he veered off the crow's intended course, it flew at his head with a vicious cry.

A frigid wind began to buffet him, keeping him from heading too far up the mountain. Whatever he had drunk made him tired. Hungry. He wanted to be where it was warm. He had to find the small woman. *Ivy.*

The third time the crow came at him, he swung his arm wide, knocking the crow to the dirt.

Ahead, the trees seemed to beckon, parting with light.

CHAPTER SIXTY-ONE

HEARING TRIPP SHOUTING from the porch, Lila sprang from the couch to press against the front door to listen. The back of her head throbbed and bled, but it was nothing compared to the way her heart pounded in her chest. How had Tripp not noticed? The fall against the table had dizzied her, but hadn't knocked her out. Certain that Tripp would leave her alone eventually, she had played dead the best she could. The troopers' arrival was just luck.

She looked around for the gun. Of course he would have it with him. Her choice was between chancing a run out the front door past him, or out the back.

He would kill her either way.

What if *he* was waiting in the woods? Surely he had followed her. He was so fast. Inhuman. But he hadn't caught her again. Despite the bath at the trailer, she could still feel his rubbery skin against hers, smell the sour-sweet odor of decay that clung to him. She knew she could douse herself in gasoline and it would never go away.

There wasn't really any choice about what she had to do. Tripp was insane. If he caught her, she would die anyway.

Lila ran to the back door and slid it open as quietly as she could. Her bare foot was so numb that she could hardly feel the cold of the stone patio beneath it. She pressed herself against the outer wall of the cabin. As she followed it, she let one hand trail against it as though doing so would keep her from being sucked into the endless forest a few yards away. The shouting continued as she crept, but the words were lost to the blood pulsing in her ears.

When she reached the corner of the cabin, she saw that the front yard was a field of gray, misty light, broken by the stubby outline of a man in a suit and overcoat.

That thing lying in the glare of the truck's headlights. The thing that had brought them all to this place. She had wanted to vomit when she saw it. But given all she had seen since then, poor Claude Dixon's body might have been a bad fake from a carnival freak show.

"Bring her out here, you bastard, or I'll kill you myself!"

Lila felt the shell of her nightmare shatter inside her, and she was almost driven to her knees with pain. But she forced herself out into the yard, screaming Bud's name.

◄ ◄ ✦ ► ►

"Lila!" Tripp's voice rose over Lila's as she stumbled across the winter-browned grass toward the wall of cars and police.

The voice inside his head was back. It mimicked him cruelly: *LilaLilaLilaLilaLilaLila! Stupid cunt! Shoot her!* The voice was metal scraping against his brain.

She had fooled him again. He had always been her fool, like in one of those idiotic fifties songs his mother was always singing.

Puuuuuuuuussy whipped!

Lila, his love, didn't want him. Didn't understand. He was going to die without her. He saw her as she was in the picture on his phone, laughing, loving him, even as she had fallen on the ice. Like they were kids. Her breath had been warm on her lips as he kissed her. How had she forgotten?

"Lila!" he screamed, raising the gun.

Lila ran, oblivious to the cold and the grass and the sharp gravel, oblivious to everything but the certain knowledge that Tripp was going to kill her. Ahead, Bud was being forced to the ground by two troopers. When she was within a few yards of him, she heard Tripp yelling her name a second time. She reached out for Bud, who was struggling to get to her despite the two giants holding him down, and almost touched him as she stumbled to the ground.

As the gunshots rang out above her, her mind automatically counted: one, two, three, four, five, before they became a thunderous blur.

CHAPTER SIXTY-TWO

"YOU'RE NOT GOING TO FIND HIM," Lila said. The words felt heavy on her tongue. "He's going to kill us all."

The chaos following Tripp's death - a blur of trooper uniforms and terse orders - had subsided. His body lay on the porch, waiting for the coroner to arrive. She found she couldn't look back at the cabin.

Why can't I feel anything?

One of the EMTs, a woman with calloused but tender hands, was treating the wound on the back of her head. *What about inside? What about the pictures of hell in my head? The smell of that animal on my body?* Those things were hiding now but she could feel them waiting for the moment she closed her eyes. The EMTs had wanted her to get in the ambulance, but she told them she wasn't going anywhere without Bud, who was still in handcuffs. Lila hated how worn he looked. She hated that she had done this to him.

The detective, Burns, told her about Danelle's murder, and that Bud was in custody because he had shot a police dog and obstructed an investigation. There was also something about his escaping custody, which she wasn't quite able to process.

"Detective Johnson and some uniforms are on their way over to that woman's trailer," Burns said. "There's nobody who can't be caught. Eventually."

She expected him to look at Bud, but he had the sense not to. Bud had practically given himself up. One of the troopers had taken off Bud's cap, one she'd never seen before. Usually his closely shaved head made him look intimidating. Intensely masculine. Now all she could see was vulnerability. What if she was the strong one in the end? He had spent all his time taking care of her, and she had done nothing but hurt him.

"I know who he is," Bud said. It wasn't a loud exclamation, but everyone around them paused and looked at him.

"How?" Lila said.

"Dwight knows him."

"What's his name?" Burns said. He drew a pen and a small notebook from the inside breast pocket of his overcoat.

"Anthony," Lila said. "Ivy called him Anthony."

"*Saint* Anthony," Bud said. They held each other's gaze across the few feet separating them.

"A saint, huh?" Burns said. "Maybe you or Mr. Yarbro can give me a last name?"

"I don't know, but it doesn't matter," Bud said. "He's dead. Dwight killed him."

Lila gasped. Was it possible? How long had it been since she left Anthony back at the trailer?

"Were you with Mr. Yarbro when this happened?" the detective said. "Telling us the location of the body would be a good thing, Mr. Tucker."

"I can't tell you because it's not there anymore. Dwight killed him the night he got into town, maybe a week or two ago. Cut him up. Buried him here on Devil's Oven. Apparently Dwight used to do that kind of thing for a living."

"Oh, God." Lila bent over, clutching her arms against her stomach. *He's been inside me. Death has been inside me.*

The EMT grabbed her from behind to steady her.

"Mrs. Tucker needs to be in the hospital," she said.

A brown SUV pulled up the driveway. Lila could hear staticky voices coming from one of the troopers' cars. She wanted to be somewhere else, away from this hellish mountain.

"Couple of weeks ago?" Burns closed his notebook. "I don't have time for this, Mr. Tucker. Right now, it seems like you're trying to tell me some kind of story to keep yourself out of jail."

"Ivy Luttrell dug him up. Sewed him back together."

Lila had known. Somehow she'd known he wasn't human.

Burns shook his head. "Give me a friggin' break," he said.

The sound started as a slow rumble, like thunder, coming from the west. They turned as one. With the sound came a wall of light, a silver dawn that rushed at them through the pines.

Lila broke free of the EMT and ran to Bud, throwing her arms around his neck. She hid her face against his chest, praying that whatever was happening would happen quickly. If it took them, it would be all right because they were together.

Helpless in the cuffs, Bud pressed his face into her hair. Later, when they were safe, far away from this place, he would remember the mineral taste of it against his lips, how the mountain had stripped it of its sweetness.

A great moaning filled their ears, as though the heart of the earth was breaking. The ground quavered and rolled, knocking Burns and one of the uniforms off their feet. The uniformed trooper would be blind for months from the searing light. Across the yard, the upper timbers of Tripp's cabin yawed. The porch roof detached from the rest of the cabin with a sound like a thousand branches snapping, and collapsed onto his body.

CHAPTER SIXTY-THREE

W'RE GOING TO FIND HIM!
The girl, Jolene, led the way up the narrow trail as though she had spent her life on the mountain. The sun was almost fully over the horizon, but the pearl light still surrounded her - a Jolene-shaped outline that drove the shadows from the brush and brambles straining toward the path.

She was so familiar. When she first came to the house, Ivy's instinct had been to drive her away. The light around her was achingly bright, as though an angel had entered the front door without any warning. There had been times in her life when she saw people swathed in faint colors: pink around a little girl at church, turquoise blue around a nurse at the doctor's office, wavering green attached to the rude man who came to fill the propane tank. She had told Thora about them, but Thora had looked at her queerly and then laughed. So she hadn't told her about Jolene.

When they neared the place where she always stopped to rest, Jolene stopped even before she did.

"Listen," Jolene said.

The sound of distant sirens broke the quiet.

"Ivy."

Jolene reached out her hand.

When Ivy took it, all vestiges of the recent night disappeared, and the sun was high above them. Early spring was overtaken by full summer. Leafed-out branches and tendrils of poison ivy strained onto the path.

Ivy felt smaller than she could ever remember feeling.

As they continued up the mountain, she glanced up at the woman whose hand she held. Her mother's pale white hair, identical to her own, swung at her shoulders, and she had a daisy tucked behind one ear. Her gauzy, blue broom skirt fell in tiers from her hips, and her sandals were rough and brown, sturdy enough for hiking. Across her chest was a long strap with a canteen at the end of it.

Ivy hurried to keep up and held fast to her mother's hand. She didn't want to be left behind. Their walks up the mountain had gotten less and less frequent, because her mother seemed worried. Unhappy. She was most unhappy when Ivy's father was home. He had begun closing himself in their bedroom in the trailer, and the noises coming from behind the door frightened them all. Thora stayed away from the trailer as much as she could.

Her mother looked down at her and smiled.

"Come on, baby. Let's get there and back before everyone gets home."

Ivy was as anxious as her mother to get to the cabin site. In her other hand, she carried a bouquet of daisies and zinnias from the garden they had planted down by the barn. She remembered that she had used to give her father flowers, but now he hated them.

When they reached the cabin site, Ivy ran to the hearthstone and laid down the bouquet. The ground around the stone was bare. Nothing would grow here, her mother had told her. Too much sadness.

Ivy knew that the right side of the hearth was where the cradle of the baby who had once lived there had sat during the day. "At night, he would sleep at his mama's bedside so she could reach him when he cried," her mother had told her. She loved to hear the stories about how the baby's sister would dance with their mother in the yard, their mother singing songs - in French, no less - that would make the birds in the trees jealous. Ivy had tried to tell Thora the stories, but Thora wouldn't listen.

They sat on the hearthstone and ate the grapes and graham crackers her mother had packed into the pink gingham rucksack she'd sewn for Ivy. When they were done, her mother plaited Ivy's hair and had her hold the end of it while she got up to look for some flexible stem or plant to secure it with.

While she waited, Ivy took Lolly Dolly out of her pocket and sat it beside her so the doll could watch her trace letters in the dirt with her fingertip. Her mother had shown her how to write her name, trailing the end of the "y" off and adding tiny fingerprint leaves so it looked like real ivy.

Hearing her mother's voice, she looked around, but couldn't see her.

She jumped up.

"Mama?"

She peered around the wild hedge of rhododendrons that grew at the western edge of the site. Her mother stood facing a man who looked like a giant. The giant was staring at her mother, smiling. But it wasn't a good kind of smile. He looked like he wanted to eat her.

"Don't worry, baby," her mother called to her. "He's not going to hurt you. I promise."

Should she believe her? Her mother didn't lie. Not even about Santa Claus or the Tooth Fairy or if there were peas in the shepherd's pie. Still, there was something wrong with the man. He wasn't someone they knew. Strangers up on the mountain weren't safe. Thora told her all the time that there might be strangers on the mountain who could hurt her. She knew she should run.

But she wouldn't. She didn't want to leave her mother there with the man. She crawled in among the branches of the rhododendron, trying to hide herself.

"Mama," she whispered.

Her mother's voice came back to her. Not in her ears, but inside her head, like a whisper.

"I won't leave you."

The man stepped closer to her mother. His chest and neck were torn and ragged like the rotting deer carcasses they sometimes found in the woods. He wasn't talking. Ivy could tell her mother was talking to him, but she couldn't hear the words. She wished her father were there. He would make the man go away.

It was so quiet, she could hear her own breathing. Even the birds had gone away.

Her mother held out her hands to the man. His ugly smile got bigger.

Ivy screamed for him to stop, but he didn't.

Her mother's voice in her head again: "Shhhhhh. Be brave."

The forest around them darkened, the light slipping away, and Ivy wanted to run to her mother's arms, or home and hide beneath her bed.

Now, the only light seemed to be coming from her mother. Ivy could only see the faint shape of her mother's body; the rest was a brilliant cloud. She looked like an angel. Suddenly, Ivy couldn't remember her mother's face. It terrified her more than anything she was seeing.

The man needed to get away from her mother, but now her mother was even closer to him. She raised her hands to his face and that ugly, ugly smile. Ivy thought his smile was even uglier than her own misshapen lip.

Then his smile was gone. He looked confused and afraid. Ivy almost felt sorry for him. *Almost.* As the light from her mother grew, it began to cover him as well.

The ground beneath Ivy started shaking, and a sound like a million coal trucks barreling toward them filled the air.

She screamed for her mother, but her mother and the man had disappeared into the light, which was spreading everywhere. It wasn't daylight, but another kind of light, glittering white and cold. Colder than the water at the lake where her father took them fishing.

In front of Ivy, the ground began to break open and she was sure they would all be swallowed up. Tree limbs cracked and fell around her, and she clung tightly to the rubbery branches of the rhododendron. The ball of light that held her mother and the man hovered over the crack in the earth. Ivy turned away, hiding her face and squeezing her eyes shut. Behind her, the earth seemed to cry out like an angry animal. *I'm not brave!* She couldn't save her mother, or herself.

Then it was done.

Ivy opened her eyes. Dawn - a true dawn - had come. High in one of the nearby trees, a squirrel scolded. Such a normal, familiar sound. She wanted to laugh with relief.

She eased herself out of the rhododendron, with much more difficulty than when she had first hidden inside it.

Jolene stood some ten yards away, her black hair tangled, her shoulders rounded with exhaustion. She sank to her knees.

"Anthony?" Ivy ran to where Jolene knelt.

Anthony lay on the ground, naked to the waist, his hair flecked with dirt, his handsome face peaceful in a way Ivy had never seen before.

She knelt beside him, and took his left hand in hers.

Beside her, Jolene was sobbing.

Anthony's hand was soft, softer than she could have ever imagined. She ran her fingers over his wrist. The stitches she had sewn so carefully (not so carefully, it turned out; he had been awkward with that hand) had disappeared. So had the wounds to his chest and neck. His skin was smooth. Unmarked.

Resting his hand gently on the ground, Ivy touched his neck. Here, too, the stitches were gone. He was perfect. She had never seen such a perfect man.

They walked the trail in silence. It was full morning, and clear. This time, Jolene followed a step behind Ivy. As they approached the trailhead, they could see the police cars parked close to the trailer.

"What if he's gone when we take them up there?" Ivy said.

"He's not going anywhere. He's dead."

Ivy nodded, feeling suddenly shy. She tucked a hand into her pocket to stroke the homely, armless little doll she had found lying in the dirt. It made her feel safe.

Jolene touched Ivy's other hand, but didn't try to hold it. "I'll be right there with you," she said.

Epilogue

LILA PULLED HER GOLF VISOR LOWER onto her forehead. She wasn't yet used to the relentless southern sunshine that poured from the sky from early morning until evening. The nearby sandhills weren't mountains; the tall pine trees offered little cooling shade. It was nothing like home.

She glanced up on her backswing. It was a terrible habit and put her off balance every time. She didn't have the concentration for golf. She hadn't had it before, but it was worse, now. Lowering the club slowly, she watched as one of the assistant pros--Todd--crossed the cart path, coming toward her. She looked past him to see if Barbara, the soft-voiced, patient assistant she had worked with for weeks, was behind him. There was no one else anywhere near the driving range.

I can do this.

The words in her head weren't any kind of match for the sudden clench of her stomach.

I will stay here.

"Mrs. Tucker."

Lila forced herself to hold out her gloved hand. She forced herself to smile.

"Barbara had a family emergency, and asked me to take

over your lesson today."

Todd was deeply tanned like the starters and everyone else who worked around the golf course. He had an easy, self-deprecating smile. But his teeth were too white in the sunshine. His mouth too big. When he took her hand, she felt her insides go rigid. If he noticed the change in her, he hid it well.

I can't do this.

Fifteen minutes later, sitting in her car with the air conditioning blasting from the vents, she tried to remember what she'd said to Todd to excuse herself. Around her the sunlight spiked off the other cars in the parking lot like so much white hot fire. Her memory was blank. Overwhelmed. She prayed that she could get home without having to call her mother-in-law or the housekeeper to come and get her.

Lila drew herself a lukewarm bath and sank into it. The tub wasn't as large as the one in the master suite, but neither she nor Bud had been comfortable at the thought of moving into his parents' old rooms. His mother had decamped to the guest house after Bud's father died, saying that she wanted something smaller. Her kindness to them after Lila's ordeal--including inviting them to take the house--had stunned both Lila and Bud. Still, the suite sat empty. Bud had talked about remodeling it, but talking about it was as far as they'd gotten.

For a month after the assault, Lila had showered in her clothes. Even now, over a year later, she could hardly bear to look at herself naked. Months and months of therapy had yet to make any kind of difference.

"Lila?"

Bud tapped lightly on the bathroom door and let himself in.

"Hey," she said. "You came back."

He smiled. "Of course I came back," he said. "I always come back."

Back from there. Back from Alta. Back from seeing
Jolene, who had stuck by Ivy through the investigation and the
plea deal. Lila didn't know why. Maybe it was out of some mis-
guided idea of friendship. She thought there was something
seriously wrong with both women. They weren't like other
people, with their secrets and bizarre attachment to the mountain. Bud had told her that Jolene had *come from the mountain-*
*-*whatever in the hell that meant.

Bud didn't need to tell her that he'd seen Jolene, and
Lila never asked. She believed him when he told her that there
was nothing sexual between him and Jolene. She knew her
husband well enough.

"I signed the sale paperwork on the club," he said.
"And I think we've got a buyer for the house."

"Since you're back, you should call your mother and
see if she wants to come over for dinner," Lila said. Anything
to keep from talking about that place. "Will you grab me a
towel?"

He watched her get out of the tub with a frank, un-
ashamed stare. His eyes weren't playful, like they used to be.
She knew she was the one who had killed his playfulness. But
he wasn't trying to make her pay. At least not on purpose.

"I thought you should know that Ivy's out of the men-
tal health center," he said, handing her the towel.

"Oh," Lila said.

Ivy's lawyer had successfully argued Stockholm Syn-
drome, but Lila knew better. Ivy had scammed everyone with
her crazy little seamstress act. She had let that animal into her
house, and served him like she was his slave. It didn't matter
that he had finally shown up dead on Devil's Oven. He had
no marks on his body. There was no clue that he was anything
more than a killer who had found his way into the mountains and murdered Claude, and Thora, as well as the man
the police found under the stage. Why? The police had never
established a motive or found a trace of him in the system.
No one who mattered had bought Bud's story about Dwight

killing Anthony days and days before Claude's death. They all assumed that Dwight had lied. But Lila believed. She also suspected that Tripp had known, that he was more involved than any of them understood.

Tripp. The snake in her Eden.

She had tried to hate him. Really tried. But all she could muster was pity.

She looked up at Bud. How long was she going to feel pity for herself? She prayed that wasn't what she was feeling for him.

No. There has to be more. Bud deserves better. We both do.

Lila shivered in the damp towel.

"Ah, Red." Bud stroked her hair. "Come here."

He held her close until the shivering stopped.

LAURA BENEDICT is the author of the dark suspense novels *Isabella Moon, Calling Mr. Lonely Hearts,* and *Devil's Oven.* She also edits the *Surreal South: an Anthology of Short Fiction* series with her husband, Pinckney Benedict. Her work has appeared in *Ellery Queen Mystery Magazine, Thrillers: 100 Must-Reads, Noir at the Bar,* and a number of other anthologies. She lives in the southernmost wilds of a midwestern state, where she is surrounded by coyotes, bobcats, and many other less picturesque predators.

Visit her website at www.LauraBenedict.com